CW00835764

Therian Promise
ALL RIGHTS RESERVED
Copyright © 2018 Cyndi Friberg
Cover art by Dar Albert
Editor: Mary Moran
ISBN: 978-1986789813
Electronic Book Publication, June 2017
Print Book Publication, March 2018

1

Therian Promise

Cyndi Friberg

Therian Heat, Book Three: Kyle is the youngest feline-shifter ever to sit on the Prime council and he's determined to prove himself worthy of the honor. A latent female with unbelievable potential has been identified by the wolves, so Kyle sets out to find her before his enemies make her one of them.

Terrified and alone, Ava manages to stay one step ahead of her pursuers until a disturbing vision leaves her weak and confused. She steps out into the cool mountain morning and a gorgeous stranger pulls her into his arms.

From the moment they first touch, passion erupts between the unsuspecting couple. Kyle is attracted to Ava's quick wit and feisty spirit while his cat wants to touch her, taste her and make her scream with pleasure. Trust doesn't come easily for Ava. Her past has taught her to be wary, but she senses a soul-deep connection with Kyle. Each secret they unearth reveals a more challenging conflict, yet together they can face any enemy.

Note from Cyndi: Many plot elements in *Therian Heat* continue on from book to book. Each couple has secured their happy ending by the end of the book, but the series is more fun if you read the books in order. Also, this book was published a few years back under the same title and author name.

Chapter One

Ava Seymour sprang up in bed, heart slamming against her ribs as anxiety jolted her awake. She carefully scanned each corner of the shadowy bedroom, visually searching the dimness, and listening for sounds that didn't belong. A branch scraped against a window and the furnace cycled on, but nothing was out of place in the calm spring night. So why was she shaking?

Carissa. Ava sensed her sister's presence as if Carissa had just walked into the room. Closing her eyes, Ava allowed the vision to unfold within her mind. When visions first assailed her months before, she'd been frightened by the disorienting pull. But her efforts to resist the spinning only intensified the vertigo, so she no longer fought their power or doubted their accuracy.

A cheerfully decorated room came into view, like a classroom meant for children. Carissa sat on the edge of a large table, legs enveloped by the full skirt of her dress. A dark-haired man knelt in front of her, more or less between her legs. He spoke in a deep, calming tone, but Ava couldn't make out his words. Despite the intimate position, they were both fully dressed.

Ava could sense the trust and affection flowing between Carissa and the dark-haired man. This was Carissa's lover, which made no sense. Her sister didn't have a lover or she hadn't six days ago, which was the last time Ava had seen her.

In the distance, a lion's roar was echoed by other feline growls. Carissa raised her head and smiled, obviously reacting to the unusual sounds. Where the hell was she? There were no lions in Colorado! Unless she was at a zoo or some sort of exhibition hall. The vision offered no other clues to Carissa's location, so Ava refocused on the images available to her.

This wasn't the first time Ava had inadvertently spied on her sister's life, but this vision felt different. The immediacy she'd experienced in other episodes was lacking now. This was an echo, a memory. Had Carissa been with this man the entire time Ava had been running for her life? She ignored the pang of annoyance and concentrated on the image. Who was the man and how had he come in contact with Carissa?

"She's ready, boys," a female announced from somewhere beyond the vision's perspective.

Ready for what? And "boys" indicated more than one male was about to participate in whatever this was. Then Ava felt them, sensed other powerful beings standing slightly back, waiting, ready for their turn...at Carissa? Why wasn't Carissa frightened? She just sat there, staring at the dark-haired man as if she wanted to devour him.

"Get moving," the unseen woman advised. "She won't be manageable for long."

Manageable? What an odd description. Carissa could be spirited and stubborn. Ava always paused to consider ramifications and judge risk factors while Carissa dove headlong into any adventure. Even so, neither of them were ever unmanageable.

A tall blond man approached, his angular features intense and serious. Bending to one knee beside Carissa, he said, "I willingly offer my life. We have waited so long for your return. I am honored to be part of your definition."

Definition? What the hell did that mean?

He pushed to his feet and offered Carissa his wrist.

Anxiety twisted through Ava, but she was lost in the vision's hold, unable to change the events unfolding before her. What was he doing? He sounded so serious, so...

Carissa grabbed his arm with both hands and lowered her mouth toward his wrist. No freaking way! She wasn't going to... Carissa bit down hard, blood streaming out from under her lips. Hunger, savage and demanding, burned through Ava. Carissa wanted this, needed it with an elemental longing that transcended rational thought or quantification. Ava felt herself being drawn deeper into the vision as desire spread through her soul. She was meant for this. *They* were born for this. How had they lived without it for so long?

No. This was a vision, which meant the images had been sent for a reason. Shuddering, Ava struggled to distance herself from the images and ignore the lingering ache. Were they vampires? Had Carissa fallen in with a coven of—

Ava shook away the fanciful thought. Vampires didn't exist, but witches did! Was this some sort of blood magic or... She couldn't even finish the thought, had no idea what they were doing. Carissa appeared to be participating willingly, but *why* would she do something so disgusting?

Before Ava could unravel fact from impression, the scene faded, releasing her from its thrall. She felt queasy and shaken, but worse was the realization that what she'd just seen had actually happened. Sometime in the past six days her sister had bit into a man's arm and drank his blood.

Ava didn't understand the ritual's purpose, but it didn't matter anyway. Trepidation urged her onward and she intended to obey. She tossed back the covers and swung her legs over the side of the bed. The last time she'd shrugged off one of these feelings two of her father's thugs had abducted her right out of the safety of her own house. She'd managed to escape them by playing the terrified victim, but now they knew she wasn't helpless. So they'd be even harder to elude.

Crossing the bedroom in darkness, she rushed across the cool wood floor. The rental cabin was small and rustic, but she'd thought the secluded mountain setting would offer her a reprieve from the people pursuing her. She hurried into the tiny bathroom and closed the door. There were no windows in the room, so she turned on the lights, relatively sure it wouldn't alert anyone to her location.

Ava's childhood had been filled with stories of Osric, her abusive father. Her mother, Willona, had been convinced the only way to protect her daughters from Osric's obsessive violence was to stage their deaths and leave everything and everyone they'd ever known behind.

Willona had died believing she'd escaped her past and built a new life for her girls. But six days ago Osric resurfaced, yet he hadn't even cared enough to come himself. Like some arrogant dictator, he'd sent teams of "his men" to collect Ava and Carissa.

Ava wasn't sure what Osric wanted or why he'd waited so long to reenter their lives. All she knew was Willona's fears had been justified and her desperate actions no longer seemed rash.

For the first few days Ava had been completely focused on evading her pursuers. She had a general feeling that Carissa was safe, but she hadn't understood her certainty. Two nights ago, she'd briefly touched her sister's mind and was again reassured by her composure. The most recent dream was disconcerting, but even during the bizarre ritual, Carissa had seemed unharmed. At least physically.

With a heavy sigh, Ava pushed away the past and focused on the situation at hand. If her father's men had found her again, there wasn't much she could do about it. Hopefully, her intuition had given her enough warning that she could make a clean getaway.

She took a deep breath to reinforce her resolve then gathered her toiletries and splashed water on her face. After hastily binding her hair at the nape of her neck, she rushed back into the bedroom.

Each night before she went to sleep, she laid out clean clothes and packed her belongings, so she could be ready to leave in under a minute. The vision had slowed her down, but not for long. She had to put some distance between herself and this madness. She couldn't help Carissa if she became the next victim.

Focusing on the conclusion, she unlocked the side door in the bedroom and stepped out onto the wraparound porch. Dawn had just arrived, making the treetops glow and casting a crimson haze across the horizon. She acknowledged the beauty without becoming lost in its majesty.

She'd stashed a motorcycle in back of the cabin. The enduro was powerful enough to tackle most mountain trails while not drawing attention to her on legal roadways. There wasn't a door leading where she wanted to go and the stone path that wound around the other side of the cabin was too visible. She climbed over the porch rail and dropped to the ground a few feet below.

Settling her backpack over her shoulder like an oversized purse, she headed for the motorcycle. She'd avoided the house she shared with Carissa, as well as their sporting goods store in the heart of Breckenridge, suspecting they were being watched. But circumstances left her no choice now. She needed her car and she needed more clothes if she was going to disappear for good.

She ducked around the corner and a large hand covered her mouth. A long, muscular arm wrapped around her waist, pinning her arms to her sides and plastering her back against a tall, hard body. Terror blazed through her mind and she screamed, twisting desperately against the man's grasp. The backpack slid to her elbow before his forearm stopped its descent.

"I won't hurt you, Ava." His voice was deep and insistent. "I am *not* one of your father's men."

The words should have soothed her, but panic blasted through her mind. She was breathing too fast and her skin prickled. Then pressure built deep inside her, rushing up through her torso like a geyser. Pain pushed against the backs of her eyes, blinding her as it set the world in motion. She screamed again, the sound so raw his hand barely muffled the cry.

Heat pulsed through her head and sound roared in her ears. His arms tightened as her legs collapsed, leaving her limp within his embrace. She heard his voice near her ear, but his words were lost in the building cacophony. Clutching his forearms with both hands, she clung to the only solid object in her heaving world.

Then reality shattered and light blasted out of her, propelling her beyond the mountain scene. She screamed and screamed, but the sound only existed in her mind. Both his arms banded her now, holding her snugly against his chest. Why was he still here? Wasn't death a journey meant to be taken alone?

The earth rushed up to meet them. He twisted violently as if to take the brunt of the collision, but her shoulder slammed into the ground and something even harder punched into her side. Pain exploded through her, driving the breath from her lungs then slicing down her arm.

Scrambling to his knees, he took his weight off her as she instinctively rolled to her back. The simple movement sent a fresh wave of agony washing over her. She gasped and lights flashed before her eyes. She could barely think past the roaring in her ears.

He arched over her, hands on the ground beside her shoulder. "Don't try to move," he directed. "We landed really hard. Catch your breath and make sure you're not hurt badly." He wasn't touching her now, but the position still felt menacing.

"Can't. Breathe." He reached for her and she shoved his hand away. The small rebellion sent pain ricocheting through her torso, but she couldn't make a sound.

"I'm going to touch your side. Only your side. You might have punctured a lung or worse." His voice was calm and firm, leaving her no room for negotiation.

Carefully keeping her arm angled over her breasts, she watched him through a haze of pain. He had the most unusual eyes, rich forest green with distinct flecks of gold. He lifted the hem of her t-shirt and slipped his hand beneath. His warm fingers touched her skin and she shivered.

"Try to hold still. I'm not going to hurt you."

His warm fingers pushed up along her side until they rested against the bruise. He shifted position several times and gradually increased the pressure. Heat sank into her flesh, tingling then burning. The pressure suddenly released, as if he'd slit the laces of an antique corset, then she drew a cautious breath. Though a faint ache remained, she could breathe again.

"What did you do?" She took a deeper breath, amazed by the change.

"Feel better?" He smiled, drawing her attention back to his handsome face. His nose was straight, if a bit narrow. His cheekbones were high without being hollow and distinct brackets framed his mouth. He shifted position and his leather jacket creaked, the early morning breeze playing through his dark blond hair.

"I thought I'd snapped half my rib cage. I literally could not breathe." Keeping her arm pressed against her chest, she managed to sit without moving her injured shoulder, and scooted backward until she rested against the trunk of a nearby tree.

"How bad is your arm?" A hint of challenge threaded through his even tone. "Or did you hurt your shoulder?"

"It can wait." She glanced around. There was no obvious path through the trees, no indication of where they were or how they'd arrived. "What the hell just happened? Where are we?"

"I'm pretty sure we teleported and I have no idea where we are." He rocked back onto his heels then stood, watching her intently. Sunlight filtered through the trees, revealing golden strands in his dark blond hair.

She stared up at him, her shoulder throbbing unmercifully. Teleportation only existed in the movies. Yeah, so did psychic healers... Her mind refused to accept his conclusion, so she returned to the basics. "Who are you?"

"Kyle Lashton. Our mothers were best friends back before you were born. We heard what Osric was planning and couldn't allow it. I've come to take you home." The emphasis he put on the word "home" assured her he hadn't meant her house in Breckenridge.

He pulled a cell phone out of his jacket and turned in a slow circle. Apparently, he couldn't find a signal because he slipped it back into his pocket and looked at her. "You're obviously still in pain." He knelt beside her again, resting his hands on his thighs. "Is it your shoulder or your arm?"

"Explain what you did to my side first." She wasn't sure why she didn't want him to touch her, but he definitely made her feel...not threatened or afraid, just hyperaware. His eyes were too green and his features too appealing. And she wasn't even going to consider how hard and strong he'd felt wrapped around her.

Before they smashed into the ground, of course.

"You feel better, don't you? Does it matter how I did it?"

He was right. If he hadn't touched her side, she'd still be fighting for breath or unconscious. "You're some sort of 'healer'?" She couldn't believe she'd said the word. She was the sensible sister. Carissa was the one who loved sci-fi movies and paranormal fantasies. Ava liked gritty crime dramas and complicated mysteries.

One corner of his mouth quirked, but his eyes remained serious. "Call it what you like. I can take away your pain, but the energy won't pass through anything inorganic. My skin must touch yours if you want me to heal you. And it will be a whole lot easier if I can see what I'm doing."

"You want me to take off my shirt?"

His features tensed and impatience narrowed his gaze. "Do you honestly think I planned this entire incident so I could see you in your bra?"

It did sound rather ridiculous when he put it that way. "I'm not sure I can get my shirt off unless you help me."

He chuckled, honest amusement warming his expression again. "Which was my wicked plan all along." He moved closer and held the hem as she pulled her uninjured arm free of the clingy t-shirt. After easing it over her head, he gingerly worked the wadded material down her other arm. He gathered her hair to the side and whistled. "That is one hell of a bruise."

His gaze remained on her injured shoulder, despite the plunging angle of her lace-trimmed bra. She braced her hand against the ground as the world swayed. The throbbing had become a burning ache as soon as she sat up. Her stomach heaved and closing her eyes only made the nausea worse. *Please don't let me throw up on him*! She couldn't imagine anything more humiliating.

Infuriated by her helplessness, she allowed him to shift her body away from the tree. "You gonna be okay like this? You're not going to pass out on me, are you?"

"I guess we'll find out."

His hands were strong, yet each motion was surprisingly gentle. He supported the center of her chest with one hand while the other swept up and down, across her shoulder and down her arm. Despite the mundane nature of his task, awareness arced between them.

The forest was cool, the ground rough beneath her, which made the heat of his hands all the more apparent. He shifted position, carefully supporting her shoulders as his hand splayed directly over the bruise. His lids lowered and his expression tensed.

"What are you doing?" she whispered, half afraid of disrupting his concentration.

"Scanning." After a pause, he added, "Healing isn't my primary ability. I can usually sense what's wrong, but my healing pulses aren't strong enough to mend bone. I was able to stabilize your cracked ribs and ease the pain, but you'll need to be treated by one of our real healers once we arrive at the sanctuary." He looked up and Ava gasped. The golden flecks in his eyes were glowing. "Your shoulder is slightly out of place, but the rest is an impact contusion."

"Which means?"

"It's a really nasty bruise, but we're in luck. I should be able to ease it back into place and make you a lot more comfortable."

He sounded so casual, as if healing pulses and glowing eyes were nothing out of the ordinary. His hand lowered, palm barely grazing her skin. Heat erupted and spread, dragging another gasp from her dry throat.

"Relax," he coaxed. "Try not to fight it."

After one searing burst of sensation, the pain receded, but the heat remained. Waves of soothing warmth rippled across her chest, tightening her nipples before pooling between her thighs. Her core tightened and her clit tingled, the feeling unmistakable and intense. She squirmed, desperately trying to ignore the unwanted side effect of his touch.

"That's...enough." If he didn't stop soon, she'd come, and the thought of moaning and shivering was nearly as humiliating as throwing up would have been. He moved his hand away and the heat slowly fizzled, leaving her stunned and tingling.

"Better?" Their gazes locked and time paused. Awareness hot and electric hung between them, humid and full of promise. His eyes narrowed, the golden light even more intense than it had been before. His nostrils flared and he leaned toward her, lips slowly parting.

Not ready to add sexual conquest to his list of accomplishments, she turned to the side then pushed to her knees, quickly reaching for her shirt.

He'd done it. Her shoulder was still discolored, but the pain was gone. "Thank you." She kept her back turned as she pulled the t-shirt into place. Even so, it was too easy to imagine his lips pressed over hers, moving and parting as his tongue explored.

"If there's aspirin in that backpack, it might be a good idea to take some, just in case. As I said, healing isn't my primary ability."

She nodded and reached for the backpack, half expecting the pain to return as soon as she moved. "If healing is more or less a hobby, what *is* your 'primary ability'?" The pack had landed a short distance away, but she was able to pull it toward her without leaving her knees. She unzipped one small compartment and then another as she searched for a pain reliever.

"I've had men watching your house and your store, so where'd that come from anyway?"

Her hands froze and she looked into his eyes. Not only had he sidestepped her question, he'd just admitted he'd been spying on her. "I thought you didn't work for Osric."

"I don't." He stood and brushed leaves and pine needles off his jeans. Then he slipped his hands into the pockets of his bomber jacket, looking anything but relaxed. His gaze alternated between visual scans of their surroundings and assessing sweeps of her.

She shifted back to her seat and folded her legs in front of her. "Then why were you stalking me?" Despite her attempt to seem calm, her voice sounded sharp and thin.

"I've been trying to protect you, but you're one slippery female."

Her mother would have been pleased by the description. All Ava felt was tired. She was tired of being afraid and tired of avoiding relationships. Even lasting friendships could be dangerous. Carissa was the only one— Carissa! "Do you know where my sister is? I haven't seen her since this nightmare started."

"Carissa's fine. She's safe and she's with my people. Now tell me where you got the supplies."

If her visions hadn't confirmed his casual statements, she wouldn't have allowed him to shift the conversation so easily. Give a little to get a little. She could play nice until she found a better option. At least figured out where the hell they were. "I got the supplies from the man who owns the cabin. I told him Carissa and I had a terrible fight and I needed some time on my own. He's never been one to ask questions and this is his off season, so he gathered what I'd asked for from my store and told me I could stay as long as I liked."

"Nice guy."

"He is. And there are damn few left in this screwed-up world."

A beam of sunlight touched his eyes and gleamed in his hair, making him appear more hunk-next-door and less stalker-in-the-alley. He definitely seemed less tense yet still watchful. "Your mother obviously taught you how to hide. How much did she tell you about your people?"

"My people?" She watched him closely, hoping to determine which impression was the real Kyle. "As in the nationality of my ancestors?"

"In a way. Have you ever heard of the Therian nation?"

She found a small packet containing two pills and ripped it open with her teeth. Then she dug out a water bottle before tossing the pills into her mouth. After swallowing the pills, she held up the bottle. "Do you want some?"

"Not right now." He kept his distance, calm and still. Like a cat with a cornered mouse. The lion's roar echoed through her memory. Why was she fixated on felines? "We should be careful with all of our resources until we have a better understanding of where we are."

She looked around, not that she could see much from her position on the ground. "Pine and aspen trees on steep, rocky slopes, cool clean air. I don't think we've gone far."

"Hopefully." He pulled out the phone again, holding it at various levels as he slowly turned around. "But Colorado doesn't hold the patent on pine-covered mountains. This could be Wyoming or Montana, even Canada."

"And you think we teleported here?" How else could she explain suddenly being in a different location? She'd been having visions for weeks. Was this really so much different? Yes! Her visions were nothing more than souped-up dreams. Teleportation was an entirely different scientific discipline.

"If we didn't teleport, how'd we get here?" He echoed her thoughts as he returned the phone to his pocket.

"You're the one with magic powers." She gestured toward her shoulder. "You tell me."

"I think your Therian energy spiked when I touched you. You felt threatened and your body attempted to remove you from the danger. It was a defense mechanism."

"I have no idea what you're talking about." But his explanation fit her strange symptoms a little too well. *Therian* nation. *Therian* energy. Was that word supposed to mean something to her?

"Why were you screaming right before this happened?"

Annoyed by his persistence, she sat a bit straighter and said, "Gee, let me think. I was dragged out of my house by armed men claiming to work for my father. I managed to outsmart them, but before I could relocate you showed up. Makes a girl jumpy."

"You weren't jumpy, sunshine. You were in pain, serious pain by the sound of it."

Sunshine? She'd never had a nickname before, had always thought they were childish, so she tried not to like it. Besides, he was right about the pain and they both knew it, so she abandoned her pointless denials. "Okay, so I felt like my brain was going to explode out my eye sockets. What does that have to do with us ending up here?"

"A spontaneous energy spike strong enough to flash two people would hurt like hell. Especially in someone untrained to deal with the intensity." His brows arched, accenting the challenge in his words. "I might be a second-rate healer, but I can't teleport at all."

"But I have only your word for that." She pushed to her feet and planted her fists on her hips. "Maybe this was the only way you could get me away from the others."

"Then wouldn't I have a car waiting or at least a couple of horses?"

"Why didn't this 'defense mechanism' teleport me away from Osric's men? I've been in danger since this mess began."

"It might have taken awhile for your energy levels to build up or... I don't honestly know. Teleportation is a rare gift. I don't know that much about it."

He'd healed her! She could barely absorb the reality. With nothing more than the touch of his hand, he'd eased her pain and realigned her shoulder. And addled her brain.

Pressing her hand over her rapidly thumping heart, she took a deep breath and then another. This day just got weirder and weirder.

"*How* we got here is really irrelevant," he went on. "We need to figure out where we are."

She looked at him then nodded. His eyes were no longer shining with the strange, inhuman light, but no one could misinterpret his hot, hungry expression. She wasn't the only one who had been affected by the exchange of energy.

Not yet ready to deal with his obvious arousal, she automatically lowered her gaze. Which only took her on a visual tour of his body. His well-worn brown leather jacket encased broad shoulders and hinted at muscular arms. It was way too easy to remember how those arms felt wrapped around her, supporting her. *Restraining* her.

She could not be taken in by a handsome face and strong body. He could be one of Osric's goons, for all she knew. Brute force had failed, so they were trying a subtler approach? Her mother had taught her never to trust anyone at face value and to independently verify everything she was told.

Well, standing here glaring at each other wasn't accomplishing anything. "If we hike to the top of one of these peaks, maybe you can find a signal for your phone."

"My thoughts exactly." His gaze lingered on her mouth, hinting at thoughts that had nothing to do with hiking.

"Even if I can't get a signal, we'll have a better view of our surroundings."

She glanced to where she'd left her backpack then noticed that Kyle was wearing it. "I can carry that myself."

He grinned. "If your pain returns, I'll be carrying you and your pack. There's no shame in accepting help."

Acknowledging his opinion with a nod, she said, "Lead on."

They started up the nearest slope, wending their way through pine trees and around rocky outcroppings on their way to the summit. There was no obvious trail, no sign of human infringement on the wilderness. Ordinarily she'd have enjoyed the pristine beauty, but today it made her feel isolated and wary. Though an avid hiker, she was no survivalist.

"If our mothers were such good friends, why did my mother never mention yours?" Without the pain distracting her, she became more and more aware of her companion. His jacket ended at his waist, leaving her an unobstructed view of his denim-covered ass and muscular thighs.

"Did your mother ever talk about her past, what life was like before she married Osric?" He glanced back at her then paused to help her past an especially steep rock formation.

His fingers wrapped around her wrist and he effortlessly pulled her up to the small ledge on which he'd paused. "She told us that both her parents were dead and she was an only child, but that was about all." They stood so close his body heat sank through her clothing. It wasn't unpleasant, just a bit intrusive.

"Then why does it surprise you that she never mentioned my mother?"

"You mentioned a name before. Something nation."

"Therian nation?" His hand remained on hers, but he made no other move to touch her.

"What is the Therian nation?"

An enigmatic smile curved his lips and he shook his head. "I better not get into all that until our footing is more secure."

They continued the climb in silence, Ava doing her best to keep up with his long strides. His legs were powerful and he moved with sure-footed agility, obviously at home in the challenging terrain. "You said Carissa is with your people. What does that mean? Where is she?" Her visions had given her a unique perspective of Carissa's situation. She was relatively certain Carissa was safe, but she wanted to see if Kyle's information would correspond with the images in her visions.

"I promise you, she's fine. Your father's men never touched her. She's with a good friend of mine. His name is Quinton Jenaro and he'll keep her safe."

"What does he look like?"

He glanced back, clearly surprised by the question. "Tall and burly, dark hair and eyes. Why do you ask?"

"I dreamed about her last night." It was more or less true. "She was with a dark-haired man. He looked sort of like a lumberjack." He'd looked more like someone who would have been featured on the lumberjack edition of the hunk-of-the-month calendar, but that was beside the point.

Kyle chuckled and turned back to the mountain. "Lumberjack fits Quinn as well as anything, but don't worry. He isn't nearly as mean as he looks."

Kyle hadn't seemed at all surprised that she'd dreamed about her sister. Were psychic powers common among Therians? "Where did Quinn take her? How do you know they're safe?"

"Last I heard they were out at the sanctuary, which is where I'll eventually take you. We have electrified fences and video surveillance, as well as physical guards."

She wasn't sure if his list made her feel more or less secure. "Why do you need all that security? Are kidnappings common among your people?"

"You need to stop saying 'your' people." Another chuckle rumbled in his chest, but this time he didn't turn around. "We're the same, sunshine. My people are your people. We're both part of the Therian nation."

NEHEMA USHERED "TEAM Leader" into her neat suburban two-story and directed him toward the living room. Masquerading as a soccer mom had worked remarkably well as she gradually allowed her appearance to mature, but circumstances had changed. Too many in the Front Range knew too much. It was time for a new strategy.

"The cats captured Gage," she told her companion. He crossed the room with three long strides and sat in the middle of the flower-print sofa, each movement illustrating his impatience.

"I heard." Though he was dressed in jeans and a pullover shirt, his bearing was unmistakably militant.

The illusion of anonymity amused Nehema so she allowed it to continue. In truth, she'd learned his name and much of his background hours after their "chance" encounter in 1979. And their relationship hadn't changed much in all the years that followed. Similar goals kept them on parallel paths, yet they both knew they weren't actually working together. She kept hoping he'd trust her enough to tell her his true identity. Instead, he hid behind a nameless mask and treated her like a fool.

He tapped his thumb against his thigh as his expression turned thoughtful. "Anything Gage knew is compromised. A mind sweep from any the cats and that coward will piss his pants."

"I was never overly confident in Gage, so he knows very little." She waved away his concerns and sat in the armchair facing him.

"He knows your name."

She shrugged. "If the cats don't know my name by now, I've given them far more credit than they deserve. What Gage has done is focus attention on me and I can't tolerate that."

"I'm not sure I understand." He scooted to the edge of the sofa, blue gaze searching hers. "If the shifters know who you are and what you're trying to accomplish, why don't they just shut you down?"

"Because—up until now—they haven't known where to find me."

"Gage knows where you live?" One of his gray brows arched, accenting the question.

She rolled her eyes. Was he going out of his way to annoy her today? "Would we be sitting here if he did?"

"But he knows enough to predict your next attack?"

"I don't attack. I *liberate*. I save helpless females from the demonic nature forced upon them by ruthless men! The females are innocent and the evil practices of the Therian elders must be abolished."

"Their practices become pointless if I find a cure." Though he didn't raise his voice, there was steel in the statement. "I haven't given up on my program."

"I'm less convinced that a chemical can permanently bind their demons, but I'm still willing to let you try." She pushed to her feet and motioned toward the stairs. "That's why I asked you here today."

He looked a bit leery, but he followed her up the stairs and to the second bedroom down the hallway. She pushed the door open but didn't enter. Warning him to remain quiet, she nodded toward the bed across the room. Three female Therians rested side by side, sleeping soundly, thanks to a strong sedative. She wasn't sure if they were sisters, but similar features and coloring identified them with a common clan. The youngest was perhaps eight the oldest in her late teens or early twenties.

"You may have the oldest," she told her sometimes partner. "The other two are mine."

"Sorry. I need all three," he said without pause or negotiation.

"No." She closed the door before continuing. "The oldest was going to be a parting gift. I'm relocating and I've decided our partnership ends here."

"All the more reason for me to take all three."

Indignation washed away her shock. She shoved him backward, the unexpected force sending him stumbling nearly to the stairs. "You ungrateful bastard. Get out of my house!"

He tapped the device nestled in his ear, his stance tense and hostile. "I need backup. Top floor by the stairwell." Within seconds four masked soldiers, dressed all in black and armed with compact automatic weapons stomped up the stairs and crowded her hallway. One backed her into a corner and kept her there with lethal efficiency. The other three slipped into the bedroom and emerged a moment later carrying one of the girls each. Her sometimes partner watched it all with silent amusement.

"You bastard," she sneered as the last soldier headed down the stairs. He'd won this round, there was no way she could salvage the situation, but she knew who he was, knew the location of his precious compound and the identities of his partners. "Enjoy it while it lasts, *Milliner*. This is far from over."

Chapter Two

Kyle stood on the summit of the nondescript mountain and scented the cool, crisp air. The smells were familiar—pine, damp earth, grass, deer, elk, *prey*... He paused and fought back a smile. He was hungry and his Therian nature was making damn sure he acknowledged the fact. The mountain had been steeper than it appeared from the base, but Ava kept up without complaint and minimal assistance. She'd marched along like a tough little soldier, all focused determination and confidence.

He'd been chasing Ava for the past six days. Well, to be more accurate, he'd been chasing the men who'd been chasing Ava. His primary concern was her safety, but he'd also needed a better understanding of Osric's strategy and the true scope of his influence. Ava was a crucial piece to the puzzle, but she wasn't the only element of this conflict requiring Kyle's attention. So, he'd watched from the shadows for the first few days, ready to swoop in if the others got too close. Instead, she took them through a twisting maze of false trails and backtracking leads until Kyle began to wonder if her escape had been a ruse and his rivals were having fun with him.

Then three days ago, Ava simply disappeared. Kyle's grand ambition to become her savior evaporated and he felt the first tingle of fear. His one advantage in this mess had been Osric's inflated ego. Osric had been so confident in his power that he'd trusted wolves to do his dirty work for him. Delegation was becoming a Therian weakness. Too many alphas didn't want to be directly involved in enforcing the decisions they made, which left them at the mercy of their muscle.

Locating someone who didn't want to be found was infinitely harder than trailing a frightened woman as she frantically outran her pursuers, but Kyle had learned all he needed to know about Osric's "organization" and he'd been determined to reach her before the wolves. In the end, Carissa had pointed him in the right direction. He'd been relieved to finally have control over the situation, but apparently fate wasn't finished screwing with him.

He turned to Ava and paused. He'd meant to ask if she had anything edible in her backpack, but her eyes were wide and bluer than the sky. Her face was flushed and an unmistakable combination of panic and dread tensed her lovely features. Protectiveness surged within him, drawing him closer, preparing his body for a physical confrontation should anything threaten this female.

He glanced at the panorama, trying to understand her reaction. Mountains stretched into the distance, some rolling and graceful, others starkly etched and rugged. This was home for his cougar, the sort of setting his cat craved when Kyle was too inundated with network business to shift and run free.

But Ava couldn't shift yet. She was still bound by human limitations. "Does anything look familiar?"

"As you said, it could be Colorado, but it could just as easily be half a dozen other places." She squared her shoulders and straightened her spine as determination pushed through the weaker emotions. "We better keep moving. Unless your phone picked up a signal, we're seriously screwed."

He shook his head, hating to deflate what little remained of her hope. "No such luck. I already tried it twice." It was more like twice in the last ten minutes. He'd been checking it off and on all morning.

"Then pick a direction." She turned in a slow circle. "Looks like we're a long way from anywhere."

"Which means we need to be smart with our supplies." There was another option available to them, but she wasn't ready to consider a Therian alternative to hours, perhaps days of arduous hiking. Besides, it was a long shot at best. He'd let the reality of their isolation sink in a bit longer then he'd offer the creative solution. "What all do you have stuffed in that backpack?"

"Trail mix, protein bars, change of clothes, a mini first-aid kit, flashlight, lighter." She shrugged. "The usual. I expected to be on a motorcycle, not an extended hiking trip."

"Well, our expectations have obviously changed." He paused and smiled at her. "I'm presuming you intend to share your supplies with me. Technically, I'm the one who's completely unprepared for this."

She looked at him through her lashes, the expression inadvertently flirtatious. At least he thought the flirting was inadvertent. She'd been anything but approachable before. "I suppose it's a reasonable presumption after healing me."

Damn. Did she practice that not-quite-a-smile expression? His entire body reacted with heat and...*hunger*. No, it wasn't her. Well, she was the focus of his spiking instincts, but she didn't realize she was the cause. Healing her had left him drained, and Therians became progressively more predatory when their needs, or the needs of one under their protection, were neglected. Patience might not be an option, but he had to find a better location than this mountaintop.

"Good." The word struggled past his dry throat. "I'm starving."

"What would you like? Trail mix or a protein bar?"

He pictured her naked on her back with trail mix sprinkled all over her ivory skin. He'd start at her knees and nibble his way to her neck... "Protein bar."

She went behind him and rummaged through the backpack until she produced a foil-wrapped bar. "You better have a drink of water too." She handed him the water bottle. "Your voice sounds sort of scratchy."

He quickly took a sip of water, hiding his guilty smile. He could think of something warm and slick and luscious that would coat his tongue and soothe this scratchy throat. He'd have her straddle his face and he'd—

"Are you all right?" She crossed her arms over her chest, staying carefully out of reach. "Your eyes are starting to glow again."

He rubbed his eyes and cleared his throat, knowing neither was likely to ease the ache rapidly spreading through his body. "Healing you left me hungry, but I'll be fine."

For a long, tense moment she stared at him, speculation narrowing her eyes, then she muttered, "He's standing there in the midday sun, so he can't be a vampire. But why was she drinking their blood?"

"You said that out loud," he revealed as gently as possible.

"I know." But the bright red flush on her cheeks said otherwise. "In my dream Carissa..."

"It was just a dream." She needed to understand the fundamental truths of her existence before she focused on details like a blood ritual. He didn't want to intentionally mislead her, so he quickly guided the conversation in a safer direction. "Let's head back down and I'll start at the beginning. Deal?"

"Deal, but let's go a different direction than we came up. We already know what's down there. Trees."

"Fair enough." He swept his hand in a semicircle. "Any preference?" Therian dreamers were generally clairvoyant in other ways as well, but she was still latent. It was surprising that any of her abilities had manifested before her animal nature was defined. More proof that Ava was no ordinary Therian. He inhaled deeply when she offered no opinion. The air smelled slightly fresher to his right, which likely meant water. Rather than explain his hunch, he provided a more conventional suggestion. "If we head west, we'll have the sun at our backs for most of the day. It's easier to see that way. Do you have a compass stashed in one of those compartments?" He motioned over his shoulder with his thumb.

She disappeared behind him again then returned with a small flashlight. Before he could remind her what she'd been looking for, she flipped it around and showed him the compass recessed in the flashlight's handle.

"Very clever." Another hunger pain cramped his gut and he quickly turned away, not wanting her to witness his distress. He breathed in through his nose and exhaled slowly through his mouth, consciously controlling his reaction to the pain. She touched his arm and he had no choice but to turn around or heighten her suspicion.

"Are you sure you're just hungry? You look sort of pale."

He tried to smile and failed. "Too much sun and not enough food." He tossed the flashlight from hand to hand as the spasm gradually receded. "I know you have no reason to trust me, but I need you to promise you won't run away. No matter what happens. I can't keep you safe if you take off on me."

"'No matter what happens'? What does that mean?"

"I'll answer all your questions, do whatever it takes to earn your trust, but I need your promise now."

She searched his gaze, glanced away then looked at him again. "I take promises seriously. I'm not sure I can say that and mean it."

"All right. How about this, as long as you have no reason to doubt me personally, regardless of how insane the situation seems, promise you will not run away."

"What are you afraid will happen?" He hadn't meant to agitate her, but she was clearly upset. "Just tell me."

"Trust me just this far and I'll earn the rest."

She huffed out a breath and crossed her arms over her chest. "You're insane. You want me to trust a crazy person." She paused and he was scrambling for a better justification when she said, "Fine. As long as you haven't given me a reason to mistrust you personally, no matter how crazy things get—though I can't imagine things getting any crazier than they are right now—I promise I will not run away from you."

"Thank you. You won't regret it." He glanced at the compass then headed toward the smell of the water, which was more or less west.

"So what's a Therian?" she prompted, obviously anxious to begin her orientation.

They descended single file, which put them at eye level when he looked back. "We're shapeshifters, Ava. Most Therians can only shift into one animal. A select few can shift into several, if all their manifestations are similar. Like Quinn, the man protecting your sister, he can shift into a black jaguar and a cougar."

"My sister's lover is a feline shapeshifter?" She stopped walking and gaped at him.

"I never said they were lovers. What did you see in your dream?"

She ignored his question and started walking again. Her features hadn't yet registered her reaction to his claim. "What do you change into?"

"A mountain lion," he said, not in the mood for cougar jokes.

"Show me." He glanced back and she grinned. "Turn into a mountain lion." It was obvious from the sparkle in her eyes that she thought she was calling his bluff.

"I'm going to shift for you, but I can't do so right now."

"Of course not." She dismissed the possibility and brushed past him, continuing down the mountain in the lead.

"When I healed you, because I'm not a trained healer, it sapped my energy. If I shift right now, it's likely I'd be trapped in cat form until my levels regenerate. I can protect you in cat form, but I'm not much for conversation."

"How long will it take for your 'levels' to 'regenerate' enough for you to shift safely?" Her tone was clipped and cool, and she didn't spare him so much as a backward glance.

"A couple of hours. If we had plenty of food and weren't mountain climbing in the midday sun."

They reached a stone ledge wide enough for them to stand side by side and she stopped again. "So what's the alternative? Am I supposed to believe your ridiculous claim just because..."

"Because I took away your pain and you have psychic dreams and we spontaneously teleported to an unknown destination? Therian energy fuels all of these abilities. We *are not* human. Is that really so hard to believe?"

She rubbed her eyes and shook her head. "I don't know what to believe anymore. You're right. I can't explain how we got here or where the hell here is, but shapeshifting? Even if it's true, I don't see how one leads to the other."

"Ending up here was an exaggeration of your fight-or-flight response. You've been isolated from Therian males, so when I touched you, your energy spiked."

"Osric's men grabbed me and shoved me into the backseat of a car. Why didn't that trigger my fight-or-flight response?"

"I'm not sure. There had to have been something different about this morning, but I don't know what it was. Give me twenty-four hours and I'll prove that what I'm telling you is fact not fantasy. Listen with an open mind and I'll—"

"You mean there's more?" She looked out over the verdant valley that stretched off to their left. They were halfway down, but the view was still spectacular. "What could be more fantastic than teleporting feline shapeshifters?"

He wasn't sure if she had accepted his offer or if she was just passing time, but hopefully her attitude would change once she saw him shift. Which meant he needed to feed ASAP. "Feline shifters are the most common kind, but the Therian nation is made up of all sorts of clans, wolves, bears, even raptors."

She chuckled and motioned for him to take the lead. "People shift into dinosaurs? Must be popular at birthday parties."

He ignored her sarcasm and continued their descent. "Not dinosaurs, birds of prey. And to my knowledge, Ian isn't popular with anyone. Except maybe my mother."

"You said we're both part of the Therian nation. Are you going to try and convince me that I'm one of these shapeshifters too? If I could turn into a leopard or a lioness, I'm pretty sure I'd know about it."

His response was interrupted as a section of the mountain required their undivided attention. They faced the rock wall and chose each foothold and grip with utmost care. Kyle reached the bottom first and steadied her as she completed the final few steps. She was agile and strong, just like a Therian female should be. A faint smile curved his lips as he reluctantly released her waist and stepped back.

The last section of the descent appeared gradual and hilly, far more hike than climb. Trees shaded them again, the coolness welcome after hours in the blazing sun. Hopefully he could keep his mind on her orientation rather than imagining all the erotic things he'd rather be teaching her. But her jeans rode low enough on her hips to reveal a teasing inch of bare midriff. Not to mention the way they hugged her nicely rounded ass.

Forcing his attention away from her body, he resumed his explanation. "Female Therians are born latent. The ability to shift is within them, but the specific animal into which they'll shift has yet to be defined."

Her steps slowed and her eyes widened. "In my last vision, Carissa..." She shuddered, unable to complete the thought.

"When a female is ready for her nature to be defined, she drinks the blood of the male she has chosen. His DNA becomes the pattern her body uses to define her animal nature. Is that what you saw? Was Carissa drinking blood?"

"I'd hoped it was just a dream, but... Carissa is a shapeshifter?" She shook her head and hurried on ahead as if she could outrun the truth. He kept pace with her anxious strides but allowed her time to absorb the information. Suddenly, she stopped short and faced him, her expression a tense mixture of confusion and dread. "If Quinn is her lover, why did she choose the blond man for her transformation?"

"I wasn't there. You'll have to ask Carissa to explain her decision. Still, you need to remember one important fact. Defining a female is not a sexual act. The ritual often stirs emotions that lead to sex, but sex is not necessary for the ritual's success. Many females are defined by their lovers, but many are also defined by prominent members of their parents' clan. It depends if the clan alpha wants to create a bond with another clan or increase his clan's numbers." He knew more about Carissa's situation than he was letting on, but Ava would accept the complexities more easily if her sister explained.

Speculation narrowed Ava's gaze and she moved closer, managing to appear fierce despite the difference in their sizes. "What does the clan alpha have to do with it? You said the woman decides who defines her."

Damn, she was perceptive. This was the part he'd been dreading the most, the part she would find the most offensive. "According to the Charter, the set of rules governing the Therian nation, a female has until her twenty-first birthday to name her guide, that's the male she wishes to participate in her definition."

"And if she hasn't decided by her twenty-first birthday?"

"Her father or her clan alpha can petition the council for permission to define her by force. I don't agree with the practice and I'm leading the push to have the policy changed."

"Glad to hear it." She started walking again, her steps stiff and purposeful. She might not know where she was going, but she intended to get there fast.

"Ava." A pause in her marching stride was her only response. "There's another policy you need to understand."

"I'm listening," she assured him even though she didn't turn around.

They wove their way between trees and around rock formations, following the gentle undulation of the ground. He ignored the persistent tightening in his belly and the pain intensifying with each step. He could not give in to his hunger until she understood the conflict surrounding them. "Once a female has been defined, she has until her twenty-fifth birthday to choose a mate."

"And if she refuses to name her mate, her father or the clan alpha can petition the council for permission to mate her by force?" Bitterness made her tone brittle and she suddenly stopped and faced him again. "Osric was forced on my mother, wasn't he? That's why she ran away from your precious Therian nation. She was protecting us from...all of this bullshit!"

"I already told you I don't agree with the practice, but we are not human. Our biological needs are different, more demanding than anything you've experienced before. Females need to be claimed for their own safety. Once a male and a female bond, their bodies synchronize and her heat cycles will no longer affect other males. But until she's in sync with one man, she is fair game for any unbound male."

"Oh that sounds delightful. Where do I sign up?" All of her feisty heat suddenly sputtered out and the color drained from her face. "This is why Osric is after us. We just turned twenty-five."

"The Alpha Council granted Osric's petition for an official intervention." They'd reached the crux of the conflict and his cat surged in response, hungry and demanding. He'd hoped to give her a little more time, to approach her with more finesse. But he was out of options. He needed energy now. "I don't know who he's chosen as your mate, but if the wolves had caught up with you instead of me, you'd be on your way to the Therian version of a shotgun wedding."

CARLY IDES STARED THROUGH the double eyepiece of the microscope, too frustrated to analyze the newest sample. Osric had entered the lab twenty minutes ago and casually sat down at the small round table. He didn't say a word, but she could feel his eyes roaming over her body and knew it was only a matter of time before he made his next sexual demand.

Submitting to him had seemed like the only way to learn what the backers expected her to learn. In fact, they had suggested she make herself available to Osric, hoping he would open up to a lover. The problem was they weren't really lovers. She was a toy, an amusing object for him to position, ogle and manipulate.

Under ordinary circumstances... She didn't let the thought go any further. There was nothing ordinary about this situation. She was locked in a secret research facility somewhere in Colorado's Rocky Mountains. At least she thought she was still in Colorado. She'd arrived by helicopter, so it was hard to determine exactly how far they'd flown.

She was a willing captive, however, having agreed to the unusual arrangement in exchange for a once-in-a-lifetime opportunity. Along with a select group of other scientists, she studied a species the vast majority of humanity didn't know existed. Shapeshifters. Therians, as they preferred to be called, were not only real, they were utterly amazing. So, if she had to put up with the lecherous behavior of one of her supervisors, it was a small price to pay to participate in the program.

Besides, if she were brutally honest with herself, once her pride was silenced, she enjoyed their little games.

"Turn around and lift your lab coat. I want to see if you're still in compliance."

Her hands clutched the edge of the workspace and she took a deep breath. The challenge was not responding to his touch, it was concealing the true depth of her pleasure as her body came alive. He'd insisted she wear only skirts with nothing underneath. It left her vulnerable, *accessible* for whatever he chose to do.

She'd encouraged Osric's advances at the direction of the backers, the mysterious three who oversaw and funded the Therian project. They expected her to slip beneath Osric's defenses and learn his true motivations. But Osric would never confide in her. She was a mere human and he was Therian. He was an invaluable resource, even if the backers didn't trust him, and she was expendable.

Pausing for a moment, she considered her next move. She was getting nowhere with her current strategy. He thought she was weak and malleable, which meant there was no reason to respect her. She'd observed the mating habits of predators often enough to know females frequently challenged males, forcing him to prove his strength before she submitted to his demands.

"I'm bored with these games." She kept her tone even and carefully erased any hint of emotion from her expression before she pivoted on her stool and faced him. "We were both curious and now our curiosity has been sated. I think it's best if we move on. No hard feelings. No regrets."

He pushed to his feet and stalked toward her, his tall, lean body moving with inherent grace. A shiver of excitement raced down her spine. Oh yeah, she had his attention now. He claimed to have a daughter in her mid-twenties, so he had to be pushing fifty. Yet not a speck of gray marred his dark hair and his skin was unlined, somehow ageless.

He grabbed her knees and forced her legs apart, or as far apart as her narrow skirt allowed. "Is that really what you want?" He grabbed the back of her hair and tilted her head until their gazes locked. His dark brown eyes were filled with lust and just a hint of cruelty. "I've been gentle with you so far. Humans tend to be fragile. Perhaps that was a mistake. Shall we see if you can take—"

The lab door banged open and General Milliner stormed into the lab. Carly had no idea which army employed him or if general was a fictitious title. It didn't really matter. His authority was unquestionable and most people simply called him "sir". One third of the mysterious backers, General Milliner had appeared numerous times on video screens, but this was the first time Carly had been in the same room with him. He was dressed in jeans and a long-sleeved pullover shirt, but casual clothes couldn't hide the autocratic tilt of his head or the unrelenting strength in his posture. With buzzed gray hair and cold blue eyes, he appeared to be in his late fifties.

Osric stepped back and let her slide off the stool. She quickly straightened her skirt, but the general's upraised brow assured her that he'd noticed the intimate position.

"General," Osric greeted in a calm, cool tone.

Ignoring him entirely, General Milliner looked at her. "Have you made the appropriate adjustments to the formula?"

"Of course, sir." She took a step away from Osric before adding, "But I was hoping for a new test subject. The results will be more accurate if the test subject hasn't been exposed to any of the earlier combinations."

Milliner's expression didn't change. He stared at her with steely expectation. "I am nothing if not efficient. Delivering three new test subjects is what brought me here today. Two are younger than I prefer, but the Therians are taking every precaution, which makes test subjects harder and harder to acquire." Before her brain could fully register the repugnance of his casual statement, he moved on. "Osric lost one of the twins, so the compound is now our top priority."

"What are you talking about?" Osric put himself back in Milliner's line of vision.

"According to my contact, a total of six males from various shifter clans gathered at the cat sanctuary two nights ago." He turned toward Osric, his gaze expressing the displeasure his casual tone concealed. "Rebel activities can be orchestrated using video conferencing and email. There's only one reason they all needed to be there in person."

Osric shook his head, clearly in denial. "They would never attempt the ritual this soon. There's no way Carissa would allow it. She grew up believing she was human."

Carly didn't know what ritual Osric meant, but he sounded traumatized by the development.

"If what you've told us is true, she didn't need to be a willing participant." Milliner sounded almost bored. "Didn't you force this awakening on her mother?"

"We did and our attempt failed." Osric shook his head. "Why would they have acted so quickly?"

Milliner laughed, the sound harsh and caustic. "To protect her from you. From us. Even if the ritual failed, her animal nature is doubtlessly established. Carissa is no use to us now."

"But Ava is still a possibility." Osric straightened his shoulders and glared at Milliner. "Ava is my daughter. I'm not giving up. I know we can create a true Therian."

Waving away Osric's conviction, Milliner said, "I don't honestly care if we have one person who can shift into ten animals, or ten who can each shift into one. I'm interested in the transformation itself and the abilities each shifter develops once their animal nature is mature."

"But you've never seen a true Therian. You have no idea—"

"We've decided to focus on known abilities, rather than dreaming about some mythic super-shifter who might or might not exist." The proverbial "we" meant the three backers, and the pronouncement took the wind out of Osric's sails. He fidgeted, rebellion still burning in his dark eyes, but he could find no adequate argument.

Barns, the head of security, tapped on the open door, drawing their attention. "Sorry to interrupt."

"What's the matter?" Osric asked even though Milliner was actually in charge.

"Something tripped one of the perimeter sensors. We don't have cameras out that far, so I dispatched a team to check it out. I doubt it's anything serious, but I thought I'd make you aware."

"Could the sensor have malfunctioned?" Milliner asked.

"It's possible," Barns admitted. "But it's more likely an animal triggered the alarm. Just wanted to keep you in the loop."

Osric nodded. "If you learn anything conclusive, let me know."

"Of course." After nodding to the general, Barns left.

"Does that happen often?" Milliner's gaze remained sharp and suspicious.

"We're in the middle of a protected wilderness. It's a wonderful deterrent for humans, but the wildlife creates its own challenges."

Milliner's gaze shifted to Carly as he motioned Osric toward the door. "Go supervise the follow-up. Any possible threat is too important to leave to an underling."

No one was fooled by the comment. Osric had been dismissed so Milliner could speak with Carly alone. Osric shot Carly a warning glare but kept his mouth shut as he stalked from the room.

"Have you learned anything new?" Milliner waited until Osric's footfalls had faded before he asked the question.

She glanced pointedly at the surveillance camera. "Is it safe to talk?"

"I took the system offline shortly after I arrived. I'll restore it before I leave the complex."

Accepting his explanation with a stiff nod, she said, "I'm not sure there's anything new to learn." She fiddled with one of the buttons on her lab coat as she composed her expression enough to meet his penetrating stare. "You apparently know more about what's going on than Osric does."

"The setback with Carissa is bound to make him reckless. It's more important than ever that you find a way to make him trust you. We're certain he's hiding something important, but we haven't been able to determine what it is."

"I understand. I'm just not sure he'll ever tell me what you're hoping to learn. To be blunt, sir, I'm human. To his way of thinking that makes me insignificant and suspect."

He moved closer, hands clasped behind his back. "We understand the challenges. That's why we've decided to up the ante. If you succeed in learning his endgame, we'll lift the restrictions listed in your contract. You'll be able to come and go as you please, which will enable you to enjoy the monetary rewards we've already promised you."

Dread twisted her stomach into a formidable knot. He made it sound so simple, so attainable. She knew it was far more complicated than he realized, but being able to leave the complex was a serious temptation. Money didn't mean much while she had no way to spend it.

Perhaps she'd given in too easily. Osric was a predator. He thrived on the chase and she'd fallen into his arms like fast-food. She needed to tease and tempt, surrender a bit and then pull away. "He has access to every room in the facility. I have nowhere to escape him, no way to refuse his advances."

"And predators enjoy the hunt as much as the feast," the general mused.

"Exactly."

"I'll have the codes to your living quarters and your office changed immediately. Is there anything else you need to make this work?"

"If I think of something, I'll let you know."

He nodded, cool blue eyes stark and assessing. "This is extremely important to us."

"I'm aware." She smiled as she began formulating a new strategy. "I'll do my best, sir."

"That's all we ask."

AVA JUST STARED AT Kyle, unable to pluck one thought out of the whirlwind assailing her mind and form a coherent sentence. Osric had been forced on her mother and now he intended to force a mate on her. This wasn't the Middle Ages. How did he expect to get away with rape and coercion? Her gut clenched and bile rose into the back of her throat. "Carissa wasn't forced to..."

"No. She has been defined, but she participated in the ritual willingly."

Her vision confirmed his claim. Carissa hadn't just been willing, she'd reveled in the savage ritual.

Needing a distraction from the overwhelming dread, Ava focused on a random detail. "What sort of shifter is Carissa now?" Ava was reluctant to believe any of it, but the evidence was mounting. "The man I saw in the vision was really tall, with sharp features and strange gold eyes."

"Therian eyes all turn gold as our true nature surges."

That was a deflection if she'd ever heard one. "Who defined my sister and why are you so reluctant to talk about him?"

Kyle sighed, but the tension in his features remained. "It's likely you saw Ian Douglas, he's the Therian raptor I mentioned before. He's old and powerful and—"

"This man wasn't old, thirty-five, maybe forty at the very most."

"We don't age the same way humans age. We mature slower and decline faster. A Therian remains in his or her prime for at least a hundred years. Some have lived much longer. Your sister's definition was special, unique. I honestly think it's best if she explains what happened and the decisions she's made because of all she's learned."

It was as close to a straight answer as he'd given her, but she couldn't help feeling he was still evading something important.

The stillness of the forest mocked her anxiety. She needed to think, analyze what he'd told her once her emotions had stabilized. "I'm giving you twenty-four hours. If we haven't made it out of this wilderness by then, you tell me everything that's happened to Carissa."

"Ava."

She looked at him and grimaced. His skin looked pale and distinct creases now framed his mouth. "What's wrong? You look terrible."

He shrugged off the backpack and stalked toward her, golden veins shooting through his green eyes. "I'd hoped it wouldn't come to this, but I can't wait any longer."

Matching him step for step, she backed up until her hips hit a rock formation. "You can't wait for what?"

"Energy." His arms shot out and pulled her toward him. "I need you now."

She shoved against his chest and twisted her face away. "Let go!"

He wrapped one arm around her waist and tangled his other hand in her hair. "Look at me."

"No." His fingers tightened and he slowly pulled her head back around. She shut her eyes, refusing to be mesmerized by his gold-threaded gaze.

"I don't want to hurt you." His mouth brushed against hers, his breath warm and moist against her lips. "Don't fight me, sunshine. I can't be gentle if you make this a battle."

She tried to turn her head, but his hand held firm. "Why do you need to kiss me to...refuel?"

"You're still latent, so your instincts will resist. It will be almost impossible for me to access what I need unless you're very distracted."

Before she could reply, his mouth covered hers. He tilted her head back and slid his lips over and against hers. Her arms were trapped against his chest, maintaining some distance between their bodies. Still, she was surrounded by his warmth and controlled by his strength. The combination stirred something deep inside her, something dark and primitive.

His tongue traced the seam of her lips, his intention obvious. She clenched her teeth and pressed her lips together. If she surrendered to his kiss, how much more would he expect? She hadn't asked him to heal her. *But healing you is what left him weak.*

Damning her conscience for a meddlesome bitch, she slowly opened her eyes. "Will you stop with just a kiss?" He hadn't pulled back and her lips brushed against his with each word.

"I'll try." The shimmering gold had taken over his gaze, as if a mountain lion looked out from his human face. "But I need to touch you. Energy can't transfer through clothes."

He'd had to touch bare skin before he could heal her. It stood to reason that this would be the same. Besides, he'd already seen her in her bra, so what difference did it make. "If this doesn't fill your tank, you're out of luck. I'm not having sex with you."

His only response was to nip her lower lip and reluctantly let go. He took off his coat and spread it over the rock behind her then did the same with his shirt. She watched the muscles in his chest flex and his abdomen ripple. Damn. Fully dressed he'd looked athletic, but his torso was utterly ripped. She settled back against the leather-padded rock and enjoyed the view.

"Now you." His voice sounded gruff and dry, reminding her that their undressing had a higher purpose. She raised her arms and he pulled her t-shirt off over her head then let it fall to the rock behind her. "The more you enjoy this, the easier it will be for me to access what I need." He wrapped his arms around her and eased his knee between her legs.

She placed her hands on his thick upper arms and heat cascaded through her body. He wasn't bulky like a bodybuilder. Every inch of his physique was sculpted and lean. His head descended slowly, eyes glowing, lips parted.

"Don't be afraid," he whispered against her lips. "I'm not going to hurt you."

She wasn't afraid, exactly, just tense beyond belief. She closed her eyes and silenced her mind, trying to relax so she'd stop trembling. He needed this because he'd healed her. It was only fair that she... His mouth covered hers and her thoughts scattered as sensations erupted all over her body.

Her nipples tingled, her bra gently rasping as he slid her up and down on his thigh. Her core felt tight yet liquid, ready for more than a kiss. Aching desire sped her pulse and heated her blood, making her anxious and needful.

His tongue teased its way past her lips as his fingers traced her spine. She took her cue from him, exploring with cautious abandon. He was hot and hard everywhere she touched and not just with her hands. The unmistakable ridge of his erection pressed into her belly, assuring her this was more than just distracting for him.

Taking the kiss deeper, he echoed the sensual rhythm of their hips with the possessive stroke of his tongue. One of his hands grasped her bottom, maintaining the steady rocking, as his other unfastened her bra. She murmured a protest against his lips as his hand slipped beneath the loosened material and cupped her breast. He teased her nipple with his thumb while his fingers gently massaged her fullness.

This was more than just a kiss, far more than a simple distraction. The ache between her thighs became a distinct pulse and her clit seemed to echo her heartbeat. She arched into the next rotation, pressing hard against his thigh. He pinched her nipple and the sharp sensation zinged down to her clit. She gasped, inadvertently separating their lips as the tension wound even tighter.

He lifted her to the rock and tossed her bra aside. Sunlight touched her breasts for a moment before his lips closed around one nipple and his hand covered the other. Her skin tingled and warmed, her desire for him burning hotter than the sun.

This was insane. She'd never been this turned-on before and they'd done little more than kiss. He latched on to her breast, the slow, demanding suction accentuating the persistent throb between her thighs. Her head dropped back on her shoulders and she pressed herself deeper into his mouth.

What he was doing felt good, but she needed his kiss. Wanted the slide of his tongue against hers and the intoxication of his taste. Grasping his face between her hands, she drew him up until his mouth hovered over hers. His gaze burned into hers, but his lips remained just out of reach.

"Say it." The demand was firm yet whisper soft. "Tell me what you want."

"Kiss me."

As soon as the words passed her lips, he pulled her forward and wrapped her legs around his waist. She clutched his back as his mouth claimed hers in a starkly sexual kiss. Her breasts flattened against his chest and his tongue thrust in and out of her mouth, mimicking a bolder penetration.

Her skin came alive with tingling heat, over-sensitized yet pleasurable. His hands moved over her back and arms, drawing the tingles into her chest. She couldn't breathe, couldn't think, could only feel the sizzling currents he stirred within her.

He tore his mouth away from hers and they both gasped. Hot tendrils of energy flowed from her into him as pleasure radiated through her body. She shivered and groaned, clutching his back with her arms and his waist with her legs.

Leaning forward, he braced her against the rock without releasing her from his embrace. "Are you all right?"

She nodded then rested her head on his shoulder, not quite ready to disentangle her body from his. It had felt similar to an orgasm yet distinctly different too. She still felt sort of muddled. "Did you take enough?"

He chuckled, his breath stirring her hair. "Are you offering more?"

Easing back just far enough to look into his eyes, she used their closeness to hide her naked breasts. "No. I just want to make sure this was worth it."

His brows arched at the subtle slur but amusement gleamed in his green eyes. "I'll have to try harder next time."

"There better not be a next time." She wasn't sure why she kept challenging him. He'd done nothing to deserve her attitude, but the impulse popped into her mind before logic could temper the reaction.

"You don't need to piss me off." He grasped her hips and rubbed his erection against her sex, gaze narrowed and bright. "Just say the word. I'll be glad to finish what we started."

"I'm sorry." She unhooked her ankles and started to scoot back, but he caught her knees and kept her pelvis flush with his.

"If you're ready for more, we might be able to get the hell out of here."

She stilled, painfully aware of her hardened nipples and flushed skin. "What do you mean?"

"If you're willing to keep going, I should be able to trigger another spike like the one that brought us here."

"Or I might teleport us to Antarctica."

"You're no longer in danger." He swept his hand down her arm but his gaze remained on her face. "If I help steady the surge, all you'll have to do is visualize the destination."

"There isn't any other way to trigger this power surge?"

His lips curved into a sexy smile as his hand repeated its light caress. "Pleasure, pain or fear. I'm pretty sure you're not afraid of me. Would you rather experiment with pain or continue—" He jerked his head to the left and his body tensed.

"What's—"

He halted her question with an upraised hand, head cocked as he listened for the subtlest sound. "Get dressed. We've got company." He stepped back and helped her down from the rock. Snatching her t-shirt off the rock, she pulled it on without bothering to find her bra. He donned his shirt but slung his jacket over his shoulder as he handed the backpack to her. "Don't put it on. If we need to run, drop it. Understand?"

She nodded, still unsure why he believed someone was out there. Finally she heard the distant growl of an engine. But there were no roads. There was probably enough room for a small vehicle in-between the standing trees, but that still left the fallen trees and forest debris.

The noise faded as suddenly as she'd identified it and still Kyle didn't relax. "Keep walking as if nothing's wrong."

"I don't hear it anymore," she whispered.

"It's idling, but it's still there."

More of his "Therian" abilities? He'd heard the engine long before she had.

"Halt!" Two uniformed soldiers emerged from the trees on their right. One pointed a compact assault rifle at Kyle as the other one spoke. "This is a restricted area. How did you get back here?"

In the blink of an eye, Kyle's demeanor changed. Gone was his ultra-cautious tension. His shoulders stooped and he ambled forward, apparently oblivious to the threat. "Dude, we are *so* lost. Just point us in the right direction and we'll get out of your hair. Promise."

The armed soldier took a menacing step forward and snapped, "Hands up. Now!"

"Whoa, chill out, man." Kyle raised his hands as he inched farther forward. "There's no need for threats and stuff. Is this like, private property or something?"

"We're with the Forest Service," the spokesman claimed. "Accompany us to our vehicle so we can verify your identities. We have no choice but to document this infraction, but you should be free to go once we've determined who you are."

"Sorry, dude. No can do." Kyle lunged at an angle, taking his body out of rifle range as he jerked the weapon out of the shooter's hands. In a blur of aggressive motion, he slammed the stock against the side of the gunman's head and spun to confront the speaker with the pilfered rifle. "Hands up!"

With obvious reluctance, the soldier complied.

"Who sent you?" Kyle tucked the rifle more snugly against his shoulder, punctuating the question with the subtle threat.

The soldier just glared at him in mutinous silence, so Kyle swung the rifle again, knocking the second soldier unconscious with one well-placed blow. "Let's get out of here."

"And go where?" Ava cried, not sure the violence had improved their situation. "We have no idea where we are. How do you know they aren't from the Forest Service?"

"Forest rangers don't carry M16s." He checked the safety then swung the rifle onto his shoulder and reached for the backpack. "At least they spoke English. Chances are good we're still in the States."

"Chances are even better that whoever sent them to question us will send someone else when they don't return."

"All the more reason for us to get moving." His gaze narrowed and he nodded toward the fallen men. "Check their pockets. See if they're foolish enough to carry identification. And toss me their radios."

Her pulse kicked up a notch as she approached the unconscious speaker. He'd landed on his side, so she patted his back pockets before rolling him onto his back. "Nothing. Not even dog tags." She unhooked his two-way radio from his belt and tossed it to Kyle.

"I'm not surprised. Their uniforms are generic." He placed the radio on a large rock and smashed it with the butt of the rifle.

As she patted the shooter's back pocket, she felt the telltale bulk of a wallet. She pulled the wallet out and unfolded it. "Silly man. Colorado Driver's License." She looked up at Kyle and smiled. "Told you we hadn't gone far."

"I'm glad you were right, but there are places in Colorado that are still dangerously remote. What's his name?"

"Daniel Edgewater. Does that mean anything to you?" She tossed the shooter's radio to Kyle as well.

Kyle caught the radio and shook his head. "I'll have Eli run a background check on him, see what he can uncover."

She had no idea who Eli was and there were too many other questions she needed answered first, so she didn't ask. She stood and brushed off her knees. "Can you still hear their vehicle?"

"Yep." After smashing the second radio, he headed off through the trees.

She quickly followed, more than ready for the adventure to end.

The Jeep lacked any official markings, but it was stripped down and utilitarian, obviously meant for military use. Kyle slung the backpack onto the floor behind the driver's seat then placed the rifle on top of the pack. After covering the weapon with his jacket, he climbed in and closed the door. Ava hurried to the other side and sat in the passenger seat.

The Jeep had left an obvious trail as it approached. Kyle shifted the vehicle into gear and took off in the opposite direction. Ava wholeheartedly supported the decision. If it was the policy of whoever sent the soldiers to ask questions at gunpoint, Ava had no interest in meeting them.

They found a swift-moving stream and followed the water downhill. Hopefully the stream would empty into a river and the river would lead them back to civilization. The grassy bank was just wide enough for the Jeep. Occasionally Kyle steered into the water to avoid a tree or rock formation. The vehicle dipped and swayed with nauseating force, but it was much better than being on foot.

The stream was a tributary just as Kyle had hoped. The river wasn't much bigger than the stream, but the wide, rocky bed indicated a greater capacity. It also allowed Kyle to travel faster than he'd driven along the mountain stream.

They rounded a bend and found a charming railed bridge spanning the river. "It's dirt, but it's a road," Kyle muttered as he carefully maneuvered up the steep embankment and on-to the road. Continuing his downhill strategy, he wended his way along the dirt road.

Lengthening shadows and cooling air warned of impend-ing twilight. After an hour or so, Ava relaxed enough to stop looking behind them. The mercenaries were likely on foot and Kyle had destroyed their radios, but it was possible they weren't the only team combing the valley.

She blew out a shaky breath and settled back in the seat. If the mercenaries had arrived a few minutes earlier, they would have been treated to quite a show. What was wrong with her? She'd never made out with a man she'd just met. Even if the primary purpose had been transferring energy, the method had been undeniably sexual.

A guilty flush crept up her neck and she looked at Kyle. His face was ashen, jaw clenched, and he gripped the wheel with both hands. "What's wrong?" He looked even worse than he had before.

"Hunger's back." The throaty growl in his words sent a shiver down her spine.

Damn it. That's what she was afraid he'd say. She looked around the secluded road for any sign of civilization. There was none, but even if they pulled over and tried again, why hadn't the transfer worked the first time? "Can you...take more from me?"

"I might have to." He groaned, clutching his abdomen with one hand while he maintained control of the Jeep with the other.

"Pull over and let me drive." He didn't argue, further proof his distress was real. She waited until they'd switched seats before she spoke again. "Are you afraid you'll hurt me? Why don't we just do it now?"

"I thought a snack would get me through until I could eat a proper meal." He slumped in the seat, arms crossed over his belly, head resting back against the seat. "Apparently, I need more than a kiss can release. Without a trained feeder, I'd need a full-body connection."

"You mean—"

"Sex." His eyes squeezed shut as his body convulsed.

She watched in helpless alarm. Even if she was willing to have sex with him, he didn't appear capable at the moment.

The spasm passed and he took a deep breath. "I need to be inside you to fully access your Therian energy." He relaxed enough to open his eyes and added, "I know that's not what you want." He wiped his brow with his forearm then motioned toward the road. "So, drive. I'll fight it as long as I can, but eventually my cat will take control."

Chapter Three

"I need another beer," Nate Fitzroy snapped and his youngest son Dhane scooted out of the vinyl booth and rushed toward the bar dominating the far wall of the dimly lit room.

"Was I ever such a kiss ass?" Bruce, the oldest of Nate's three sons, asked as he tossed back a shot of whiskey. Bruce was ambitious and mean and couldn't be bothered with pleasantries.

Years of necessity had taught Nate how to temper his impatience with diplomacy and he'd about given up hope that Bruce would ever learn to control his violent tendencies. A Fitzroy had been Blue River Pack alpha for seven generations, but times were different now, far more complicated. Strength and aggression were no longer enough. An alpha also needed stealth and strategy. It was a lesson Bruce needed to learn if he hoped to survive, much less rise to power.

Dhane returned with a bottle of beer in one hand and a shot of whisky in the other. Trying to rack up points with his big brother as well as his father? Nate fought back a smile. Bruce was right. Dhane was a world-class kiss ass.

The bar was teeming with people, most of them human. If this had been an official pack meeting, they'd have gathered at the Clubhouse, a private hideaway where Blue River

58

Pack was free to indulge their wilder appetites. But Nate wasn't sure what he wanted to do next and he never allowed his pack to see his indecision. An alpha must be strong and decisive, always in command.

Dhane slipped back in beside Bruce and slid the beer across the table. "If you don't believe Robert's explanation, what do you think happened to Ava?"

Robert claimed that he'd finally found the cabin where Ava had been hiding, but before he could capture her she'd literally vanished right before his eyes. "I think Kyle Lashton beat us to the finish line and Rob is afraid to admit it. I've heard stories of cats who can teleport, but I've sure as hell never met one. Besides, Ava is still latent, which means Rob is full of shit." Nate took a drink of beer while his sons reacted to his statement.

"Then Rob should be afraid," Bruce sneered. "He begged for the opportunity to prove himself. If he fucked this up, the others will make him pay."

"I'll decide what happens to Robert," Nate stressed. "We need to reposition our efforts, refocus. If my sources are accurate, and they usually are, Carissa has been defined."

"I said all along that we didn't need Osric. All he did was slow us down."

Nate waved away Bruce's conclusion. It was more evidence of his narrow-minded view of life. "If it weren't for Osric, we would have been kept in the dark."

"As usual," Dhane muttered. "Cats dominate both councils. We only have what power they allow us. It isn't right."

It was an oversimplification. There were more cats on the Alpha Council simply because there were more cat clans. As for the Prime Council, two of the four members were cats. But Kyle's strongest ally was Ian Douglas and he was a bird.

Rather than correct his son, Nate said, "That's why it's so important that Bruce define Ava."

"What?" Bruce set the shot glass down, gaze narrowed and intense.

It was time for a test, a final exam, one that would prove Bruce worthy of his heritage or leave him at the mercy of his own failings. The mission Nate was about to propose would require a calm, strategic mind. If Bruce rushed in filled with blind arrogance, the cats would destroy him. But if he took his time, gathered facts and chose his course wisely, he would secure a prize coveted by every unmated male in the Therian nation.

Controlling an Omni Prime would shift the balance of power like nothing else could. Nate would do it himself, but it would have to be done by force and Nate had never possessed the stomach for rape. Bruce, on the other hand, was not only amoral enough to commit such a loathsome act, he'd probably enjoy it. But first, he'd have to steal Ava away from Kyle Lashton.

He looked into his firstborn's cold hazel eyes and fought back a shiver. "We've screwed around long enough. I want you to take care of this personally. Figure out where Kyle has taken her and then fuck her into submission. And I mean *only* fuck. I still want to try the ritual, but I'll choose the six men who participate. I'll say it one last time. Fuck her as often as you like, but if you define her, I'll kill you."

"I get it. She can drink my come just not my blood. At least not yet." Cruel anticipation made Bruce's eyes gleam.

"Lashton isn't just going to let this happen and he's got the backing of the Prime Council. Do I have permission to kill a network Prime?"

"They'll declare war on us," Dhane muttered, his gaze shifting from his father to Bruce and back.

Already disappointed with the direction of Bruce's thinking, Nate kept his expression blank. This was the right thing to do, the only thing to do. Bruce needed to prove himself once and for all or pay for his impertinence. "The cats already have one of the sisters. We cannot let them control both. I'll deal with the consequences. All you have to do is bring me the girl."

CARLY SQUELCHED THE last twinge of pity stubbornly compressing her heart and pushed the needle into the IV tubing. Before her conscience could resurface, she squeezed the syringe and watched the light blue liquid flow toward the patient. The new test subjects were all so damn young. She'd chosen the oldest of the three, the one who appeared least traumatized by their capture, and still the girl was little more than a child.

"What will this do to me?" The young woman stared up at her with wide green eyes. She was surprisingly composed given the circumstances. She'd been darted like an animal and brought to a paramilitary complex. Now she was strapped to a treatment table while an unknown chemical flowed into her vein. Through it all there had been no hysterics, no pleas for mercy or terrified tears. This one had been protective, frequently using herself as a shield when the guards or technicians ventured too close to the other two.

According to project procedures, Carly wasn't supposed to answer questions. She was supposed to give directives and remain emotionally detached. "You'll be fine." The lie tasted bitter on Carly's tongue, but *Life as you knew it is over. You're now the property of the backers* sounded so pessimistic.

"Will I be released when you're finished with me or do these tests end with an autopsy?" Her lips trembled and tears gathered behind her thick lashes. Somehow she managed not to cry.

Carly rotated her body so her back was to the camera then whispered, "If you die, I'll be punished. We need you alive." It was the only reassurance she could offer and she wasn't even sure it was a mercy. Before the girl could speak again, Carly snatched her tablet computer off the foot of the bed and hurried from the room.

Damn it. She could not let herself be affected by their plight. Their suffering was for the greater good. If their mutative powers could be understood, and ultimately reproduced in humans, the possibilities were endless. At least that's what the backers were fond of saying. Scientific advancement never came without sacrifice. She could not lose sight of the long-range goals.

She rounded a corner and collided with Osric. Her computer slipped from her hands and she gasped. He caught the tablet half a second before it crashed onto the floor.

"Where are you off to in such a hurry?" He loitered in the intersection, teasing her with the small computer.

"My office." She straightened and smoothed her skirt then stuck out her hand with obvious expectation. Milliner had promised to change the security code to her office and her apartment so Oscric couldn't barge in on her. She was anxious to find out if the general had kept his word. "I just injected the refined formula into one of the new test subjects."

"That's right. Milliner dropped off three new test subjects, didn't he?" The announcement about Carissa's definition had likely distracted him. "Are they male or female? Have you been able to identify their clan?"

"They're tigers." *Just like you, asshole.* "Maybe you know them," she added with a casual shrug.

"I better not know them." He seemed anything but amused by the possibility. "The backers assured me that no one from my bloodline will ever be touched unless I approve the acquisition."

"All I know is they're from one of the tiger clans and all three are female." He stared off into the distance, clearly lost in thought, so she quickly snatched her computer from his grasp. "I need to transfer the girl's information and then type up my observations, and I left my external keyboard in my office. Call me old-fashioned if you like, but I still can't type worth crap on the touch screen."

"So upload the readings off your tablet and use the desktop in the observation booth to document your findings." It wasn't a suggestion. She heaved a sigh and fell in step beside him. "Have you been avoiding me?"

"I've been busy." She hadn't intentionally set out to avoid Osric. Preparations for the next phase of testing had made her less accessible than usual. But the change in her schedule worked perfectly with her new strategy. Operation Hard to Get had officially begun.

"Your workload hasn't kept you from me before. Perhaps I should reassign some of your responsibilities."

He sounded petulant, and it was all Carly could do not to laugh. Every child wanted most whatever they were forbidden. "I thought we settled this before. I'd prefer to keep things professional between us."

They stepped into the observation booth and the door closed behind them before he responded to her statement. "And I'd prefer you naked and on your knees."

"Then I'm afraid we're at an impasse. You want—"

The phone rang, the distinct tone identifying the caller as someone from security. With a muttered curse, Osric pushed a button and activated the speaker. "What's so urgent?"

"Delta team just returned with Charley team in tow," Barns informed him. "They've got a fascinating story. Figured you should hear it for yourself."

"Send them here."

"Yes sir. They're on their way."

"Who is he talking about?" She figured it had something to do with the tripped perimeter alarm, but Barns could be even more secretive than Osric.

"Charley team was sent to check out the phantom intruder, but they never returned. Delta team was dispatched to figure out what happened. This better not be bad news. I'm really not in the mood."

Two uniformed guards arrived a few minutes later. They nodded politely to Carly then waited for Osric to speak.

"What did you find out? And what the hell took you so long?"

The younger soldier had a nasty bruise on the side of his face. On closer inspection, Carly discovered that the older man's temple was bruised as well.

"We found two hikers, sir. One female, one male," the older guard began. "They pretended to be lost until I told them to accompany us to the vehicle so I could verify their identities."

"And then they jumped you?" Osric's tone verged on flippant. He really could use a class in non-confrontational communication.

"Yes sir." Though the soldier's posture was stiff and his shoulders squared, his gaze remained downcast. Was he humiliated by his failure or did Osric make him uncomfortable?

"Were they armed?"

"Not in the conventional sense."

"What's that supposed to mean?"

The soldier raised his chin, but he stared straight ahead. "The male was inhumanly strong and fast, sir. I believe he was one of the shifters."

"And the female?"

"We had no actual interaction with her, but Barns showed us a picture of Ava Seymour and this female looked very much like her. We also found this." Hand trembling, he held out a white, lace-trimmed bra. "Apparently we interrupted their activities."

Osric stepped closer and snatched the bra out of the guard's hand. "Describe the male." Menace infused every word.

The guard swallowed hard then licked his lips before he answered, "Dark blond hair, light eyes, either green or blue. I'm honestly not sure which. He was about my height and a whole hell of a lot stronger than he looked."

"Too vague," Osric snapped. "Did he have tattoos or scars? Did Barns show you an image of Kyle Lashton?"

"He did, but I couldn't be sure. I'm sorry, sir."

"Spent more time looking at the woman than the man?" The guard didn't respond to the provocation. "Did they leave on foot?"

The soldiers exchanged wary glances before the older one admitted, "They took our Jeep, sir. Barns has people trying to track them, but they've got a good head start."

"Unbelievable." With the bra crushed in his fist, Osric swept the workspace with his arm, sending plastic organizers and file folders catapulting across the room. "You're useless. Get out of my sight! Both of you!"

The soldiers eagerly complied and Carly moved to the far side of the console, unsure if Osric would take out his frustration on her. A long moment passed in tense silence. Carly split her attention between Osric and the door, trying to calculate her chances of slipping past him.

He raised the bra to his nose and inhaled deeply then growled and threw the undergarment across the room. "She was here!" Osric pushed his hand through his hair as he shook his head in disbelief. "She was on this property and those fools let her get away!"

Carly waited for a moment, hoping his fury would subside. Then suddenly curiosity narrowed Carly's eyes. "But what was she doing here? It seems like an odd place for a romantic tryst."

"If they kept that bastard from screwing her, I might let them live."

As usual, he was missing the point. "The guard said they were on foot. It would take days to hike back in here. Why were they out there? How did they know where to find you?"

He glared at her, nostrils flaring. "Who said they were searching for me? There's nothing connecting me to this project. I've made damn sure of it."

Was he being purposely obtuse? One glance into his cold brown eyes assured her that she was the one missing the point. Osric was nobody's fool and he knew far more about this project than she would ever be allowed to know. "Then why? You don't seem surprised, just frustrated."

"I have Kyle's sister."

This was new information. "One of the test subjects is your rival's sister? How did you get the backers to sign off on that?"

Spiteful pride curved his mouth into a thin-lipped smile. "They don't know and you're not going to tell them. She's a contingency plan, nothing more."

"If all else fails, you'll offer to trade his sister for Ava?"

"Exactly."

"Which one is—"

"I'm not a fool, Carly. You'll know what I want you to know and nothing more."

She nodded, but her gaze shifted to the double row of monitors. Which one was Klye's sister? Osric had hidden his treasure in plain sight. Her attention gravitated toward Devon's holding cell. Devon had been one of the first test subjects to be acquired. At present, she was curled up like a child, sound asleep. Relaxed and peaceful, her lovely features gave no hint of the fiery personality hidden within the compact package. Every moment Devon was awake was a challenge. Carly had often wondered why she hadn't been scrubbed from the program. Devon's body responded well to the formula, but she really was more trouble than she was worth.

But this new possibility explained so much. Osric was obsessed with Devon. He spent hours watching her, and more than once Ava had caught him pleasuring himself as he stared at images of Devon.

"Maybe they're more telepathic than we realized," Carly mused. She needed to pass on what she'd learned to General Milliner, but first she'd have to sneak away from Osric's watchful eyes. "The sister could be sending out some sort of signal, guiding Kyle to her location."

His gaze narrowed thoughtfully, but he didn't seem convinced. "Then why'd they come on foot? They can't execute a rescue without an escape vehicle. And why drag Ava along? This doesn't make sense."

He hadn't rejected her hypothesis, nor had he confirmed it. Osric seldom shared specifics about the Therians with her or the other scientists. Anything he was willing to divulge was given to the backers and they determined who benefited most from each tidbit of information. It was a frustrating and counterproductive policy, but it kept anyone from learning too much about the mysterious Therians.

"We don't know for certain it was Kyle." She'd meant to soothe him with the thought, but his reaction was anything but pacified.

His lips pressed into a thin line as he glared at Devon's monitor. "There's only one person who can tell me for sure and this time she's going to talk."

"FINALLY!" KYLE'S HANDS shook so hard he could barely operate his phone. He'd never ached this badly in his life and he still wasn't sure where he was.

"Can't they use your phone to find us?" Ava glanced at him then looked back at the winding mountain road. They'd reached pavement about an hour ago, but they had yet to stumble across anything familiar. They were headed west on Frying Pan Road and they were forty-six miles away from Basalt. But those clues didn't mean much to either of them.

"The phone's disposable," he told her. "That's probably why it's taken me so long to find a signal."

"Who are you calling?"

"Jake. He's lived all over the mountains. If he can't point us back to civilization, we're doomed."

The call connected and a female said, "Toulouse Tavern," over raucous music and overlapping conversations.

"Hey, Enya, is Jake around."

"Kyle? Where the hell are you? Half of the network is out looking for your sorry ass."

Leaning his head against the window, he smiled. Enya's familiar feistiness was a welcome reprieve from hours of confusion and pain. "It's a long story. We're west of a town called Basalt. Any clue..."

He heard Enya's muffled protest as someone ripped the phone out of her hand. "Have you passed Ruedi Reservoir?" The background noise diminished as Jake walked into an office or storeroom.

"Not yet. Last sign said we were forty-some miles from Basalt."

"They found your truck at the cabin where you were supposed to nab the other twin. Is Ava with you?"

"Yeah, she's here. We had to borrow a Jeep. Probably need to ditch it soon." Another spasm rippled through his gut and he clenched his teeth to keep from moaning.

"I'll meet you in Basalt with a couple of my guys. We'll lay a false trail with the Jeep and get you two to safety."

"Sounds perfect. We're on Frying Pan Road. Will that take use all the way to Basalt?"

"Yes. It will take you right through the center of town then hang a left on Two Rivers Road. A couple of blocks down you'll find a strip mall on your right and a ball field on your left. Pull into the strip mall. We should be waiting for you. We're closer to Basalt than you are."

"Thanks, man. I appreciate this."

"I'll add it to your tab."

Kyle ended the call but left the phone out in case they needed Jake again. Kyle had a perfectly good GPS. Unfortunately, it was on the dashboard of his truck.

"He's going to meet us in Basalt?" Ava's eyes were wide and she kept pressing her teeth into her lower lip. Though the expression was charming, her anxiety disturbed him. Even with hunger tearing him apart, he felt compelled to comfort her.

"Less than an hour and we're home free." He paused, breathing through a spasm. "Jake's going to bring a couple of his guys with him and they'll take care of the Jeep."

"Did he explain where we are?" She manufactured a smile, but her eyes were filled with worry.

He was doing his best to conceal his pain, but she was obviously not convinced. "He said he'd beat us to the rendezvous, so we must not be too far from Aspen."

"That's where Jake lives?"

"Yeah. He runs a bar there with his sister." Gnawing pain rolled over him again and a strangled groan slipped past his lips. Despite his determination to resist the urgent hunger, he was about to lose control.

"Will they be able to help you?"

All he could do was nod. The pain grew worse with each passing moment. His cat stretched and struggled against his human cage. He should have handed the phone to her, had Jake give her directions.

He gasped then forced the words out in a harsh, strained rush. "Keep going until you reach Basalt. Left on Two Rivers Road."

"Can't you navigate as we go? I'm not sensitive about backseat drivers."

"Strip mall...on right."

"Oh God, Kyle, should I pull over?"

"No!" He clutched his belly, shaking helplessly. "You promised not to run! Now tell me...directions."

She started to repeat what he'd just said but the roaring in his ears overtook the sound. Damn it. He wasn't going to make it to Basalt. He ripped his shirt off and unfastened his pants then dove toward the backseat, shifting in midair.

Oh my God. The words repeated through Ava's mind as she dragged her gaze back to the road. She had to be asleep at the wheel. People didn't turn into animals. Not in reality. Yet Kyle's long, lean body had rippled and...*flowed* right out of his pants and onto the backseat. Human one minute and— No, that wasn't right. According to Kyle, he wasn't human.

And neither was she.

She glanced over her shoulder, needing to assure herself that a large, limp cougar was now sprawled across the backseat of the Jeep. A Jeep they'd stolen from mercenaries after teleporting to the middle of nowhere. She'd thought being hunted by her abusive father was harrowing enough. Suddenly her life had gone from *Law and Order* to the *Twilight Zone.*

And he'd been right to make her promise. Part of her wanted to pull over, get out of the Jeep and run like hell.

As if sensing her thoughts, the cougar growled, but he lacked the strength to raise his head. "Straight to Basalt then left on Two Rivers Road, strip mall will be on the right. I was listening, Kyle. Really, I was. Just relax we'll be there soon." She felt like an idiot talking to a cat, but this was no ordinary cat. She'd only seen his transformation out of the corner of her eye and still the image was imprinted on her brain. Effortless, fluid and utterly surreal.

Kyle was a shapeshifter, an honest-to-God shapeshifter. Did that mean— No, she wasn't ready to continue that line of reasoning. She had to accept one revelation at a time.

Grasping the wheel with both hands, she focused on the road. It wouldn't do either of them any good if she put the Jeep in a ditch. Kyle's labored breathing assured her he was alive. Hopefully, he'd stay that way until they reached Jake.

She was part of the Therian nation. The realization echoed through her mind like the ominous toll of a distant gong. Her father was hunting her so he could control what sort of shapeshifter she would become. The explanation rang true, yet it seemed insufficient. Kyle had said Carissa's definition was special, unique. There was more to the story than Kyle had explained, details he hadn't reached before they were interrupted by the mercenaries. But each time she tried to fill in the blanks, she was overwhelmed by the possibilities.

Her mind was still whirling with speculation and confusion when she reached Basalt. Like so many other tiny mountain towns Basalt's main street was lined with narrow shops and restaurants, each pressed against the other in block-long rows. Ava paid more attention to the street signs than the storefronts and easily found Two Rivers Road. She turned left and then focused on the right until she located the strip mall.

A dark SUV was parked in the back corner of the lot. Three of the four doors opened as she approached and three large, leather-clad men piled out. The driver had long dark hair while his companions were both blond. It stood to reason that this was Jake and his men. They seemed to be expecting her. Still, a shiver of apprehension skittered down her spine.

There were a few cars parked near the restaurant at the other end of the mall, but none were occupied. She parked a couple of spaces away from the SUV and hesitated. Was she about to jump from the frying pan into the fire? Who should she trust? Was the enemy of her enemy really her friend, and how could she know for sure that they were Osric's enemies?

Something bumped her seat hard enough to rock her forward. She looked back and found cougar-Kyle's massive amber eyes watching her intently. Had he head-butted the seat or swiped it with his paw? Either possibility was so unbelievable she just shook her head and sighed.

The dark-haired man tapped on her window, but his attention was immediately drawn to the backseat. "Why'd he shift?" he asked as she rolled down the window.

"He's hungry. Are you Jake?"

"In the flesh." A roguish smile parted his lips as his thick-lashed gaze settled on her. "Ava, I presume. My hunters were starting to wonder if you exist."

She glanced at the two blond men waiting by the SUV. They were both tall and brawny. One wore a biker jacket, the other a leather vest. Both sported wallet chains and extensive tattoos. Men like these had been hunting her as well as Osric and Kyle? What made her so popular—or so hated?

Shaking away the tangent, she looked at Jake again and fought back another shiver. Without a smile, his features were sharp, his bearing watchful, his gaze downright piercing. "How should we do this?"

"Open the passenger door. I'll back up to you so he can jump in."

It made more sense than blithely walking a mountain lion across the parking lot. She looked back at Kyle and asked, "You doing okay?" He made a rumbling sound and she shook her head. Had she expected him to answer?

Spurring herself into action, she walked around to the passenger side of the Jeep and opened the door. Jake, or one of the blonds, had opened the back end of the SUV and laid down the seats. Jake backed across the parking lot until the tailgate nearly touched the open door of the Jeep.

Kyle leapt into the back of the SUV and one of the blonds closed the tailgate as the other one closed the door.

"You're with me." Jake motioned her toward the SUV.

"I'll be right there." She ran back around to the driver's side of the Jeep and dug her backpack and Kyle's jacket out from behind the seat. The rifle had slipped mostly under the seat and it would connect them with the mercenaries anyway, so she left it where it lay. "Kyle confiscated one of their guns. It's under the seat."

The blond nodded then climbed in behind the wheel. It was all neat and efficient and...strange. Had Jake told them not to talk to her or was this their idea of being respectful? It was almost as if they didn't know what to make of her. Well, the feeling was mutual. She was thrilled to be back on semi-familiar ground, but now she was surrounded by strangers.

She hurried to the passenger side of the SUV as Jake leaned across and pushed the door open for her. "Thanks," she muttered, and checked on Kyle before she locked her seat belt into place. He lay on his stomach, head resting on his crossed paws. He looked almost like an oversized housecat.

"Did he intentionally shift or was this spontaneous?" Jake waited for his men to take off before he continued on Two Rivers Road. Though dark and smoky, Jake's eyes were actually green. And he hid model-perfect features under scruffy whiskers and a bad boy's scowl.

"He weakened after he healed me." Jake shot her a side-long glance, clearly surprised by her answer. "I tried to feed him energy, but it wasn't enough. He was in pain for hours before he lost control."

"Start at the beginning. When did Kyle catch up to you and how did you end up on Frying Pan Road in a stolen Jeep?"

Kyle obviously trusted this man, but she wasn't sure she trusted Kyle. "Do you have a phone? I'd like to call my sister. Kyle said she's staying at a cat sanctuary with a man named Quinn."

He chuckled and shifted his gaze back to the road. "I guess I'd be suspicious too. What did Kyle do with his phone? It was disposable, hard to trace."

"It must be on the floor of the Jeep. His transformation sort of eclipsed everything else."

"I'll bet." He was silent for a moment, apparently lost in thought.

Ava fidgeted. His questions had been straightforward and understandable, but they made her feel defensive. She hadn't asked Kyle to heal her, certainly hadn't wanted him following her. She hadn't asked for any of this.

Staring out the window, she tried to imagine what it would be like to have friends who cared enough to come and rescue her. One phone call from Kyle and Jake stopped what he was doing and dragged two of "his men" along for the ride. Carissa loved her unconditionally, but Ava hadn't realized how isolated they were until the past caught up to their present.

"Kyle's not a healer. Was he able to fix whatever was wrong or should I arrange for someone else to take a look at you?" His tone was gentler now, less accusatory.

She pictured one of the fierce-eyed Therian men touching her, his fingers running over her bare skin and shivered. "I'm fine. We need to focus on Kyle." The corner of Jake's mouth quirked and she realized she'd included herself in Kyle's treatment. Kyle had stabilized her ribs and taken away her pain. It was only natural that she'd want to repay his kindness.

That was your justification for making out with him too, her conscience reminded. She'd kissed him and touched him, mesmerized by the texture of his flesh. If the mercenaries hadn't interrupted, how much further would it have gone? Would she have thrown caution to the wind and wiggled out of her jeans so he could screw her right there on the clothes-covered rock? How romantic.

It hadn't been romantic. It had been wild and savage and hot.

"You better think about something else." Jake's tone was deep yet tinged with amusement. "If you walk into Toulouse Tavern smelling like sex, every man in the place will think it's an invitation."

She tensed, mortified by the implication. Could he actually smell her arousal? Either he could or he could read her mind, which would be even more humiliating. She needed a distraction fast. "Toulouse Tavern? Is that your bar?"

"Yes."

Oh that was helpful. He could grill her with questions, but all he gave in return was yes and no answers? "Who is Toulouse?"

His gaze gleamed through the dimness as he glanced her way. "It's my sister's idea of irony. Toulouse Tavern sounds upscale and classy, but she pulled the name from an animated flick called *The Aristocrats*."

"I love that movie! Wasn't Toulouse the feisty orange kitten who was always getting into trouble?"

"That's him. Regular little wannabe badass."

She smiled as scenes from the movie scrolled through her mind. Such innocent amusements belonged to another lifetime, another Ava.

Glancing out the window, she spotted a road sign. They were headed south on CO 82, which would take them into the heart of Aspen. She looked at Kyle and her heart lurched. He'd rolled to his side and his eyes were closed, tongue visible between his pointed teeth. Was he resting or unconscious? "I didn't mean to hurt him. If I'd known this would happen, I wouldn't have let him touch me."

"Kyle doesn't do anything he doesn't want to do. No one is blaming you for this."

But she was blaming herself. "Is there someone at your bar who can feed him?"

"Enya, my sister. She hates doing it, but I'm pretty sure she'll make an exception for Kyle."

She refused to identify the odd tightening in her chest. It was impossible that she might be jealous. She'd only known Kyle for a matter of hours. *And he saved your life twice.* She shoved the fact to the back of her mind, annoyed once again by her conscience.

"What's your connection with Kyle?" she asked Jake.

"Different clan, same network." He looked at her and asked, "Do you know what that means? How much has Kyle told you?"

"We're all part of the Therian nation. If you're part of his network, you're a feline shifter, but you turn into something other than a cougar."

"That's the gist of it. I belong to the largest clan of tiger-shifters. Osric is my uncle, by the way. So that makes us cousins."

"We're cousins?" The revelation jarred her for a moment. Osric wasn't just a malicious bastard, he could shift into a tiger? Then the shock passed and she made the connection. Her hands clenched and looked around for a weapon. "Are you taking me to Osric?"

"God, no. I'm a rebel, just like Kyle. Me and Osric haven't been on speaking terms for years and he isn't allowed anywhere near the bar." They'd reached the outskirts of Aspen. He navigated the roundabout and jogged right on Seventh Street before turning left on Main.

Unsure how she would ever trust anyone with ties to Osric, she let her mind digress. "Other than Osric, I thought Carissa was my only living relative. This is really strange."

"She's all who's left on your mother's side of the family tree, but the Parlain side still has lots of branches."

"That's right. You said you have a sister." Ava still felt stunned. The information was so unexpected that she wasn't sure how to process it.

"I have three sisters," he corrected. "Enya's the oldest. Well, I'm the oldest child, Enya's the oldest daughter."

"Is your entire family part of the rebellion? Are your parents still alive?"

He turned down an alley and backed into a parking place near the back door of what she presumed was his bar. The building was tall and narrow, the walls muffling the music until all that remained was the distinct bass beat.

"See if you can rouse him." He pushed open the driver's door and swung his long legs to the ground.

She unfastened her seat belt and turned around, kneeling on the seat so she could reach Kyle. Her hand trembled as she reached for his triangular head. *Please God, let him still be alive.* His fur was soft and warm, and he turned into her touch, slowly opening his eyes.

Jake lowered the window then dropped the tailgate. "Can you move?" Kyle made a low rumbling sound and Jake looked up and down the alley. "It's clear." He turned and pulled open the door to the bar then swept his arm toward the opening. "Go for it." Had Jake actually understood that sound or were Therians telepathic? Kyle paused to nudge her hand then turned in a tight, rather awkward half-circle and leapt out the back of the SUV. "Want me to grab your stuff?"

It took her a second to realize Jake had been talking to her. "I can get it, but thanks." Jake closed up the back as she gathered the backpack and Kyle's jacket. "Oh my God. I forgot his pants."

"Ron and Steve will go through the Jeep before they abandon it. They're very thorough. They'll find anything you left behind."

"How are they going to return if they abandon the Jeep and why did Kyle refer to them as your men?"

"They'll call for a ride and I'm the highest-placed tiger among the rebel clan." The SUV chirped as he locked the doors then motioned her inside. "You still have a lot to learn about your new world, but let's make sure Kyle is recovering before we figure out our next move."

She hadn't forgotten about Kyle. She was just trying not to imagine how Enya would facilitate the energy transfer.

I need to be inside you to fully access your Therian energy. Kyle's words had haunted her ever since she realized another woman would be feeding him.

Jake led her up a steep, narrow staircase to the top floor of the three-level building. "Do you live up here?"

"Enya does. My house is a few miles outside town."

He led her to a bedroom halfway down the hall. A tall brunette in a black miniskirt and stiletto boots knelt next to Kyle, who was lying on his side again. "What the hell happened to him?" Her smoky-green gaze shot from Jake to Ava and back. "It's like he's been sucked dry."

"I'll explain later. Can you feed him or not?"

"Is she the one everyone's been searching for?"

Ava didn't understand the bitterness in the other woman's tone, but her resentful scowl was pretty hard to misinterpret.

"Enya, focus," Jake snapped. "Kyle needs you now. The details can wait."

"Then take her downstairs. I won't work with an audience."

At Jake's urging, Ava left the backpack and Kyle's coat on the floor and followed him down a different flight of stairs. The music grew progressively louder with each step they descended. "How did she know we were coming? Are all Therians telepathic?"

His only reply was a secretive smile.

Ava had expected a claustrophobic dance club with gyrating bodies and flashy décor. Instead the ground floor spread out to either side of the main building, creating an open, casual atmosphere. A spacious dance floor took up most of the center section. Pool tables were off to the right and a restaurant was situated on the left.

"You own three connecting units in downtown Aspen? Were your ancestors Tabors or something?" Only a silver baron could afford this sort of real estate in a resort town.

He flashed another mysterious smile. "My family settled in the area long before the rich and famous came here to ski." Motioning toward the restaurant, he asked, "Are you hungry?" He slipped out of his black leather jacket and handed it to a passing waitress. "Throw that in my office for me."

The waitress looked Ava over with a semi-hostile stare before treating Jake to a flirtatious smile. "Anything for you, Mr. Parlain."

Mr. Parlain? Did he expect such deference from all his employees?

He led her to a table in the far corner of the restaurant. The music was noticeably muted and Ava spotted transparent panels separating the restaurant from the rest of the bar. A different waitress appeared at the table before Jake could settle in his chair.

"Just coffee for me, Mary." He motioned to Ava. "Bring Ms. Seymour whatever she wants."

Ava's stomach felt tense and empty, but nothing sounded appetizing. Worry for Kyle overshadowed her appetite and made her restless. "Maybe a bowl of soup. I'm not very hungry."

"You need something substantial. You're weaker than you realize."

She glanced at the menu and cringed. How could she sit here munching a burger while Kyle struggled for life?

"Bring her a steak." He looked at Ava and added, "I presume you eat red meat. Our kind can't seem to resist it."

Nothing else sounded any better so she nodded. "That'd be great."

"How would you like it cooked?" the waitress chimed in.

"Medium rare."

"Baked potato and salad okay?"

"Sure."

"Be back in a jiff."

The waitress sauntered off and Ava looked at Jake. "Why did you presume I need to eat?"

"Therians can sense weakness in others. My tiger is going crazy because you're so drained." He scooted his chair closer to the table and lowered his voice. "I will protect you and

Kyle until you're both strong again. Now, enough stalling. Tell me what the hell happened out there."

Chapter Four

"She's still unconscious," Osric snarled as he stomped across the lab.

Carly took a deep breath and carefully controlled her expression before she turned from her computer screen and looked at him. "I told you the new formula is harder to metabolize. She might be out for a few hours yet."

"You said that a few hours ago."

When Osric's plan to interrogate Devon had been foiled by the formula's side effects, it gave Carly an idea. She'd keep Devon sedated while she attempted to notify the backers. They might not want Osric to take out his frustration on Devon if Devon were more than just a stubborn test subject. She couldn't sedate Devon indefinitely, but she'd give it a little while longer.

"I don't know what to tell you." She kept her legs tucked under her desk and tried to sound indifferent. "Giving her a harsh stimulant at this point would risk serious damage."

"Well, make damn sure no one else goes near her." He started for the door then stopped and glared at her again. "Did Milliner know about the test subjects? Did he say anything to you?"

She raised both hands and shook her head. "I have no idea what you're talking about. General Milliner delivered them, but he told me nothing specific."

"The girls are my kin, not close, but blood relatives. And I think that bastard knows it."

"Why would he intentionally provoke you like that?" Milliner was the type of person to pick at a scab until it bled. Capturing Osric's relatives for this program was well within the scope of his personality.

"You tell me. You've been all buddy-buddy with him lately."

She scoffed, folding her arms across her chest. "Yesterday was the first time I've been in the same room with him. You're paranoid."

"Maybe. And maybe I'm starting to see things clearly for the first time. I'm going out for a couple of hours. No one goes near Devon until I return."

He slammed the door behind him and Carly exhaled. Afraid he'd give it one more try on his way out of the facility, Carly accessed the security feed and watched Devon's holding cell. The door swung inward a few minutes later and Osric appeared. "So predictable," she muttered as he stalked across the small room. He patted Devon's hand and even slapped her hard enough to redden her cheek, but the young woman remained unconscious, completely limp. Carly switched to the corridor cameras and followed his progress until he left the building. "Don't hurry back on my account."

"Do you always talk to the computers?"

Carly gasped and spun around in her chair. First General Milliner and now Roberto risking personal appearances? Something about the situation was definitely escalating.

"It's been an odd night." Pushing to her feet, she straightened her skirt and offered him her hand. "Were you expected? No one warned me."

"Warned? I mean you no harm. I assure you." He pressed her hand between his, holding it far longer than necessary. "The detour was a last-minute decision. As with yours, my night has been rather odd."

He was taller than she'd realized. Videoconferencing could be misleading. But his eyes were just as dark and his features even more appealing. He wore gray dress pants and a white shirt, yet he'd folded back the sleeves, partially revealing a tattoo on his forearm. His thick brown hair brushed his shoulders and the diamond stud shimmering on his earlobe gave him a rakish air. She'd called him "the pirate" until she'd learned his name and she suspected the nickname would amuse him.

"What can I show you or are you here to see someone else?"

He moved his hand to her shoulder as he said, "Relax, *cara*, this is not a surprise inspection."

"I'm sorry. Osric has been particularly challenging today."

"Thus the reason for the parting shot?"

She smiled, ignoring the irrational urge to wrap her arms around him and press her face into the warmth of his throat. "Exactly."

His hand slid to her elbow, an unmistakable caress. "James and Tias are waiting for our call. We presumed it was important. You're not usually so persistent."

James? She pressed her lips together and started across the room. She'd heard Milliner called general so often she'd begun to think that was his first name. "I'm honestly not sure how important it is. I'll let you three decide."

His hand moved to the small of her back as they walked down the hall. The warmth of his fingers sank into her skin, the gentle pressure far more arousing than it was meant to be. Why was she so...aware of him? She sure as hell wasn't sex-starved. Osric had made sure of that. But Osric treated her like a blowup doll. He played with her when he was in the mood and walked away without a second thought.

And Roberto would be any different? Who was she kidding? If she encouraged the interest in his dark eyes, the most she could hope for was a few minutes of pleasure. She'd already compromised her self-respect to increase her standing with the backers. She was not going to do it again!

The quandary was ironic. In college she'd craved male attention, longed to participate in the sexual escapades transpiring all around her. Instead, her intelligence and ambition kept men at bay. Now her intelligence and ambition led her to a situation where she was sequestered with a group of men, vastly improving her sexual appeal.

Refocusing her mind on the present, she led Roberto to the conference room and he ushered her inside. They sat on opposite sides of the large oval table and angled their chairs toward the massive video screen. Roberto used his cell to notify the others that they'd arrived. Carly had no idea how they remotely activated the projector, but there were no controls in the conference room. Or if there were controls, Carly had no idea how to access them.

The video screen came alive, dividing into six neat segments. Tias, a striking Asian woman in her late forties or early fifties came online first. General Milliner's image appeared a few seconds later.

"What have you learned?" Tias prompted.

Carly thought the question was meant for her, but Roberto answered. "The entire convoy is lost. That wily bitch knew exactly where to strike and how to hurt us. This will set us back weeks, perhaps months."

"We don't know that it was Nehema." General Milliner was a little too quick to defend the "wily bitch" and the other two backers glared their impatience at him. "The three I took from her belong to a powerful tiger clan. This could be—"

"If anyone associated with the girl's clan knew enough about our operation to strike the supply convoy, the complex itself would be under attack. Therians don't waste time with subtleties." Tias managed to command attention without raising her voice or changing her expression. "This was Nehema and we all know it."

"Were you aware that the girls are related to Osric?" Everyone looked at Milliner, confirming Ava's suspicion that he had acted alone.

"I knew it was a possibility," he muttered. "The Therians have closed ranks. It's going to be harder and harder to get our hands on test subjects. Greater risks will have to be taken. You might as well get used to it."

"The deed is done. There is no avoiding the ramifications." Tias dismissed his defensiveness and turned to Carly. "How are your reserves?"

Rather than give Tias false hope, she took a moment to mentally inventory her supplies. "If I focus entirely on the new test subjects, I might be able to stretch my current stock out for a week."

Roberto sighed and shook his head. "Which means all of the established programs come grinding to a halt."

"We were unprepared this time," Tias admitted. "It will not happen again. I'll reroute all established supply runs and shuffle vendors wherever possible. We will not waste energy bemoaning our loss. We will move on and learn from our mistakes."

"And allow this aggression to go unanswered?" Milliner looked as if he wanted to reach through the screen and shake her. "This was an intentional provocation. I will not allow—"

"You got greedy!" Tias managed to look every bit as intimidating as her male counterpart. "We are not going to waste time and resources on your pride."

Defiance blazed in Milliner's gaze, but he said nothing more.

"I agree that our goals are more important than teaching Nehema her place," Roberto began, "but these Abolitionists have become more than an annoyance. If an opportunity presents itself, we should permanently solve the problem."

So Nehema was the leader of a group called the Abolitionists? And this group knew about shapeshifters. How odd. How many other groups of humans knew about the Therians? Maybe a better question was, are there other quasi-human species mixed in with the unsuspecting population? She shivered and released her tension with a deep breath.

After agreeing with Roberto's compromise, Tias looked at Carly and prompted, "You asked to speak with us."

The fact that they'd discussed backer business in front of her made her feel important, but she wasn't foolish enough to believe she was one of them. She was a tool, and when her usefulness had ended, they would dispose of her like any other tool.

"The guards discovered a couple of hikers, one male and one female," Carly began in a calm, clear tone.

"We were told."

If they weren't upset about the incident, she could just imagine what they were told. "Who submitted the report and what did they tell you?"

"Barns submitted the report," Milliner told her. "We were led to believe that the guards verified that the hikers were no one of consequence and then drove them a safe distance from the complex. The hikers believed they were rescued by two forest rangers."

No wonder they'd recruited a spy. How long had Osric been lying to them and how often did Barns help him falsify reports? "The truth is a little less tidy, I'm afraid. The hikers were not released. They overpowered the guards and took off in their Jeep." She waited until shock registered on their expressions but didn't give them time to reply. "And that's not the worst of it. Osric thinks the female hiker was Ava Seymour and the male was Kyle Lashton."

"Ava has been desperately eluding capture to avoid coming here." Roberto drew her attention away from the screen. "Why would she venture so near Osric's stronghold?"

"That was my question as well."

"And did he tell you?" Tias' expression remained cautious, but Carly heard hope in her soft tone.

She'd only been spying on Osric for a short time, but the backers had hoped for better results. Well, she was about to prove her worth to her demanding superiors. "Osric had no idea why Ava would intentionally put herself in such a vulnerable position, but he's pretty sure Kyle was attempting to rescue his sister."

"Osric is hiding his rival's sister among the test subjects?" Tias exchanged meaningful glances with her partners then muttered, "That sly bastard."

"He didn't intend to tell me who she is, but—"

"It's Devon." Carly wasn't surprised that Tias anticipated the punch line. She was shrewdly intelligent and every bit as ruthless as the men. "It explains his arrogance as well as his obsession with the girl."

Devon was in her mid-twenties, hardly a girl, but Carly didn't correct her supervisor. "He was infuriated by the near disaster and intended to interrogate Devon, to find out if she was somehow signaling her brother."

"Did he damage her?" Milliner scooted closer to his camera, clearly upset by the possibility. "We've accomplished more with Devon than any other test subject."

"Yes sir, I'm aware. That's why I've kept Devon sedated until I could speak with you."

"Then he hasn't harmed her?"

"No sir. Intimidation is lost on someone who's unconscious. He's impatiently waiting for Devon to 'metabolize the
new formula'. I told him it could take several more hours."

"Excellent work." Tias offered a rare smile. "I knew you
were perfect for this position."

Carly refused to think about all of the positions she'd
been in since her stint as spy began. It had been a means to
an end, nothing more. "I can't keep her sedated much longer.
He's already suspicious."

"I'll take her to another complex," Roberto said.

There were other complexes? A sick feeling took root in
the pit of Carly's stomach. The more she learned about this
project, the less she liked being part of it. "Osric will be furious and he'll immediately suspect me."

"Which is why Barns is going to take the fall for you,"
Milliner supplied. "I can't believe that scrawny bastard has
been double-crossing us."

"Devon will need to be interrogated once she's relocat-
ed," Tias reminded. "We need to know if what Osric fears is
true."

"I'll take care of it," Milliner volunteered, and Carly shivered. Would being interrogated by the cold-eyed general be
any better than what Osric had in mind?

"There's no need for you to exert yourself." Roberto
grinned. "I'll speak with her on the way to her new home."
Given a choice between Osric, Milliner and Roberto, Carly
would vote for the soft-spoken Italian.

"Is there anything else we need to know?" Tias asked.

"That's all I've been able to learn. For now."

"Avoid him until he learns that Barns betrayed him then be there to console him," Milliner advised.

She liked the first part much better than the last, but she nodded. "I understand." Tias and Milliner blinked out, leaving her along with Roberto. "I'll prepare Devon for travel. Where are you taking her?"

Laughter made his dark eyes sparkle as he pushed back from the table and stood. "No wonder Osric can't resist you. You're adorable."

Osric didn't think she was adorable, he thought she was weak and convenient. And each time he took her, ambition devoured another part of her soul. "If you take me with you, I'll find out everything Devon knows." She tried to make the offer sound playful, but she wanted nothing more. She wanted to go back to being a respected scientist who was largely ignored by men.

"You're right where we need you. For now. Make sure Osric has no reason to doubt you."

She nodded, silently accepting her fate while inside she was screaming.

"AND ALL THAT TIME YOU had no idea where you were?" Jake didn't sound accusatory. He sounded concerned, so Ava tried to relax. Reviewing the bizarre events hadn't been fun, but he'd listened without interruption, allowing her to move quickly through the sequence. She still had so many unanswered questions and a nagging sense that the danger hadn't passed. Who had dispatched the guards? And most importantly, was Kyle going to be okay?

"The only thing we were worried about in the beginning was whether or not we were being followed." She pushed aside her empty plate, amazed that she'd devoured the entire steak dinner. She'd thought she was too anxious to eat. Despite his gruff exterior, Jake had managed to put her at ease. "And once we were sure we were on our own, Kyle pointed the Jeep downhill and we hoped for the best."

"Not a bad strategy when you're shooting from the hip." Jake fiddled with one of the forks laid out on his side of the table, obviously lost in thought. "I presume you've never teleported before."

"No...or yes. I've never teleported before." Ava stirred the ice in her water glass with her straw then took a sip. She still felt dazed, as if she'd been relaying a chapter from someone else's life. "Kyle thinks it was a reflex, part of my survival instincts."

"That makes sense, but it still seems really random and not very helpful. Therian abilities, even in their infancy, tend to be more accurate than that."

Ron or Steve—the tall, stern-faced blond didn't say a word, so Ava wasn't sure which one he was—walked into the restaurant and handed Jake a plastic bag containing everything they'd recovered from the Jeep. Jake thanked him, and the guy walked away without ever making eye contact with Ava.

"Is he always so friendly?"

Jake lounged in the booth across from her, obviously at home in his domain. "He has other, more valuable skills." He opened the bag and looked inside. "Kyle's phone should be in here. Do you still want to talk to your sister?"

"Of course I do." He continued rummaging through the bag as she asked, "Is it safe to call her cell? I don't want to reveal her location."

"Osric knows where she is, but..." He looked up, hesitating over what he'd been about to say.

"Quinn claimed her so she's no use to Osric?"

"Basically." He found the phone and handed it to her. "I'm not saying she's no longer in danger. Allowing ourselves to believe that is foolish."

"He's just more interested in me now?"

"He's always been more interested in you." Jake set the bag aside and returned his gaze to her face. "Carissa's definition just widened the gap."

Rather than ask him to explain the strange claim, she activated the phone and entered Carissa's number. Still, the comment buzzed around in the back of her mind. They were fraternal twins. Why would Osric care more about her than he did about Carissa?

"Hello." Carissa's voice sounded hushed and thin.

"It's me, Car. I'm fine. Are *you* okay?"

"Thank God I answered. I didn't recognize the number, but Quinn thought it might be Kyle."

Ava smiled, soothed by the familiar cadence of her sister's voice. "I guess that means you're all right."

"I'm wonderful." She laughed. "But where are you? They found Kyle's truck out on Pine Valley Ranch. Are you with him? How did you leave the cabin?"

"Keep the information general, just in case," Jake cautioned. "You'll be with her tomorrow. You can catch up then."

Ava nodded. "Jake says to keep it short. I'll see you tomorrow."

"Don't you dare hang up!"

"I wasn't going to. It's just better if we leave the details until tomorrow."

Clearly beyond caution, Carissa persisted, "Jake? I thought you were with Kyle? Where are you?"

"It's a really long story and Jake's right. This phone is disposable, but you've had yours for years. Chances are slim that we're being recorded, but better safe than sorry. The important thing is we're both safe and we'll be together soon."

Carissa finally calmed down enough to pause. "I really missed you. This has been the worst week of my life and yet it's been the best. It's so confusing."

"I'm right there with you." Several times literally. Ava smiled.

"I love you. Please be careful."

Emotion thickened her sister's tone and Ava blinked back tears. "I love you too. And I'm always careful. You're the reckless one."

"Tell Jake to be nice or he'll answer to me."

Ava looked at the brawny tiger-shifter seated across from her and smiled again. "I'll tell him." She ended the call and handed the phone back to her host.

"You'll tell me what?"

"To be nice or Carissa will kick your ass."

He chuckled as he returned the phone to the bag. "Ordinarily I'd welcome the challenge, but Quinn's scent was all over her long before we defined her."

"'*We* defined her'?" She scooted forward and lowered her voice to a harsh whisper. "You were part of that ritual, weren't you? You were in that classroom. Carissa drank your blood." Images from the vision flickered through her mind and she shuddered. She only saw Quinn and the blond man, Ian, clearly, but she'd sensed others in the background waiting to participate. "How many were there? How many different natures did she absorb?"

"I can't believe Kyle got into all that with you. He should have made sure you were safe before he even brought it up. There's devotion to the Omni Prime and then there's outright obsession. He's moving closer and closer to obsession."

Warmed by Jake's overreaction, she quickly hid her smile with a sip of water. He was concerned about her, even to the point of being angry with his friend. But it wasn't fair to let his misconception stand. "Kyle didn't say a word. In fact when I brought up what I'd seen in my dream, he confirmed that the ritual was real then refused to talk about the specifics."

Jake stretched his arm out along the back of the booth and narrowed his eyes. "You saw the ritual in a dream?"

She nodded. "That's why I decided to run. I knew it wasn't happening live. I've had enough dreams to know the difference between real time and memory. But I was left with a sense of dread. Something was horribly wrong and I needed to get the hell out of there."

"So you threw your stuff in a backpack and headed for your motorcycle, but Kyle grabbed you when you ducked around the corner."

They'd already been through all this, so she just nodded. She was pretty sure he was thinking out loud anyway.

"What if 'fight' engaged rather than 'flight'. The flash might have taken you to the source of danger rather than away."

She scrunched up her forehead as she tried to follow his logic. "I took Kyle with me, but that wasn't intentional."

"I'm not talking about Kyle. The wolves didn't find the cabin until after you'd flashed out, so there was no real danger at the time. Kyle was there to protect you. I have a feeling your Therian side knew that all along."

"Where are you going with this?" She rubbed the bridge of her nose as a dull throb erupted behind her eyes. "What do you think the teleportation really means?"

His lips parted as if he would tell her and then he shook his head and chuckled. "I'm not sure yet. I think I've read too many spy novels or something. Just ignore me."

She seriously doubted Jake had been ignored a day in his life. He had the kind of personality that would draw people to him even if he weren't disgustingly handsome. "What's an Omni Prime?"

He shifted his forearms to the tabletop. "I can't believe I fell into that trap."

"It wasn't a trap. But the door's been opened, so I want to know more. If it involves my sister, I have a right to know."

"It's a long, complicated story and Erin, Kyle's mother, is the best person to tell you. She's our Historian. It's her job to keep all the facts straight. You'll meet her tomorrow."

"All right. A detailed history can wait, but tell me about my sister. What did the ritual do to her?" He just stared at her for a moment and trepidation sent a shiver down her spine. "Kyle told me Osric has the right to name my mate, but it's more than that, isn't it? Will I be expected to undergo this blood ritual? Am I an Omni Prime too?"

A slow smile curved Jake's lips while speculation narrowed his gaze. "I guess we'll run through the basic facts. The Omni Prime is a line of gifted females within the Therian nation. Their purpose is to balance the power of the male-dominated councils. They haven't existed, at full strength, for hundreds of years, but the potential exists within your bloodline."

"And Osric is desperate to control that potential power."

"It's not just Osric," Jake stressed. "There are many who want to control the Omni Prime. Osric just happens to have the council's backing because of the antiquated laws contained within the Charter."

Even having glimpsed the ritual in her vision, the idea didn't seem real. She felt as if they were talking about a movie or a graphic novel, something wild and unbelievable. "Carissa obviously learned about this potential and agreed to attempt the ritual."

"Yes. With Quinn at her side, she felt safe and empowered enough to reclaim her rightful heritage."

"Which brings us back to my original questions. How many of you participated in the ritual and what did it do to Carissa?"

"The ritual requires six."

"This is why Kyle was so quick to make sure I understood definition doesn't require sex. My sister didn't sleep with anyone but Quinn." She paused for a long, shaky breath, needing to remind herself that Carissa was safe and in the arms of the man she loved. She'd still feel a whole lot better once she'd seen Carissa for herself. "She just drank your blood." Ava rubbed her eyes as her stomach tightened in protest.

"I know it's hard to imagine, but I want you to know that Carissa made the decision for herself. Nothing was forced on her."

Actually it wasn't hard to imagine at all. She just closed her eyes and she could see her sister's face, the passion burning in her eyes and the wildness in her expression. There had been an elemental hunger, a primal awareness Ava had shared for a second before her logical brain drew her back from the smoldering intensity. "Then she can shift into six different animals?"

"Your sister is still learning how to control her abilities. It will be years, perhaps decades before her full potential is realized. Historic Omni Primes could shift at will into anything they desired, but we're honestly not sure what Carissa will be able to accomplish. The bloodline hasn't been maintained as well as it should have been."

"Can there be more than one Omni Prime or will I only undergo the ritual if something happens to Carissa?" Did she even want to undergo a blood ritual? Ava was firstborn, by all of eleven minutes, but firstborn nonetheless. Had Carissa... She shook away the doubt before it finished forming. They had never been competitive like that. For much of her life Carissa had been Ava's only friend and vice versa. There was no way Carissa would have done something so underhanded.

"Generally there is only one, but you two are twins so the rules are a little different. Besides Erin wants to reestablish..." His head snapped up and his gaze went blank for a moment then worry darkened his expression. "Something's wrong with Kyle. Come on."

Without further explanation, he scooted out of the booth and hurried across the restaurant, leaving her little choice but to follow. She had to jog to keep up with his long strides, but his intense expression or some telepathic warning sent people scurrying out of their way. He took the stairs three at a time, a feat her shorter legs wouldn't accommodate, and reached the bedroom several seconds ahead of her.

Jake had already crossed the room and was standing beside the bed by the time Ava reached the doorway. Kyle had returned to his human form and was sprawled on his back across the bed. The sheet was tangled around his hips, barely covering his groin as he thrashed and twisted in obvious delirium. Enya knelt on the edge of the mattress, doing her best to calm Kyle down. Much to Ava's relief, the only thing Enya had removed was her high-heeled boots.

"He won't accept my energy." She panted. Her face was pale, features tense, arms shaking.

"Then how did he shift back?"

She shrugged, straightening enough to glare at her brother. "I don't know. He roused long enough to switch, stumbled to the bed and collapsed. I've tried everything. I've narrowed the stream to a trickle, tried to sneak it past his sensors, and he still fights like I'm trying to poison him."

"Maybe you are." Jake's sharp gaze shot to Ava. "You said he fed from you right before the soldiers found you. How far did things go?"

Heat suffused her face, but she refused to shy away. "Second base." She couldn't think of a less embarrassing way of explaining the situation.

Enya crawled off the bed and Kyle quieted. His breathing grew harsh and irregular, but he gradually stopped thrashing. "It usually takes more than that for a couple to sync."

"But he'd healed her a couple of hours before," Jake reminded. "His energy would have been all through her already."

"What are you talking about? Did I do something wrong?" Tears blurred Ava's vision and she wasn't sure why. She was angry and she was terrified.

Jake placed his hand at the small of her back and Kyle made a growling sound deep in his throat. Snatching his hand away, Jake quickly explained, "Your energy mixed when he healed you and then again when you fed him. This might have triggered synchronization." Jake motioned Ava closer to the bed. "What exactly did you feel when he—"

"Don't be an ass, Jake." Enya saved her from more embarrassment. "You know what she felt and this is all new to her. She's not going to be able to decipher what did or didn't happen. There's only one way to tell if they're in sync or not." She shifted her gaze to Ava. "Get on the bed and see if he'll let you touch him."

Ava crossed her arms over her chest, hiding her hardened nipples. Just thinking about what she felt when Kyle "fed" from her made her core melt and her skin tingle.

"He's not going to bite you." Enya was starting to sound impatient. "Didn't you enjoy it before? Oh Creation, you're not a virgin, are you?"

Without responding to Enya's questions, Ava approached the bed. She reached for Kyle's arm. She certainly hadn't been this tentative in the woods, but she hadn't had an audience then. Her fingers brushed Kyle's forearm and he moaned. Then he rolled toward her and frantically reached out for her with both hands.

"Guess that solves the mystery," Enya muttered. "You're definitely in sync."

"I don't know what that means."

"It means you're the only one who can feed him," Jake told her. "At least for the next three months."

She took a step back. "I don't mind feeding him, but I'm still feeling a little woozy myself."

"She's right. We should saturate her and then give them some room," Enya suggested.

They moved toward her with obvious intent and a weight dropped into her belly. A surreal haze wrapped around her brain and she suddenly wanted to scream. Yesterday she'd been curled up in front of a fire reading a trashy novel and now tiger-shifters were about to "saturate her" so she could feed the cougar-shifter who had saved her life. Yeah, nothing out of the ordinary in that.

Except her sister was now an Omni Prime, some sort of super shifter who had taken on the animal nature of six different men in an attempt to free her true potential. A potential that existed in Ava as well, if she was able to set aside reality as she knew it and embrace this strange new world.

"Are you okay?" Jake's deep voice drew her back from her troubled thoughts.

"Sorry. I'm just a little overwhelmed right now."

He carefully placed his hand on her shoulder and waited until she looked into his eyes. Kyle growled again and grew restless, but she kept her eyes fixed on Jake. "I'm generally a big picture type of person, but today might be an exception. Focus on one thing at a time. Kyle's going to die if he doesn't get energy now and you're the only one who can give it to him. Once that problem is solved, we'll move on to something else."

She nodded and took a deep breath. "Good plan."

Enya moved up behind her and Ava closed her eyes. Jake moved his hands to her neck, supporting the back of her head with his fingers while his thumbs pressed against the underside of her jaw. Enya pushed up Ava's sleeves and clasp her upper arms. Skin against skin, as Kyle had said, Therian energy couldn't pass through inorganic material. Tingling currents pulsed from their fingertips, warming and tightening Ava's skin. She relaxed, trying to remain calm and open as her senses were bombarded with sensations and impulses. Her ears buzzed and her muscles twitched. Enya gripped her more firmly.

"Almost done," Jake whispered.

Their hands were hot against her skin, their touch starting to burn. She drew air in through her nose and released it slowly through her mouth, trying to control her instinctive reaction to the growing discomfort. Kyle only needed energy because he'd healed her. She owed him this at the very least.

Jake released her head with a groan and stepped back. Ava quickly followed. "You have to get undressed. Energy can't pass through—"

"I know."

"If he's too weak to *arouse* you—"

"Give it up already." Enya slapped his arm then dragged him from the room by his sleeve. Jake's grin was utterly unrepentant.

Ava pulled off her boots and faced the bed as she shed the rest of her clothes. Other than get naked and touch him, she had no idea what she was supposed to do. Was Kyle aware enough to help her? He'd perked up instantly when she touched his arm and reacted each time Jake touched her. Hopefully Kyle would stir again. She was ready and willing, but the able part had a long way to go.

Well, there wasn't anything she could do to instantaneously change her skill level. She folded her clothes and set them on a chair, arranging her boots underneath. *You're stalling.* Her inner voice could be such a bitch.

She blew out a shaky breath and focused on Kyle's haggard face. This was medicinal. It didn't matter that it felt a whole lot like having sex with a stranger. He literally needed this or he would die. With that thought fixed squarely in her mind, she crawled into bed beside him and carefully placed her hand on his shoulder.

MARY DROPPED HER KEYS on the hallstand and released a tired sigh as she turned back to the front door of her apartment and rotated the deadbolt. Toulouse Tavern might be in one of the most beautiful locations in the region, but that didn't make the work any easier. Her feet ached, her back... Alerted by something that didn't belong, she paused and allowed her senses to sharpen and her claws to lengthen.

Everything was quiet and calm, but the faintest hint of dog hung in the air. Shit!

"Miss me?"

Recognizing Bruce Fitzroy's deep voice didn't help her relax. He might not be a stranger, but he was equally unwanted.

She drew indignation around her like a suit of armor and slowly turned around. He was little more than a silhouette in the darkness, but she glared anyway, hoping he could see her angry expression. "What are you doing here? You lost the privilege of coming and going as you please when you—"

He spun her back around and pushed her arms up as he pinned her against the door. His body contoured to hers and his fingers banded her wrists, keeping her claws away from his face. "I always come when I please, but I promise to take you with me."

Their sexual encounters had gone on for several months almost a year ago. She'd been turned-on by his bad-boy looks and badass attitude, as well as the forbidden nature of sleeping with a wolf. But he liked it fast and rough, which was fine, some of the time. She liked a good wall banger herself—some of the time. But like a restaurant that only served one entrée, he became tedious and she'd found somewhere else to eat.

"Get out!"

"I'd rather get *in*." He whispered the claim in a throaty tone that had once sent her pulse racing.

She slowly counted to three then scrambled for the quickest way to get rid of him. The last thing she needed right now was a yappy dog. "Bruce, I am not playing here. I'm really not in the mood." He rubbed his erection against her ass and ran his hands up and down her arms. If she jerked out of his grasp, he'd take it as a challenge. She had to remain calm and unaffected by his touch. "I smell like a sweaty hamburger and I'm exhausted. Your timing couldn't be worse." A moment passed as he humped her back. She just closed her eyes and tried to ignore him.

Finally, he pushed off the door and growled, "What the hell is wrong with you?"

She turned around but kept the door at her back, not sure the battle was won. "I just worked a double shift. I'm dead on my feet."

"So sit down and kick off your shoes. I'll rub your feet."

Tension spiraled through her belly and the hairs on the back of her neck bristled. Bruce was anything but romantic. In all the months they'd been together, he'd never once held a door or brought her a gift. "I'd rather take a shower and collapse into bed—alone. Besides, if Jake finds out you're in Aspen, he'll kill you."

"I'm not afraid of Jake," he sneered.

"I wasn't inferring that you are. This is just a really bad time for you to come nosing around. Something big was going on tonight. Everyone's on edge."

His gaze narrowed with calculated interest and she recognized her mistake. He already knew or at least he'd suspected and she'd just confirmed his suspicions. Damn it. This is why he was in Aspen, why he was coming on to her. She forced her tired brain to focus. She couldn't tell him any more. Even if she had to screw him to get rid of him, she would not endanger Ava.

He stalked forward and pressed one hand against the door. "Battle plans? Should I be summoning our fighters?" She wasn't fooled by his casual tone. His cold hazel eyes revealed his determination. "What's Jake up to now?"

"Our clan has no interest in expansion. You know that."

"Then what had everyone 'on edge'?"

She couldn't un-spill the beer, but she could minimize the damage. Hoping her performance was more convincing than his, she shrugged and shook her head. "No clue. All I know is the tavern was seriously busy and everyone seemed sort of jumpy."

He looked her up and down as she did her best not to squirm. Then his gaze iced over and he stepped back. "You're right. You need a shower."

Rather than reacting to the slur, she ushered him out then closed and locked the door. After offering a hurried prayer of thanks to any deity willing to listen, she dug her phone out of her pocket and called the tavern. The restaurant was closed, but the bar was still open for another few minutes anyway.

"Toulouse Tavern, good morning."

Enya's sarcasm made Mary smile. "Hey, it's Mary. Tell Jake that Bruce Fitzroy is back in town and looking for trouble."

Chapter Five

Hunger tore through Kyle, the sudden, tight spasm trapping his breath in his lungs. He shook, muscles twitching as his body burned. He prayed for a moment of relief, a random blast of numbness so he could gather energy or catch his breath. The blessed oblivion never came. Each cramp, each creeping urge drove the need deeper and made his pain more excruciating. The spasm released and he exhaled, the whoosh of air ending in a moan.

Warm fingers brushed his forehead, his temple, his jaw. "Kyle?"

Ava. If he was dreaming again, why was the pain still so intense?

She repeated the hesitant caress on the other side of his face. Then her soft body slid against his as she settled against his side.

He trembled, holding back the urge to attack, to take what he wanted, what he needed with every cell of his starving body.

"I don't know what to do," she whispered. "I want to feed you, but I—"

With an instinctive surge of strength, he swept her beneath him and pinned her arms against the bed. "Say it again." His voice sounded gravelly and...desperate.

"Say what?"

He still hadn't opened his eyes. Part of him was terrified this wasn't real. He wasn't afraid to die. Anything would be better than this endless, burning hunger. But he knew madness would claim him if he opened his eyes and her image disintegrated.

Slowly lifting his lids, he blinked until her face came into focus. So damn beautiful. And so afraid. He eased his grip without letting go and tried to relax his muscles. "Are you really willing?"

"That's why I'm here."

"A kiss won't cut it this time. You understand what I need?"

Her smile didn't quite reach her eyes, but she nodded. She was trying to be brave. "I'm not a virgin, Kyle. I've actually seen a penis before."

The fact that she still called it a penis proved her minimal exposure to them. "If I lose control and try to claim you, scream for Jake. He's probably listening outside the door anyway."

Her gaze darted toward the door, but she whispered, "I trust you."

"Don't." He treaded his fingers through hers and gave her hands a squeeze. "I don't trust myself right now. Do not, for any reason, drink my blood."

"That would seal my definition and ruin any hope I have of becoming an Omni Prime." Her eyes twinkled as she smiled this time. "I understand the situation. Now shut up and kiss me."

On an ordinary day it would have been hard as hell to resist that invitation, today it was impossible. Kyle released one of her hands and slipped his arm beneath her neck as he lowered his mouth to hers. Her lips parted and her tongue greeted his with a silken swirl. Warmth and affection flowed into him, sweetening the kiss and driving back the urgency degree by degree.

The fiber-thin link he'd formed on the mountain vibrated, urging him on, guiding him deeper into her mind. He fit his mouth more tightly over hers and parted her legs with his knees. She opened for him, offering her body and her energy.

Humbled by her selflessness yet unable to go slowly, he found the opening to her body and eased inside. Slick, hot softness surrounded him, caressing the head of his cock as he drove steadily inward. She tensed and tore her mouth away from his.

He stopped, panting harshly. "Am I hurting you?"

"No." She drew her legs up along his sides and tilted her hips. "It's just been a long time."

He released her other hand and stroked the side of her face. "I need..."

"I know." She squeezed him with her inner muscles and smiled. "It's all right."

A fresh wave of hunger crashed over him and he gritted his teeth. He didn't want to take her roughly, selfishly feeding as she endured the ordeal, but his ravenous body was leaving him little choice. "I'll...make it up to you. I promise." He pulled back slowly then thrust hard. Pleasure burst through the pain, driving back the hunger.

Her hands moved over his arms and down his back as he rocked between her thighs. His chest grazed her breasts, keeping her nipples pebble-hard. He eased into her mind, sinking deeper with each firm thrust. Their link expanded, creating a stronger connection. He flowed through her consciousness, carefully siphoning energy as her thoughts and sensations trickled into his mind.

She wasn't afraid anymore, yet she felt overwhelmed and uncertain. He refused to allow their first joining to be traumatic, so he rolled to his back, taking her with him. Then he urged her up so she straddled his hips, his shaft still buried deep inside her.

"Ride me." His voice cracked, making the directive sound more like a plea. It didn't matter. He'd worry about his pride once his cravings were under control.

He grasped her hips and showed her the motion he needed, hoping she'd feel less vulnerable if she controlled their movements.

She didn't need help for long. Bracing her hands against his chest, she found a rhythm that sent pulses of pleasure surging through them both. She arched her back, drawing his attention to her breasts. High and round, the mounds quivered each time she brought her hips down and took him deep.

He covered her breasts with his hands, enjoying the rasp of her hard little nipples against his palms. Even with their lack of foreplay, her skin was flushed and the sporadic tightening of her inner muscles assured him she was nearing orgasm.

Her energy seeped into him, stabilizing his need without assuaging the hunger. He craved the dazzling surge of energy released each time she came. This steady dribble would never ease the ache consuming him.

Easing his hand between their bodies, he found her clit with his middle finger and caressed the sensitive nub. She gasped and started then energy rushed into him, saturating his emaciated cells. Her hips moved faster and she squeezed him tighter, rubbing against his finger as she took his cock deep into her wet core.

Coherent thoughts slid from her mind as pleasure overtook her. She cried out and slammed her body down over his. Kyle fought back the need burning in his balls. It felt so damn good! But he knew he'd slip into unconsciousness as soon as he let himself come and he was far from sated.

Dazed and tingling, Ava murmured a breathless protest as Kyle lifted her off his cock and dragged her forward. One glance over her shoulder proved that he was still hard, so why had he stopped and separated their bodies?

He shifted her knees, arranging her astride his face. She gasped and fought for balance as he slid her legs outward, not stopping until her sex rested against his lips. His intention was obvious, so she didn't say a word. She wasn't sure why he'd waited until now to use his mouth, but she wasn't about to argue.

His tongue parted her folds, lazily circling her clit before pushing into the center of her body. She was already wet and sensitive from the demanding slide of his cock, making each subtle motion of his tongue all the more arousing.

Don't hold back, love. I need you to come as often as you can.

She'd felt his presence in her mind as soon as they kissed, but his words still surprised her. *Can you hear my thoughts too?*

Yes, but don't let it distract you. Concentrate on what my mouth is doing.

His tongue slid in and out a few times then he caught her clit between his lips and drew lightly on the swollen nub. Sensations spiraled through Ava's core and streamed down the inside of her thighs. She felt weightless and dizzy as tension gathered low in her belly.

He grasped her bottom and ground her sex against his mouth as his tongue swirled and thrust. His upper lip rubbed her clit and distinct spasms pulsed deep inside her. Reaching back, she steadied herself against his thighs and she cried softly as she rode out the orgasm.

Her limbs grew heavy and her eyelids drooped as he withdrew more energy. She'd offered herself willingly, had basically known what to expect, but it still felt odd to know he was drawing sustenance directly from her body.

While she was still stunned and shaky, he crawled out from under her and turned around. He urged her forward, bringing her hands to the top of the headboard as he pressed against her back. "Are you still doing okay?"

She nodded, but she wanted to see his face, needed to know her surrender was strengthening him.

He positioned himself between her thighs then grabbed her hips as he drove home in one fast thrust. She gasped, clutching the headboard as the sudden fullness took her breath away. There was no pain, but he definitely stretched her tighter than any of her other lovers.

A deep growl intruded on her thought. Then he pulled nearly out. "I'm your lover now. That's all that matters." He accented the statement with a possessive thrust and they moaned in unison.

He stayed deep inside her and ran his hands over her body. She rested her head against his shoulder and relaxed beneath his touch. His fingers skimmed over her skin, never lingering in one place for long. When her skin tingled and her core tensed with need, he placed his hands on her hips and he took her with long, smooth strokes.

She grasped the headboard, pushing back against him and raising her ass. He filled her mind as he filled her body, creating a connection far more intimate than any she'd experienced before. The past faded, overpowered by Kyle's savage tenderness. He caressed her breasts, teasing the nipples as his cock slid in and out.

"Kiss me."

Happy to obey, she turned her head and tilted her face. His mouth sealed over hers, his tongue thrusting deep as soon as her lips parted. Her cream mixed with his unique taste, the combination both new and evocative.

His fingers plucked her nipples then moved down and teased her clit. Sensations followed in the wake of his nimble fingers. Her breasts felt heavy and her core clenched, her orgasm hovering just out of reach.

Suddenly, he rotated to the side and pushed her head down as he thrust fast and hard between her thighs. He collared her neck, keeping her head low as his hips furiously pumped. Desire blazed into her mind, consuming everything but the need for fulfillment. His cock stabbed into her, driving deeper than ever before. She clutched the covers and pushed up into his frantic thrusts, exhilarated by his frenzy.

He cried out sharply and shuddered against her as he released his seed deep inside her. The hot splash of his release sent her over the edge one last time. She felt the inescapable draw as he extracted energy. The persistent suction kept her climax pulsing until she was breathless and weak.

"Thank you," he whispered as he gently separated their bodies. He collapsed onto his side then rolled to his back, sprawling across the bed.

She stared at him, too shocked to move. "Are you okay? I thought this would heal you."

"Need. Sleep." His eyelids drooped and his breathing became deep and regular.

He was breathing, so his heart was beating, but she still felt like there should be something more she could do. He looked pale and exhausted yet peaceful. "Feel better." As she eased her feet toward the edge of the bed, he caught her wrist and pulled her toward him.

"Stay." He didn't open his eyes, but his fingers remained firm against her wrist.

Warmth and tenderness welled within her as she settled against his side. He wrapped his arms around her, pulling her even closer.

Her debt was paid. She'd kept her promise, so why did she still feel drawn to him?

Were they "in sync" like Enya said? And what exactly did it mean if they were? Sex with Kyle had been amazing, but what did that prove?

It had been less than a week since she'd seen her sister, and Carissa had managed to adjust to Therian expectations. Carissa's devotion to Quinn had been obvious in Ava's vision. Was it possible that she had stumbled on to a similar attraction, or was Kyle simply the first Therian male she'd met?

Jake was better looking than Kyle. Jake was also charming and self-assured, yet she didn't feel the same connection with the powerful tiger-shifter that she felt with Kyle. Whatever the cause, her body had obviously made its choice and she feared her heart wasn't far behind.

With a weary sigh, she pressed her face against his chest and let his scent surround her. She was safe and satisfied. The combination was impossible to resist. Within minutes she was sound asleep.

OSRIC MOVED SO QUICKLY and so silently he seemed to appear out of nowhere. His fingers tangled in the back of Carly's hair and he jerked her head back. "Where did they take her!"

"I don't know." Pressing back into his hurtful grip, she tried to ease the pain. "Roberto showed up while you were gone and took Devon with him when he left. No one said anything to me about why or where."

"I don't believe you."

She had anticipated Osric's outburst and made preparations while he was gone. She hadn't expected him to stay away all night, but that was just as well. After a restful night's sleep and a hearty breakfast, she was better prepared for the challenges awaiting her.

"You're hurting me." She didn't struggle or reveal her distress. She remained passive and waited for him to release her.

With an exasperated snarl, he shoved her away and braced his hand against the countertop. They were alone in the lab, as per usual. Her two assistants had a way of disappearing every time Osric entered a room.

"First Milliner bags three of my kin when he'd agreed to leave my family out of this. Now that preening Italian transfers Devon when he knows I'm not finished with her. Can't you see what they're doing?" Veins of gold burst in his dark gaze as fury contorted his features. "They're trying to squeeze me out."

When the backers were finished with Osric, they'd kill him, not annoy him. But Carly wisely kept the thought to herself. "What do they gain by 'squeezing you out'?"

"Control."

She remained out of reach, unsure if his temper had played itself out or if he would strike again. "We've learned a lot about your people since this project began, but you still provide a unique perspective. Surely the backers realize your value."

He crossed his arms over his chest and glared at her. "How did they learn who Devon was?"

"Her transfer could have nothing to do with—"

"Nice try." He stalked toward her, his expression overtly menacing. "I only told one person about my contingency plan."

"I didn't say anything to anyone." She held her ground yet lowered her gaze. Challenging an enraged predator was just plain stupid. "Conversations in this place are never private. Who was on duty yesterday?"

He raised her chin and searched her gaze for a long, tense moment. If he didn't take the bait, he wouldn't find the video files Tias had planted. She'd used an archived file and manipulated the time-date stamp to make it appear current. Though sound was conveniently garbled, the image was quite clear.

Rather than debate the issue, Osric walked past Carly and sat down behind the communal desk. He activated the workstation and brought up the security logs. It didn't take him long to find the planted file. He watched Barns enter the conference room and his scowl darkened. "This is twenty minutes after I left the complex."

"Was there any other reason for Barns to contact the backers?" She tried to sound casual but her heartbeat was racing and her mouth was so dry she could barely form the words.

"He's head of security. He updates them on a regular basis, but this is no coincidence." Osric advanced through the file, verifying that no one else entered the conference room during his absence. "And less than an hour after his unscheduled report, Devon is transferred to who knows where." He clenched his fists, clearly accepting the false evidence. "Greedy bastard. He'll pay for this."

It was the conclusion she needed him to find, but it was where her plans for Osric began not ended. "Would you like to grab a cup of coffee? I'm ready for a break."

He whipped his head around, challenge burning in his dark eyes. "I thought you wanted to keep things professional."

She smiled, hoping her slanted glance appeared flirtatious. "I suggested a coffee break not a nooner."

"Too bad." He ran his gaze up and down her body then shrugged. "I might make time for a nooner. Coffee breaks don't interest me in the least."

"Fine by me." She started back across the room, having expected his reaction. He couldn't pursue her if she didn't run.

He grabbed her upper arm, bringing her up short. "You gave up too easily."

"I don't have time for games." She tugged against his hold, secretly thrilled by the strength of his grip. He might look like a man nearing middle age, but she knew from experience that his body was lean and muscular. If only a kind person resided within that buff body, these games would be a lot more rewarding.

"I think you enjoy games every bit as much as I do." He pulled her toward him with slow, steady insistence. "You pretend indifference while your body begs for more."

"You treat me like a sex toy." She took a deep breath and looked into his eyes. It was a dance, a balancing act. She had to encourage his interest without actually giving in.

"And you enjoy every minute of it." He reached for the top button on her blouse, but she twisted away. "Is this where you try to convince me you aren't willing?"

"I'm not that big a hypocrite." She straightened her shoulders, giving him a better view of her cleavage. "My body responds to your bullying, but my mind is appalled by my weakness. I have more pride than to let it go on indefinitely."

"So this is about assuaging your pride?" He chuckled and released her arm. "I seldom fuck any human more than once. The fact that I'm still interested should make you feel better."

What an arrogant jerk. If not for the backers, she never would have let Osric touch her in the first place. He was a means to an end. Nothing more. But she couldn't let him realize how she really felt. "That's the problem. You're not interested in me. You're interested in my body."

A dark smile curved his lips and he leaned toward her. "Come to my room and I'll prove you wrong."

"Do you really think I'm that stupid? As soon as the door closes behind me, you'd be all over me."

His brows shot up while lust smoldered in his gaze. "Have I forced anything on you?"

"That's not the point. I don't want to sleep with you again, so going to your room would be foolish."

"Don't trust yourself?"

"Yes, I don't trust myself."

That seemed to please him. "How can I earn your trust if you avoid being alone with me?"

"Do you want to earn my trust?"

It took him a moment to reply and he seemed almost surprised by the answer. "I do."

She just stared up at him, letting the tension build. He would never follow her lead. He needed to make the next move.

"We both seem fond of games," he said a short time later. "I propose a challenge of sorts."

"I'm listening."

"I'll go to your room and stay until you ask me to leave."

Smoothing down her lab coat, she kept her face averted. "We already established that I have a hard time resisting you."

"Then what do you suggest? What will it take to make you more comfortable with our encounters?"

Finally! An angle she could use. "I'd like to know more about you. You're always so secretive."

His gaze narrowed on her face as he considered the suggestion. "And what do you offer in return for my personal history?"

She started to reply then licked her lips instead. It had to be his idea. "What do you want?"

"Obedience. For every question I answer, you comply with one directive."

"I won't sleep with you. We need to start over, allow this to develop gradually."

"My clothes stay on unless you remove them."

There was a hell of a lot he could do without removing his clothes, but she had to keep his interest. "And you'll still leave as soon as I ask you to?"

"Of course."

His triumphant smile only added to the tension gripping her belly. Could she suppress her own desires long enough to interrogate him or would they end up in bed together? The challenge excited her as much as the pleasure he was likely to give her. This was as close to control as he'd allowed her to have and she intended to use it to the fullest.

"Deal, but no one-word answers or evasions. I'll obey as long as you're honest and open."

He motioned toward the door, his gaze fixed on her mouth. "Lead the way."

It only took a few minutes to reach her quarters, but she used the time to prioritize her questions. This was about gaining information. She could not lose sight of her goal. She locked the door behind them and activated the privacy jammer. "No one can hear you but me."

"And no one can see you but me."

She wasn't sure why the distinction was important but she nodded. "Did you approach the backers or did they recruit you?"

"I thought you wanted to learn about me as a person."

"I do. This project is our common ground. I'm trying to understand how you fit in with what the backers are trying to accomplish."

"Fair enough." The apartment was compact and his large body made it feel even smaller. A privacy curtain separated the bedroom from the living area. He strolled around the room, looking at the sparse decorations with bored indifference. "They recruited me."

"How long have you worked with them?"

He shook his head and smiled. "I say nothing more until you're naked."

She had three quick-dissolve tablets in her pocket, but she needed to slip them into something he'd actually drink. Once he ingested the chemical cocktail, he'd be far more accommodating. "You only answered one question. That entitles you to one article of clothing."

"This isn't strip poker, sweetheart. If you want answers, you do as you're told."

If she obeyed without question, she was no longer a challenge. "Top or bottom? You can't have both."

He looked as if he'd argue then he shrugged. "Start with the top."

Slipping out of her lab coat, she draped it over the back of a kitchen chair and made sure the pocket with the tablets was easily accessible. "Can I get you something to drink? It's early, but I think I'll have a glass of wine."

"I thought you wanted coffee." He sat in the sleek black chair across from the kitchenette.

"Wine goes better with naked breasts." She smiled as she unbuttoned her blouse and placed it on top of the lab coat. *Come on. Try the wine. I'm not sure I can pull this off if we're both sober.*

"White or red?" Except for the occasional gleam in his eyes, his expression remained stoic.

"Which do you prefer? I have both."

"Bring the bottles here so I can find out."

She wasn't sure what he had in mind, but she didn't see a way around it. Retrieving the half-full bottles from her refrigerator, she brought them to him then quickly stepped back.

"You're still wearing your bra."

"Sorry." She unfastened the front clasp and took off the undergarment.

"Come here."

"Why?"

"Because I'll tell you how I met James Milliner if you do."

She licked her lips, desperately wanting to cover her breasts. But she wasn't here to entertain him. She was trying to learn as much as she could about her mysterious companion. "Tell me first then I'll obey."

Osric chuckled and pulled the cork out of one of the wine bottles. "I want to find out if I prefer red or white. Now stop being so contrary." He set the corked bottle on the floor and reached for her hand. She reluctantly moved between his legs as he scooted to the edge of the chair. Then he raised the open bottle and drizzled red wine over her left breast.

The cold liquid streamed across her warm skin and Carly shivered. Her nipple hardened as the liquid followed the contour of her flesh. He caught the red droplets with the tip of his tongue then retraced the wet path until her skin was clean.

Thinking he'd finished with phase one of his "experiment", she exhaled and started to retreat. He caught her hips as his mouth fastened on to her nipple. She stood perfectly still and he moved his hands, only touching her with his mouth. The long, firm pulls drew heat into her breast and made the tip tingle.

He released her suddenly and her nipple sprang free, wet and tightly puckered. "Very nice. Now hand me the white."

She took the open bottle from him and exchanged it for the other. Trickling white wine over her right breast, he sampled the new offering. He sucked harder, scraping her with his teeth. She tried to ignore the sensations darting from her nipple to her clit, but he knew how hard to nibble and always managed to pull back just as pleasure turned to pain.

"Red," he decided, and scooted back in the chair. "Unless you want to continue the experiment. White might be more suited to your navel or those adorable dimples on your lower back. But I suspect red's sweetness will balance out the salty-sharp taste of your sex. Shall we find out?"

Shaking off the sensual haze, she grabbed both bottles and hurried across the apartment. "How did you meet General Milliner? You promised to tell me." She retrieved two wineglasses from the cupboard and set them on the table near the chair with her lab coat. Blocking his view with her body, she pulled the tablets from her pocket and dropped them into one of the glasses then covered them with wine. Swirling the wine around in the glass, she waited until the tablets dissolved then returned to her guest.

He accepted the glass but didn't take a drink. "I told you the backers recruited me, but that's not exactly true. One of Milliner's teams captured me eight years ago. I was treated like the others, examined, tested, experimented on."

Shocked by the revelation, she couldn't think of anything to say for a moment then questions bombarded her mind. "Then why in the world would you help them? Why subject others to the same mistreatment you'd endured?" *What did they give you that was worth betraying your own people?*

"You're a scientist," he snapped. "You understand the cost of medical advancement."

She needed to be more careful. The last thing she wanted was to piss him off and have him clam up on her. He fiddled with his glass, but he still hadn't raised it to his lips. "Were the other two backers involved back then? How long has this project been going on?"

"I'm not sure exactly. Milliner met Roberto in the eighties. Tias joined the club a few years later. The project was in full swing when they captured me."

The project had been underway for perhaps forty years and they still didn't understand what enabled Therians to shift? That wasn't accurate. The backers had a basic understanding of the biological processes. They just couldn't recreate the abilities in humans.

She took a sip of her wine, hoping Osric would do the same. He rested the base of his glass on his thigh and stared off into space. "How did you go from being a test subject to participating willingly in the program?"

He finally took a long drink of wine then set the glass aside. Damn. Would enough of the drugs reach his system with only one drink? "If you want more, lose the skirt."

He'd seen her naked before and she wasn't ashamed of her body. This could only be humiliating if she allowed it to be. She unzipped her skirt and stepped out of it, draping it across the chair back with her other garments.

"They learned what they could from me then turned me loose. It wasn't until a few months later that I realized they'd tagged me."

That wasn't surprising. It was standard procedure to tag test subjects. Of course he wouldn't have known their procedures back then. "That didn't really answer the question. How did you end up helping them?"

"Take off the rest. I want you completely naked."

She kicked off her shoes and rolled down one of her stockings. She started to roll down the other then stopped. "You're not talking."

His gaze traveled the length of her half-naked body as a fresh wave of lust formed his expression. "Therians mate for life. Once our bodies sync with our mate's body, we are incapable of—"

"Wait." She tossed her stockings over the chair and paused with her thumbs hooked under the waistband of her panties. "What does that mean? How does your body 'sync' with your mates?"

"We're shapeshifters, *Doctor* Ides. Our bodies literally shift, becoming more attractive to and compatible with our mate's physiology."

"And your body retains that change for as long as your mate lives?"

"Yes. Once the mating bond is formed it's permanent, but while a female is still searching for her mate, synchronization lasts three months with each potential partner."

"Then it's the female's responsibility to find her mate?" That didn't seem quite fair.

He chuckled and his gaze focused on her exposed breasts. "Females go into heat, which announces to every unbound male that she is physically ready to be claimed. It's the male's job to convince her that he is the strongest and most capable of satisfying her every need."

"Being physically capable of reproduction doesn't mean anyone is ready for a lifetime commitment." Yet having strong, demanding males vying for her attention sounded like a sexual fantasy. Except she'd be expected to spend the rest of her life with whomever satisfied her best. Maybe being human wasn't so bad after all.

"You're human." He made it sound like a disease, but she'd already decided she was thankful for her humanity. "You'll never understand the intensity of mating fever."

He said no more, so she dragged her panties down to mid-thigh then turned so all he could see was her bare hip. "What does this have to do with your joining the program?"

"My mate…" He picked up his wineglass and drained it with several deep gulps. "She was weak and selfish and terrified of her destiny."

She let her panties slip down her legs then she kicked them aside. The pain in his eyes was even more disconcerting than his usual lechery. "You're obviously not incapable of being with other women now, so what happened to her?"

"Willona's mother, Maggie, had three mates and she could shift into numerous animals. Maggie wasn't technically a *true* Therian, but she was damn close."

Feeling foolish just standing there naked, she walked to the couch and sat. But he shook his head when she reached for the throw blanket folded over the back. She sat up straight and kept her thighs pressed together. "I've heard you use that term before. What do you consider a 'true' Therian?"

"I have reason to believe Therians were once true shapeshifters. I think we changed forms as easily as humans change their clothes."

"When and why did Therians lose the ability to shift into anything they wanted to?" She was fascinated by the details, but Osric had likely told the backers his theories already. She needed current information, specifics he'd be reluctant to share.

"It happened gradually over countless generations. Cats grew suspicious of dogs and dogs saw weakness in the smaller clans. It became the norm to mate within one's own clan, so the ability to shift into other forms dwindled away."

"What made you think Willona would still have this ability?"

"Her mother was defined late in life and she took on three animal natures. I knew Willona would be even more receptive to a multiple definition if she was defined while her spirit was still fresh and strong." His gaze dipped to her breasts then sank lower. "Open your legs."

Carly swallowed hard. He was moving closer to the present, closer to the inner workings of the Therians. Besides, the drug should be kicking in soon. She inched closer to the edge of the sofa and parted her thighs.

"Wider."

Slowly, she complied and heat crept across her skin. She always felt humiliated after they played these games, but her body responded to his demands more readily than any lover she'd ever known. "You said Willona was weak and afraid. What happened to her?"

He rubbed his eyes and then his nose. Good. Facial numbness was a common side effect, but this was taking forever. "No one believed me. They all thought Maggie was a fluke, that her abilities were some random trick of nature." He left his chair and knelt on the floor in front of her. His hands cupped her knees and pushed her legs up and back until her heels rested on the edge of the sofa. "Sam didn't believe me either, but he agreed to help me try."

"Who is Sam?" She was naked and spread before him, her core creaming beneath his watchful eyes.

His breaths came faster and he kept blinking his eyes. She thought he'd succumb to the drug and then he pushed two fingers into her and smiled. "You missed me." He pumped slowly, watching his fingers disappear inside her body and reappear coated in cream. "So wet and hot."

"Tell me about Sam." Despite her determination to resist his careless stroking, her body responded. Tension gathered low in her belly and her clit began to twitch.

"Wolf pack alpha." His voice sounded slightly slurred, but his hand kept up the steady motion, teasing and arousing her. "Willona refused to name her guide, so I got permission to define her."

She tensed, easily reading between the lines. "By force?"

"She only struggled in the beginning. We didn't want to hurt her, but definition brings out the animal in Therian males."

"You took turns...you and this wolf alpha?" What little desire he'd managed to stir sputtered out. She pushed his hand back and scurried off the couch, but there wasn't anywhere to hide. The bathroom door didn't lock and the bedroom was only separated from the main room by a curtain. "Did she survive?"

He turned and sat down, leaning back against the sofa. "I feel...weird."

Finally. She darted into the bathroom and grabbed her robe off the back of the door. By the time she returned, his eyes had glazed over and his mouth hung open. Roberto had given her the drugs and told her they were amazingly effective. If the combination worked as promised, Osric would provide truthful answers to her questions and wake up with jumbled memories of a sexual encounter.

"Did Willona survive the forced definition?"

His head came up, but his gaze remained clouded. "Yes. She hated us and refused to shift. I'd never heard of anyone strong enough to suppress their animal nature, but Willona was."

"What happened to her? How did she die?"

"We were looking into ways to force a shift when she realized she was pregnant."

"That's right. She gave birth to twins." The two young women he'd been so determined to find.

"Not technically twins." His voice became a monotone drone, but he answered without hesitation. "Ava is mine. Sam fathered Carissa."

"I see." She hadn't realized multiple father...litters were possible with Therians. They looked so human. It was easy to forget how truly different they were. "Is Sam still alive?"

"No. Willona was starting to thaw toward him so I killed him."

Holy shit. Had he just admitted to murder without flinching? She'd always sensed a darkness in Osric, but she hadn't expected this. "And how did Willona react to Sam's death?"

"She contacted the Abolitionists and arranged to be 'rescued.'" He sneered as he went on. "As if she could be rescued from her own nature. I wouldn't have bothered to track her, but she took the girls with her. That was inexcusable."

She was dying to ask him about the Abolitionists. Did he know Nehema? But she didn't want to lose her train of thought. "Only Ava is your blood kin. Why were you searching for Carissa?"

"Both girls possess Maggie's blood so either can be defined with multiple animal natures."

"Is that what Milliner was talking about when he said alpha males from all over the State had showed up at the cat sanctuary?" A million details were waiting to be filled in, but she hadn't learned anything new and she wasn't sure how long the drugs' effect would last.

"Carissa has been defined. I don't know if the attempt was successful, but Ava is my only hope now."

"How did Willona die?"

"Car accident. I think it was arranged, but I haven't been able to prove it."

He had admitted to murder without batting an eye. Maybe her questions should be more direct. "Is it your intention to betray the backers?"

"I serve Zophiel. I cannot betray those who do not hold my allegiance."

Well, this was interesting. She wondered if the backers would share his rationalization. "Who is Zophiel?"

"Spy of God. Angel of Devine Justice. Mistress of this unworthy slave."

Mistress? Angels tended to be asexual or male, but this was clearly no ordinary angel. "Does Zophiel go by any other name?"

"That is not for you to know. Before you are worthy to bask in her light, you must be cleansed by fire."

That didn't sound like fun. "What does she look like? I don't want to offend her if I happen upon her someday."

"She has beauty beyond compare. Flowing blonde hair so light it is nearly silver and crystal-blue eyes that shimmer like stars. Her features are nothing short of perfection and her shape knows no equal. If you wandered into her presence, you would tremble at the sight."

The drugs were supposed to make it all but impossible to lie, so Zophiel had to be imaginary. Didn't she? "When did you last see your Mistress in person?"

"Unbeliever! May Zophiel have mercy on your soul." He folded his knees beneath him and pressed his palms together as he rocked back and forth, chanting in a soft, singsong language.

Apparently Zophiel's influence had overridden the drugs' effect. Roberto had warned her that she would have approximately half an hour before Osric was overcome by the need for sleep. She'd learned more than she ever hoped, so she decided not to push her luck.

She moved in front of him and pressed his face into the valley between her breasts. "Let's go to bed." He remained stiff and unresponsive for a long time then one of his hands skimmed up the back of her leg and squeezed her bare behind.

Chapter Six

Something soft brushed against Ava's cheek, drawing her back from the most decadent dream of her life. She'd been making love with Kyle, exploring his amazing body with her hands and her lips. And he'd returned every caress, mirrored every lick and nibble. The images were so appealing she didn't want to open her eyes.

The featherlight caress danced along her jaw then teased her upper lip. A rich, sweat scent filled her nose and she sighed. Rose.

She opened her eyes and found Kyle sitting on the edge of the bed, brandishing a long-stemmed rose like a paint brush. "Good *afternoon*." Startled by the implication, she looked at the blind-covered window and he chuckled. "We were beginning to wonder if you'd ever wake up."

"What time is it?" She pulled the sheet up and tucked it under her arms. He was dressed in jeans and a t-shirt, which made her feel more naked somehow.

"A little after one." He stroked her shoulder with the rose then ran the bloom down her arm and slipped the thorn-less stem into her hand. "I hope you're hungry." She closed her fingers around the stem and raised the flower to her nose, enjoying the fragrance as he set a large wooden tray across her lap. "I wasn't sure what you liked so we made a bit of every-thing."

"We?"

"Enya was my sous chef. She knows the kitchen better than I do." He lifted the plate cover and set it aside.

Ava looked at the generous array of breakfast selections and groaned. "You don't expect me to eat all of this, do you?" Cheese melted into a mound of scrambled eggs. French toast had been arranged beside a stack of pancakes while bacon and sausage balanced out the plate.

"You saved my life. This is the least I could do." His eyes appeared particularly green as he poured her a cup of coffee. "How do you feel? My control was pretty lacking last night."

She spotted the empty vase and returned the rose to the container. "You didn't hurt me." He held out the coffee mug and she was glad for the distraction. His gaze was too percep-tive, too penetrating. "I never knew...never imagined that sex could be like that."

Her confession seemed to please him, but his gaze was still guarded as he looked into her eyes. "I know Enya told you that our bodies are in sync. Do you understand what that means?"

Setting down the coffee mug, Ava picked up her fork and started with the scrambled eggs. "I'm pretty sure I experi-enced the difference, but I'm not sure I understand the de-tails. Jake and Enya tried to explain it to me, but I was pretty distracted last night."

"I didn't intentionally trigger the change, but I'm afraid I am to blame. Our energy melded when I healed you and then again when I fed from you on the mountain. The combination confused our bodies, made our animals think we were trying to mate."

Heat spread across her face and she was certain her cheeks were bright red. "I understand how that could be confusing."

"We didn't form a mating bond, so this synchronization isn't permanent."

For just an instant disappointment crept across her mind then logic kick started her brain. Did she want the connection to be permanent? She barely knew this man. "How long will we feel like this?"

"About three months. But it's important that you understand this doesn't happen unless a couple is attracted to each other in the first place. Our responses are amplified, our needs more intense, but the basic appeal is natural."

Her nipples tightened beneath the sheet and tension built between her thighs as memories of the night before scrolled through her mind. "Can we talk about something else?"

"Of course." His smile was a little too knowing and his gaze caressed her face. "I didn't mean to embarrass you."

She returned his smile then busied herself with breakfast. "How long will it take to reach the cat sanctuary? I can't wait to see Carissa again."

"They're coming here instead."

"Why the change of plans?" She didn't really care where the reunion took place as long as she saw her sister face-to-face. Her visions were becoming more detailed and more frequent, but she wouldn't be completely convinced Carissa was safe and happy until they were in the same room.

"Your spontaneous teleportation."

"What about it? You freaked me out and I overreacted."

"Jake is convinced it was no random flash and I'm starting to agree with him. Therian abilities tend to be specific. Like your visions. You didn't understand what you saw, but the images were detailed. Right?"

"I suppose." She didn't want to seem like a coward, but she'd been looking forward to a place far away from danger, secluded and secure. "I have no idea where we were. Does Jake?"

"He's established a likely radius. We're hoping Ian can search the area and figure out where the guards came from."

"Ian's the raptor?" It was hard to imagine a bird with human—no Therian intelligence, but that's what Kyle's suggestion implied. "How much of you remains intact when you shift? How will a bird be able to search for a covert facility?"

"Instincts are stronger, thoughts less cluttered by minor details, but I'm still me. Ian will have no trouble remembering his mission once he shifts into an eagle."

She nodded and wrapped her hands around the warm enameled mug. Her appetite had gradually faded as she realized the fight was far from over. The past twenty-four hours had been a whirlwind of crisis and emotions. She'd never felt so helpless and yet so protected at the same time. These Therian males possessed the most intriguing combination of ferocity and tenderness. It felt wonderful to have someone at her back for a change.

"Are you done?" After quickly refilling her coffee mug, she raised her arms so he could remove the tray. "You look sort of spooked. That wasn't my intention." He scooted closer and reached for her free hand. "You don't need to be afraid, Ava. You're not alone. We won't let anything happen to you."

His fingers were warm and strong, his grip firm yet careful. "I feel like I've been running my entire life. Even after we settled in Breckenridge, I never felt safe. I knew someone was out there, watching me, waiting for some sort of signal I didn't understand."

"Knowledge is power. I won't pretend the danger is gone, but you know who's behind it and you're much more prepared to deal with it now." His thumb caressed her knuckles and awareness arced between them, making the air sizzle with anticipation.

He took the mug from her hand and leaned in to kiss her when hurried footfalls sounded on the stairs. They turned to the half-open doorway as Enya stepped into the room.

"We've got big trouble. Throw yourself together and get downstairs." With no further explanation, she handed Kyle a stack of clothes and hustled back the way she'd come.

Ava threw back the sheet and crawled out of bed. Kyle handed her the clean clothes and said, "I'll find out what's going on. Take the fastest shower of your life then join us downstairs."

Accepting the bundle, she nodded and headed for the bathroom. Ava quickly showered and dressed. She ran a comb through her hair and rinsed out her mouth with toothpaste then rushed downstairs. Jake was pacing the floor in the railed entryway between the bar and restaurant. His expression was thunderous as he talked to someone on a cell phone. Enya and Kyle stood off to one side, watching Jake with obvious concern.

"What's going on?" Ava whispered as she pressed in close to Kyle.

"Someone snatched three of our females," Enya replied. "One's our sister. The two little ones are our nieces."

Jake ended the call and shoved the phone into one of his pockets as he pulled keys out of another. He looked at his sister as he said, "They've been gone for hours. They could be anywhere by now."

"Why did Liz wait so long to call us?" Enya crossed her arms over her chest, looking every bit as upset as Jake.

"She didn't. Cheyenne agreed to take the girls so Liz and David could have a night to themselves. Liz went to Cheyenne's about an hour ago to pick up the girls and found an empty apartment. All three of them were gone. Liz is pretty sure they were taken some time last night, but she has no idea who or why."

Apparently Liz and Cheyenne were two of Jake's sisters and the "little ones" belonged to Liz. "What can we do?" Ava asked.

"We can't be sure this isn't a ploy to scatter our forces," Jake warned. He looked at Kyle as he went on. "Take Ava to my place. Have Ian meet you there. I'll organize the search while you and Ian investigate our theory about the teleportation."

Kyle caught the keys Jake tossed him and said, "Got it."

"What about me?" Enya asked. "Do you want me to join the hunt?"

Jake shook his head. "You need to go calm down Liz. She might be able to sense the girls if she can get her emotions under control."

"I'm on it." Enya departed without a backward glance.

"Be careful," Jake stressed. "This has trap written all over it."

WHILE OSRIC WAS SLEEPING soundly in her bed, Carly rushed to the conference room and called the backers. She'd been thrilled when she was given the security code to the conference room. It was the only room in the complex from which outgoing calls were possible. Her excitement fizzled soon after as she realized she had no one in the outside world who gave a damn about her. She'd always been an outcast, isolated by her ambition and intelligence. Her lack of family and friends was likely one of the reasons she'd been recruited for this project.

Any one of the three backers could respond to her page. Tonight Roberto came online. He wore a silk robe and his dark hair was tousled as if he'd just crawled out of bed.

"I'm sorry to bother you, sir." If he lived in Italy, as she suspected, it was likely about nine o'clock at night. "I just finished questioning Osric."

"Were the drugs helpful?" The wall behind his desk was wainscoted in rich reddish-brown wood and the edge of a large gilt-framed painting was barely visible. He'd obviously positioned his desk so that few clues to his location were evident.

"Very. It took a bit longer for him to go under than I would have liked, but once the drugs kicked in, he was extremely cooperative." She hesitated, unsure if indulging her curiosity was worth the risk of annoying her boss. "May I ask a question, sir?"

"Of course and stop calling me sir. Milliner might need his ego stroked on a regular basis. I prefer candid honesty."

"All right. I couldn't help wondering why you hadn't used the drugs on Osric before now."

"We discussed it, several times in fact. But the memory loss isn't complete. If we'd strapped him to a chair and interrogated him, he would have known we didn't trust him. This way he'll wake up in bed with jumbled flashes of a night spent with his lover."

She nodded, fervently hoping that was all he remembered.

"What did you learn?"

She'd learned that Milliner was more of a bastard than she'd thought—if that were possible. And the project had been going on far longer than she realized. "Most of what he told me was not new. Osric likes to brag. But I asked him if he had plans to betray the backers and he told me he couldn't betray someone unless he'd sworn allegiance to them first."

"Did he tell you who held his allegiance?"

"He said he served someone named Zophiel."

"Zophiel?" His dark brows drew together over his aquiline nose. "Surely that isn't a real name."

"According to Osric *she* is God's spy and the angel of Divine Justice."

"A female angel?" He chuckled and ran a hand through his hair. "This gets better and better."

"I pushed for more details and he went into some sort of trance. He rocked back and forth and chanted in a language I'd never heard before."

"We all sensed that he was up to something. We never dreamed it was this creative."

"She's likely a figment of his imagination. He was abandoned by his mate and ostracized by his people. Then he was captured by Milliner and treated like a guinea pig. That's enough to make anyone create a loving mistress who values and adores him."

"If that's all she is." He was quiet for a moment, his dark eyes narrowed and intent. Then his expression reset and he smiled at her. "As usual, you've performed extremely well."

"Then will I be able to leave the complex?" Her heart thudded and her belly clenched. The promise of freedom is what kept her going, allowed her to survive Osric's cruel treatment.

"We need to determine if this Zophiel is a legitimate threat or simply an imagined companion." His eyes turned cold and unapproachable. "We haven't forgotten our promise, nor do we intend to renege. We just need more time."

Suspicion dropped into the pit of her stomach, but she managed to nod. "If he tells me any more, I'll let you know."

Roberto nodded and the screen went blank.

CARISSA FLEW ACROSS the living room and wrapped her arms around Ava. Both women cried out with happy enthusiasm and Kyle couldn't help but smile. He glanced at

Quinn and found a similar smile softened the perpetually somber expression of his best friend. It had been a very long time since Kyle had seen Quinn so relaxed.

"I know it's only been a week," Carissa said, "but this has been the longest week of my life!" She gave Ava another hug before stepping back and inspecting her sister from head to foot. "You're really all right?"

"I'm fine." Ava laughed. "You're the one who managed to rearrange your entire life while we were separated." She blinked back tears and motioned toward Quinn. "Introduce us."

"Quinn, this is my sister Ava." She made a sweeping motion toward her sister then reversed direction and said, "Ava, meet Quinn."

Ava crossed to Quinn and shook his hand. "You make her unhappy for any reason and I'll come after you."

Quinn chuckled and his smile widened. "You have nothing to worry about."

"Why don't we give them a few minutes to catch up?" Erin suggested. She stood next to Ian, not far from the front door. The imposing raptor-shifter observed the scene in silence, his gold-veined blue eyes ever watchful.

Ava and Carissa sat on the sofa and immediately began a lively conversation. Kyle led his mother, Ian and Quinn through the sunny kitchen and out onto the wide, multi-level deck. Jake's house was large and orderly, but the expensive furnishings and stylish décor revealed nothing about the sole inhabitant. Jake might sleep beneath this roof, but he lived at Toulouse Tavern.

"Where's Jake?" Ian asked as Kyle slid the glass door shut behind them. Afternoon sunlight bathed the backyard, yet the breeze was surprisingly cool. Jagged peaks surrounded them, the Aspen Mountain visible in the distance. It was easy to understand why so many flocked to this area. The setting had just the right balance of grandeur and tranquility.

Dragging his gaze away from his surroundings, Kyle answered Ian's question. "Cheyenne and Liz's daughters were taken from Cheyenne's apartment sometime last night. There were signs of a struggle, but Liz has no idea who would take them or why."

"Oh my God. Jake and Enya must be frantic." Erin shook her head, worry and compassion obvious in her bright green eyes.

"Abolitionists?" Quinn's expression instantly hardened taking on a lethal edge.

Kyle shrugged, the gesture born of frustration not apathy. "I can't imagine anyone else who would dare such a thing, but they haven't been this aggressive in years."

"Unless you count Gage trying to kill me and Ian." Quinn arched his brow, challenging Kyle to contradict the point.

"Gage's actions weren't sanctioned by Nehema," Ian said. "In fact, she was furious when she learned what he'd done."

"Who the hell is Nehema?" Kyle looked at Quinn then back at Ian. "For that matter, who is Gage?" Apparently there had been some interesting developments while he was incommunicado.

"Gage is the Abolitionist who 'rescued' Willona and set her up with a new life," Ian explained. "He took a shot at either me or Quinn and hit Carissa by mistake. We captured him as he was setting up for a second try."

"Did you take him alive?"

"Of course." Ian's smile was chilling. "He did his best to resist my scans, but in the end I learned everything he knew. Which wasn't nearly as helpful as I'd hoped. A woman named Nehema calls the shots, but Gage had only spoken with her on the phone. His direct contact was a man he referred to as Team Leader. I have his image, but little else."

"The kidnapping could be retaliation," Kyle suggested.

"I'd agree if they'd taken someone from your clan. Jake had nothing to do with Gage's capture."

Ian had a point. Kyle sighed and reviewed the events, searching for patterns or subtle clues. "We're back where we started. If this wasn't Abolitionists, who had a grudge against Jake or benefited from the crime?"

"Has there been a ransom demand?" Quinn motioned toward the mansion beside them. "Everyone knows the tigers are loaded."

"I still think Abolitionists are our best bet," Erin said. "Three females, one nearing definition. It's not really a departure from their MO."

Ian didn't look nearly as convinced. "Liz's girls are, what, eight and ten? They're years away from definition."

"But Cheyenne isn't," Kyle reminded.

"Cheyenne lives alone." Erin's brow remained knitted, her lips compressed. "They probably came for her and had no choice but to take the girls."

"No choice?" Ian sneered. "Are you crazy? There are always choices."

"I'm not defending them." She sounded shocked by Ian's conclusion. "Why are you so testy?"

"Sorry." He raked his hair with his hand as he took a deep, calming breath. "There have been too many attacks. Too many unanswered questions. I need an objective or better yet a good fight. Just ignore me."

"You're tired and frustrated." Erin wrapped her arm around his waist and gave him a maternal squeeze.

"At least we know Devon's safe," Quinn offered. "That's one less unanswered question."

Ian didn't argue, but Kyle spotted suspicion in his gaze as he glanced away. "What are you talking about? Did Devon come home?"

"She sent me a video message this morning," Erin explained. "She said she'd come back as soon as the Charter was changed and forced definitions were abolished. I want to believe it, but something about it still feels wrong."

"Prisoners of war are forced to create video messages all the time." Ian looked at Kyle as he went on. "I've had a bad feeling about this from the beginning. This might have started out as a protest for Devon, but she would never be this cruel."

"How did she look in the video?" Each time Kyle tried to sense his sister he crashed into her mental shields. His mother had reported the same problem. Wherever Devon was, it certainly seemed like she didn't want to be found.

"The video was damn convincing," Ian admitted, "but it's all a bit too convenient. As Erin said, it just doesn't feel right."

"I haven't called off the search and I won't until she's found," Kyle assured them. "It doesn't matter if she's protesting or if this is beyond her control. We will find her."

Ian's stiff nod was mirrored by Erin.

"What's being done to find Cheyenne and the girls?" Quinn asked after a tense pause.

"Jake knows we'll help in any way we can, but we have a different mystery to investigate right now."

"What mystery?" Quinn prompted.

Kyle motioned toward the patio furniture grouped at one end of the spacious deck. He sat across from his mother, flanked by Quinn and Ian. "Ava had a vision about Carissa. She saw the ritual."

"Did she think we were hurting Carissa?" Quinn was clearly upset by the idea.

"The vision was detailed enough that Ava realized Carissa participated willingly. However, she was still left with a sense of dread, as if something horrible was happening or was about to happen."

"Go on," his mother urged.

"She grabbed her stuff and headed for the motorcycle stashed behind the cabin. I grabbed her as she came around the corner. I didn't want her to scream or run. The next thing I knew we teleported halfway across the State."

"Ava can teleport?" Erin sounded intrigued, not surprised while the two men stared at him with obvious skepticism.

"It was a spontaneous reaction to my touch."

Quinn laughed. "And I thought I repelled females."

"She thought she was in danger and her instincts spiked?" Ian ignored Quinn's attempt at humor. "Was the location random?"

"I thought so at first, but we encountered armed guards in the middle of the forest."

"They weren't forest rangers?" Quinn asked.

"With M16s?" Kyle shook his head. "We *borrowed* their Jeep and drove until we found a road. Jake gave us directions then brought us here and ditched the Jeep."

"I'll scan Ava's memory then search from the air and see if I can find whatever they were guarding." Ian started to push back his chair but Kyle stopped him.

"You can't touch her. She hurt herself when she landed and I had to heal her. It left me incredibly weak."

Ian's gaze narrowed, his tall body tense and agitated. "What does that have to do with my scanning her mind?"

"We exchanged energy a couple of times and it triggered synchronization."

Ian folded his arms over his chest and glared from Quinn to Kyle. "It's mighty convenient that both of Maggie's granddaughters ended up bound to cats."

"We're not bound," Kyle stressed.

"Yet." Ian shoved back his chair and moved to the deck's railing, turning away from the table. "This gives you three months to convince her to mate with you. Just like Quinn you've shut out the competition."

Kyle knew it hadn't happened like that, but he also knew how it looked. "I was dying, Ian. I didn't have a choice."

"There are always choices," Ian muttered then turned around and retreated behind an expressionless mask. "An aerial search is our best bet of figuring out what the guards are protecting."

"I agree." Kyle understood Ian's strategy. Even if he'd intended to court Ava, there was nothing he could do about it until her physiology reset. Fixating on a situation beyond one's control was an utter waste of energy. Besides, the safety of the tiger females had to come before personal agendas. "Jake figured out a rough perimeter and the most likely areas within the search area."

"Show me."

Rather than retrieve the map from Jake's office, Kyle sent the image to Ian telepathically. He also transmitted his memory of their conversation and as much as he remembered about the actual escape.

"You saved her life." Ian's expression didn't change, but his tone softened a bit.

Kyle hadn't purposely shared the intimate details of his interaction with Ava, but Ian was the strongest telepath he knew so it wasn't surprising that he'd absorbed more than Kyle had intended. "And she saved mine in return. The rest just happened."

"Or the rest was meant to happen," Erin added with a cheeky smile.

Ian glared at her while Quinn and Kyle rolled their eyes. Erin might be the network Historian, but she'd always been a hopeless matchmaker.

"I'll see what I can find." Ian tugged off his boots and stuffed his socks down inside them. Erin rose to collect his garments as he continued to undress. He pulled off his shirt and she folded it neatly and set it on the table. "I should return by nightfall. If not..." He shrugged. "I'm probably screwed."

"That's not funny." Erin gave him a quick hug and Ian moved to the middle of the deck. He spread his arms and raised his face to the sky. The golden streaks in his hair glistened and his skin began to glow. He leapt into the air and his shape blurred, transitioning from human to bird in a smooth, flowing motion. Wide, majestic wings spread, propelling him higher with each strong rhythmic flap. He soared then swooped then glided, sailing gracefully upon the cool mountain wind.

AVA SANK BACK INTO the corner of the couch, stunned and nearly numb from all the things her sister had told her. "It all sounded ridiculous when Jake told me about it, but you've confirmed everything he said."

"Do you understand why Mother ran? What Osric and Sam Collins did to her?"

Drawing her legs up before her, Ava wrapped her arms around her knees. "She was terrified and resentful and they still forced her to endure the blood ritual."

"Osric only knows enough about the Omni Prime to be really dangerous. What happened to Mom was nothing like what happened to me."

"I know." Ava smiled. "I saw enough in my vision to understand the difference."

"Why didn't you tell me you were having visions?" Carissa sounded hurt.

"Would you have believed me?"

"Probably not. My concept of reality has been significantly changed since I met Quinn." A dreamy smile bowed her lips for a moment then she refocused and said, "You've seen Kyle shift and you've experienced power exchanges. Do you still have questions about any of this?"

Ava laughed and tucked her hair behind her ear. "I still have questions about *all* of this, but I know I'm not human. I started feeling different as soon as Kyle touched me."

"Are you two lovers?"

"I don't know what we are. Lovers seems too simplistic, too casual for how I feel when I'm with him. He says we're 'in sync'. Do you know what that means?"

Carissa nodded, a contented smile lingering on her lips. "Quinn and I synchronized almost from the beginning. It's a little frightening at first, but it's wonderful too."

A musical chime echoed through the house, drawing their gazes to the front door. "Jake wouldn't ring the bell. It might be Enya."

"I thought she went to comfort her sister."

They both stood but neither approached the door. Someone tried the knob then Ava heard the scrape of a key slipping into the lock. The visitor had a key, so why was her heart still pounding? She glanced toward the kitchen and the deck beyond. Should she call for Kyle? Wouldn't it be better to—The door pushed inward and a young brown-haired woman paused in the threshold.

"Hi." She looked at Carissa and Ava with obvious reluctance. "This is my day to clean. Should I come back?"

Before Ava or Carissa could respond, the maid was shoved inward and a burly man kicked the door shut. Brown, copper and gold combined in his longish hair and his jaw was shadowed as if he hadn't shaved for a couple of days.

"Have a seat." He motioned the maid toward a chair with the pistol in his right hand then his cold hazel eyes shifted back to the sisters. "Which one of you is Ava?"

"I am." Carissa stepped forward before Ava could speak.

Kyle, we have an armed visitor. Can you hear me? She couldn't drag her gaze away from the gun in his hand.

We're already in position, love. Just play along.

She wasn't alone. No, *they* weren't alone. Carissa was no longer her only companion. "She's trying to protect me. I'm Ava."

The intruder glared at the maid. "Which one is which?"

"Don't know either of them." She seemed remarkably composed being that she was an armed man's hostage. Unless she wasn't human. Was she waiting for the right moment to shift into something more dangerous? Like a tiger?

"Who are you?" Carissa asked the intruder.

"I'm Ava's mate." He smirked. "She just doesn't know it yet." Without shifting the gun from Carissa, he looked at Ava. "Get over here or your sister dies."

"You're too late," Ava insisted. "Kyle claimed me last night."

His nose twitched and his eyes narrowed. "His scent isn't strong enough. He might have fucked you, but you're still un-claimed."

"If you say so." What were the men waiting for? Her stomach was knotted and sweat beaded her upper lip.

"To me. Now." His eyes gleamed as he parted his lips, displaying his elongated fangs.

Kyle had said to play along, but the stranger's weapon was pointed at Carissa. Ava took a slow step forward then stopped. "Let them go and I won't fight you."

He laughed. "Get your ass over here or I'll shoot them both and teach you to obey. You're still latent, which means you're no match for me."

"But I am." Carissa dove for the floor, shredding her clothes as she released her human form.

The stranger fired, but the bullet flew high, missing Carissa by at least a foot. Carissa's feline body was sleek and black with vivid white stripes.

An enraged growl erupted from the stranger as Carissa's head connected with his groin. He sank to his knees, the pistol dropping to the carpet as he crossed his arms over the injured area. The maid darted forward and grabbed the weapon. She stepped back and covered the intruder as Carissa slowly circled him. Their movements were confident and smooth, as if the attack had been orchestrated. And Ava had never felt so useless in her life.

For just a moment she thought the fight was over then the stranger lunged to the side and shifted with a furious snarl. His body shrank and compacted, bones snapped and fur sprouted through his skin. The change was grotesque yet fascinating, far less...graceful than Carissa's shift had been. With a long snout and sharp-looking teeth, he was much larger than any wolf Ava had ever seen.

A feline cry drew Ava's attention to the kitchen as Kyle, in cougar form, came bounding into sight. Carissa moved closer to the maid, respectfully yielding the fight to Kyle.

The wolf seemed pleased by his new opponent. He charged Kyle only to connect with one of the cougar's powerful claws. Bloody slashes parted the wolf's fur from shoulder to chest. The wolf yelped, knocked sideways by the force of the blow.

Kyle was bigger and more controlled, but apparently the wolf wasn't ready to accept defeat. The wolf charged again. Kyle caught him by the throat and flipped him over, pinning him to the floor. The wolf flailed, twisting and kicking as Kyle's teeth sank deeper into his flesh.

"Kyle!" The maid's voice snapped with sudden authority, her stance suspiciously militant. "Bruce spilled no blood. Nate deserves the opportunity to discipline his son."

After a long, anxious moment, Kyle released his shift, smoothly transferring his hand to the wolf's throat as his body changed. "Would Nate hesitate if one of his females were threatened?" Blood smeared his lower face and both hands. His eyes still glowed with amber light. Ava shivered. He looked every bit as savage as he had a few minutes before.

Carissa had released her shift as well and Quinn quickly wrapped her in a blanket. They stood near the archway leading to the kitchen. Erin on Carissa's other side. They all stayed back and remained silent. This was Kyle's choice to make. Kyle's woman had been the focus of the attack. It was his right to seek retaliation. The realization sent another shiver down Ava's spine. Kyle's claim on her might be temporary, but for the next three months she was his to protect, his to pleasure and enjoy.

"It doesn't matter what Nate would or would not do." The woman remained poised and ready, pistol now aimed at

Kyle. "If you're a man of honor—as you claim—you'll abide by the rules."

After another long pause, Kyle stood, utterly unconcerned with his nudity. "Why did you let him use you? You're one of Jake's sentinels. You could have overpowered him at any time."

"Exactly." She grinned and lowered the gun. "That idiot mistook me for a maid and I couldn't resist. I knew he was up to no good. I just needed to find out exactly what he wanted." She picked up Bruce's jeans and moved closer to the panting wolf. "Shift back, asshole. Daddy is going to be very upset with you."

Chapter Seven

Ian returned shortly after sundown. Ava's mind was still reeling from the events of the day. It was wonderful to see Carissa, to know she was safe, happy and very much in love. But all of Ava's choices still lay ahead, threatening to shape her life into something she no longer recognized. She stood by the sliding glass door in the spacious country kitchen, watching the sun sink behind the mountains. The others sat around the kitchen table, debating strategy. Light began to fade as shadows crept across the land and a sudden motion drew her gaze to the sky.

A massive bird sailed over the treetops then swooped toward the house. She shifted position, tilting her head as the bird flew nearer. Its long, powerful wings spread wide, slowing its descent as it landed on the deck's wooden rail. The eagle hopped off the rail and the outline of its body shimmered as the shape stretched and expanded, growing longer and broader in a smooth, streaming motion. Light from the house spilled onto the deck, allowing her to witness the miraculous transformation. Legs and arms stretched outward then the torso and head took on detail and definition. Regal features and rippling muscles arranged with perfect symmetry.

Ava was mesmerized by the surreal display and the masculine beauty of both bird and man. A sensual smile curved his lips and he inclined his head, acknowledging her presence—and the fact that she was staring at him.

She turned from the window as a guilty flush crept up her neck. "Ian's back."

Erin shoved her chair back and hurried out onto the deck. Ava didn't even turn around. Nudity might be an inevitable part of Therian life, but she'd been reared with human sensibilities.

Crossing to the table, she sat beside Kyle and tried to wrangle her chaotic thoughts. "Who's watching the store?" It was an incidental detail, but the concrete connection to her old life allowed her to sidestep the looming conflict and calm down. Besides, they'd worked hard to build a successful business and she wasn't willing to watch it slip away regardless of the new challenges they were facing.

"I called Amanda and let her know we had a family emergency. She closed the store for the first couple of days, but asked if she could work out a schedule with Luke until we return. It's the off-season, so I'm sure they'll be fine until things settle into a routine for us."

"And is that likely to happen anytime soon?"

Erin and Ian stepped into the kitchen, interrupting Carissa's reply. Ian was dressed and composed as he joined them at the table. "I'm pretty sure I found it." Everyone perked up, scooting closer to the table as they waited for more information. "I'd about given up when it started to get dark and I spotted lights in a secluded valley. I'd pictured a military outpost with multiple buildings and a landing strip or helipad." He shook his head and the overhead lights made the gold streaks in his hair shimmer. "It was nothing like that, just a moderate two-story building with a large vehicle shed and a clearing off to one side."

"Was there an access road? What about fortification?" Quinn asked.

"No physical barriers other than the location. I spotted two sets of guards patrolling the perimeter, but I didn't see so much as a dirt trail." He rubbed the back of his neck then rolled his shoulders. "I haven't flown that much in years. I'm going soft." He chuckled then went on. "I'd like to return tomorrow with a camera and GPS. I'll mark the exact location and see if I can verify the number of inhabitants, maybe identify patrol patterns and guard rotations."

"Without any sort of access road, this is going to be a logistical nightmare." Kyle looked at her and tried to soften the observation with a smile.

"How do we know this building has anything to do with us?" Ava couldn't remain silent any longer. This sounded like a time-consuming wild-goose chase. "You guys are basing your strategy on the fact that I teleported to that location. I was panicked at the time. I think Kyle was right in the beginning. It was nothing more than my survival instinct."

"Perhaps." Ian searched her gaze, his expression intense yet unreadable. "We'll take it one step at a time. I'll gather more information tomorrow and see where that leads us."

Everyone nodded though Ava remained uneasy. They all had much more confidence in her abilities than she did. Her visions were unpredictable at best and teleporting had been a fluke. She glanced at Carissa, still amazed by the ease with which her sister had shifted. The feline Carissa became wasn't even an identified species but some unique blinding of the six animal natures she'd absorbed. Ava shuddered. Carissa had always been adventurous and brave while Ava analyzed each possible outcome and progressed with cautious deliberation.

"We had a visitor while you were gone," Quinn told Ian.

"Do I even want to know?" Ian shook his head, a smile tugging at the corners of his mouth.

"Bruce Fitzroy mistook Natasha for Jake's maid and 'forced' her to let him into the house," Quinn explained.

"How did he know Ava was here?"

"Why do you immediately presume he was after me?" Ava's stomach tightened as the implications of Ian's conclusion sank in. The hunt wasn't over. She was still in danger, still a conduit of unimagined power. Someone worth killing to possess. She'd seen a hint of Carissa's abilities and the glimpse drove home all the fantastical claims she heard over the past few days. It was all real. The blood of an Omni Prime flowed in her veins. If she lived up to her full potential, she might be the next true Therian.

"You're the only thing here worth stealing." Ian's gaze moved over her face, the gold veins in his rich blue irises especially apparent as he searched her features.

Kyle reached over and squeezed her hand, drawing her attention away from Ian. "You don't need to be afraid. I wouldn't have let him touch you. Natasha only allowed the situation to progress as far as it did so she had concrete evidence to present to the council."

"Fitzroy mistook Natasha for a maid?" Ian laughed. "I bet she laughed her ass off about that."

"Once Bruce was secured, she wasted no time mocking him," Quinn confirmed. "But your question is interesting. How did he know Ava was here? Was the tavern open when Jake got the call about the kidnapping?"

"The bar side was basically dead, but the restaurant was fairly busy," Kyle said. "Jake was focused on the kidnapping, which is understandable. None of us thought about someone overhearing the conversation."

"Well, someone obviously did." There was just enough disapproval in Ian's voice to make Kyle tense.

"Bruce is an arrogant idiot," Quinn refocused the conversation. "He knew Ava wasn't here alone and he still tried to snatch her. But when it came time to pull the trigger, he spent so long posturing that a newly defined female took him down."

"Thanks a lot," Carissa huffed.

"You did incredibly well." Quinn wrapped his arm around her shoulders and drew her closer, chair and all. "That wasn't my point."

"What was your point?" Already her irritation began to melt. Carissa was obviously helpless to resist her lover's touch.

The affection and longing flowing between Carissa and Quinn made Ava feel empty and restless.

Are you all right? Kyle squeezed her hand and she looked into his eyes.

I'm fine. She dragged her gaze away from his face. The smoldering desire in his gaze was far too similar to Quinn and Carissa's.

"Bruce Fitzroy is an annoyance not a threat," Quinn stressed.

"Nate will either keep him on a leash or Kyle won't need to stop next time."

Erin's easy conclusion made Ava feel sick. She could still see Kyle crouched over the wolf, blood dripping off his chin.

"I'll mention it to Jake once things quiet down," Ian decided. "A customer overhearing a conversation is one thing. He needs to make sure he doesn't have a leak."

No one argued with that, so the impromptu briefing ended.

"Is anyone else hungry?" Erin asked. "I'd love a pizza, but it's probably unwise to tempt fate with a delivery."

"Check the freezer," Ian suggested. "Jake's a bachelor and bachelors always have frozen pizza."

"This bachelor owns a restaurant," Carissa reminded with a smile.

Erin crossed to the surprisingly large refrigerator and opened the freezer side. "Ian wins. Plenty of frozen pizza. What's everyone want?"

Ava slipped off her chair and went out on the deck. The night was cool and clear, the sky studded with flickering stars. She crossed her arms on the railing, needing a moment alone.

How had Carissa accepted all this so easily? Ava no longer doubted the things she'd been told, but she wasn't sure how to process her new reality. In less than a week her life had gone from a semi-boring routine to life-and-death struggles, attempted murder and kidnappings.

And what the hell was she going to do about Kyle? People in high-stress situations frequently developed intense connections, but as soon as the danger passed, the attraction faded away. She didn't want to offer more of herself than Kyle offered in return. Everything was too new, too uncertain. She couldn't let her insecurities turn him into some sort of hero.

As if summoned by her musings, Kyle suddenly stood behind her and wrapped her in a soft blanket. "I know you're conflicted and I'll give you some space. I just didn't want you to freeze to death."

She reached back as he started to leave and caught his wrist. "Please stay." His arms wrapped around her and his body heat sank through the blanket, adding to the comforting weight.

"Would you really have killed him?" she whispered without turning around.

He took a moment to answer and she felt his arms momentarily tighten against her waist. "I won't lie to you and I can't pretend to be something I'm not. Therians are predators and we're intensely protective of those we care about."

Did he honestly care about her or was he just grateful she'd saved his life? The question echoed back and reversed. Did she care about him or was she simply grateful he'd saved her life?

"Do you want me to answer that or are you just working things out in your mind?"

She smiled and rested the back of her head against his shoulder. "Once I'm defined, will I be able to shield my thoughts from you? Being this transparent obliterates my feminine mystique."

He chuckled then rubbed his cheek against her hair. "I assure you your mystique has lost none of its power. I'm fascinated by you."

"Why?" Even though it revealed her vulnerability, she couldn't suppress the word.

"Why am I fascinated by you?" He sounded disbelieving, so she turned around, dislodging his arms in the process. He moved his hands to the rail and stared into her eyes as he waited for her to reply.

"You can have any woman you want. Enya was hostile until she realized we were in sync."

"Enya was likely hostile because we're in sync."

"That doesn't change the fact that she wants you." He didn't deny it, so she went on. "Are you leader of your clan?"

"Yes."

He seemed reluctant to elaborate, but she wasn't in the mood for evasions. "Explain how all this works. Why is Ian annoyed by our connection? Was he hoping to bond with me?"

"The most powerful male in each clan becomes alpha. The twelve most powerful alphas serve on the Alpha Council. All the clans are organized into four networks. Quinn and I belong to the Rocky Mountain Feline Network. There is a Southern Feline Network, Canine Network and the Minority Network. The most powerful alpha from each of these four networks becomes their network's Prime."

"Why are there two feline networks?"

"Because there are more feline shifters in RMFN than all the other networks combined. I don't know why we've fared better than the other Therians, but it's been that way for a very long time."

"Are you your network's Prime?" She'd had no idea it was this well organized, but she'd sensed authority in both men, the sort of confidence that only came with power.

"I am and so is Ian. And you're right. He's hoping you'll join with him and become part of the Minority Network."

"Does that mean it's still my choice to make?"

"Of course." He sighed, removing one of his hands from the rail as he brushed his hair back from his face. "Nothing will be forced on you, *ever*. Even if you don't choose me, I'll make sure no one harms you or pressures you needlessly."

"If I don't choose you?" Her mind stalled on the phrase, unable to move beyond the concept. "You want me to...bond with you *permanently*?"

He ran his knuckles across her cheek and smiled. "Don't panic, sunshine. You know damn well I want you, but any permanent decision is a long way off. You don't have to be afraid any longer. Any one of us would give our lives to protect you."

"How very medieval of you."

Despite her grumbling response, he chuckled then tilted her chin up and searched her gaze. "The concept might be antiquated, but I mean it literally. We are sworn to the Omni Prime. Your life and the life of anyone within your bloodline is more important than ours."

"I refuse to accept—"

He placed his fingers on her lips, halting her words. "It doesn't matter what you accept. The choice was ours to make. And when you are ready—regardless of how long that takes—you will choose the male who best meets your needs and balances your abilities." His fingertips brushed over her face as he drew his hand away.

"I won't have abilities of any importance until I'm defined."

He nodded, his gaze lingering on her mouth. "That decision must be made sooner, but you still have time. Relax. Allow yourself to adjust to all these changes."

Carissa hadn't needed time to adjust. She'd learned all the secrets their mother had hidden from them and chosen her new life path while Ava ran and hid like a frightened rabbit.

Erin slid the door open and called, "Pizza's almost ready."

"We'll be right in," Kyle told her.

The warmth in his gaze made Ava smile. "Have you and your mother always been close?"

"Yes, but we became especially so after my father died."

She nodded. "Death seems to do that to the ones left behind." She'd thought she was close with Carissa until their mother died. Then they became inseparable, having no other family but each other. Or so they'd believed at the time.

Ava sat across from her sister as Erin set two steaming pizzas on the kitchen table. The men waited as Erin served the younger women then they attacked the rest of the gooey slices. They spoke of people Ava didn't know and it made her feel even more like an outsider when she realized Carissa understood the references. Erin tried to include her in the exchange, but the conversation quickly became too lively to control.

Quinn and Kyle enjoyed exchanging playful insults while
Ian remained quiet and watchful, his gaze frequently straying
to Ava. He was handsome and imposing, but she felt no attraction, no elemental connection like the one she felt with
Kyle. So it wasn't Therian males as opposed to human men.
She hadn't felt the overwhelming urge to jump Jake's bones.
It was only Kyle who made her irrationally...horny. She'd always hated the word, but nothing else expressed the continu-
al restlessness only his touch quieted.

"Has anyone checked in with Jake?" Carissa asked as the
men divvied up the final pieces of pizza.

"I talked briefly with Enya," Ian said. "Jake's still out in
the field."

"Any new information? Has he picked up a trail?" Erin's
eyes were the same forest green as Kyle's, Ava noticed as they
filled with compassion. "Those poor girls."

"They don't know anything yet, but Jake will keep at
it until they're found. Stubbornness is a common Therian
trait."

Stubbornness, protectiveness, compassion and ferocity,
Ava added to the list. Most modern women would consider
their attitudes chauvinistic and out-of-date. Ava found them
charming. She'd spent so much of her life trying to be strong
and self-sufficient. Knowing someone was there to protect
and care for her was incredibly appealing.

Kyle pushed back from the table and held out his hand.
"Mind if we desert you with the dishes?" he asked his mother.
"We're still recovering from our adventures in the wild."

She chuckled then winked at him. "Go on. I'm sure Carissa and I can handle it. We wouldn't want you to strain yourself."

Ava's face flamed as the others laughed, everyone except Ian. His gaze followed her with obvious interest. Kyle slipped his arm around her shoulders and ushered her from the room. "Ignore him."

"Ignore who?"

He stopped walking and turned her to face him, his hands resting on her shoulders. "Answers like that will make me think his attention isn't unwanted. Are you attracted to Ian?"

"No. I've just never had one man this interested in me, much less two."

"Better get used to it," he advised in a whisper. "Until you choose your mate, you're going to draw a lot of attention."

Kyle led her to the bedroom he'd selected for them and motioned toward the suitcase on the chair near the connecting bathroom. "Carissa brought some of your clothes and stuff."

"Yeah, she told me Quinn drove her to our house while we were lost on the mountain. I guess she was pretty upset and he was trying to keep her distracted."

"I can think of more interesting ways to keep a woman distracted." He grinned at her, but she was too busy rummaging through the suitcase to notice.

"It will be so nice to wear my own clothes." She looked at him and flashed a beaming smile. "She remembered my toothbrush!"

"It's amazing how much we take for granted. All the simple pleasures of life."

With her toothbrush in one hand and a sleep shirt in the other, she looked at the bed then nibbled on her bottom lip. "Do you mind if I take a bath before we go to bed? I really need to relax."

"Anything you want. Tonight's for you."

She glanced away while her cheeks turned pink. He loved it when she blushed. It made her seem so innocent, so untainted by the harsh realities of life. "Why is that? It's not my birthday or anything."

"You promised not to run no matter what happened."

"I kept that promise." Her brows scrunched together over her nose, creating adorable furrows in her brow. He wanted to smooth away the faint lines with his lips then kiss his way down to her mouth.

"I know you did. Now it's my turn to prove that I'm a man of my word. Last night was not what I intended for our first time together. I promised to make it up to you and I intend to keep that promise tonight." Before she could reply, he swept her into his arms and carried her into the bathroom. The large sunken tub was the reason he'd chosen this bedroom. "I was going to fill the bath and bring you chilled champagne, but you ruined the surprise."

"Sorry." She slid down his body as he released her legs. "Are you going to join me?"

"That's up to you. I'll remain your obedient servant if you'd rather just soak or I'll wash your hair and rub your shoulders if you'd rather have company."

Mischief glistened in her blue eyes and she placed her hand on his chest. "What if I'd rather have my obedient servant in the tub with me?"

He laughed. "It's your night. What would you like me to do?" He wasn't sure how long his Therian nature would allow him to indulge her, but he'd give it a try. She'd already experienced forceful and demanding. This might be fun.

"Undress for me. I was too worried about you dying on me last night to enjoy your visual appeal."

"As milady commands." He swept his arm in front of him as he bent into a courtly bow. Then he turned on the water so the bathtub could fill while he obeyed her first directive. He tugged off his boots and socks then pulled his t-shirt off over his head. Her gaze boldly followed his movements, frequently lingering in strategic areas. Therians were blessed with a higher metabolic rate than most humans, so obesity wasn't a problem. In fact the vast majority of human diseases didn't affect Therians.

Glancing at the tub, he made sure he had time before he asked, "May I undress you as well?"

"Not until you're naked." She pointed to the front of his jeans.

Desire rolled through him, fueled by the challenge inherent in her attitude. They'd barely begun and already he wanted to regain control, to rip the clothes from her body and press her up against the wall. Instead, he lowered his zipper and slowly removed his pants. Her gaze followed the descent of his hands until his shaft sprang free then her focus locked into place. Their positions the night before had kept her from seeing more than an occasional glimpse of his cock. Her rampant interest now only made him even harder.

He stroked himself with one hand, drawing heat and urgency into his groin. "See what you do to me. Would you like to touch it, sunshine? It's all for you."

She immediately reached for him, but he caught her wrist. "Not until you're naked." He used her words as a sensual taunt. So much for being passive.

Her gaze narrowed for a moment then she ripped off her shirt and tugged on one of her boots. The stubborn footwear wouldn't budge.

"Would you like my help with that?"

She sat on the edge of the tub and he removed her boots and then her socks. Pausing long enough to turn off the water, she stood and unfastened her bra. Her enthusiasm thrilled him, but it also compromised his efforts to keep things slow and easy. He unzipped her jeans and she shoved them down then kicked them aside.

Before she could touch him, he pulled her against him and covered her mouth with his. Her hands moved up and down his back, pausing from time to time to squeeze his ass. Her lips parted and her tongue lightly touched his, but he wasn't ready for a deep, breath-stealing kiss. Instead he eased her back and motioned toward the tub.

"Get in."

She laughed. "I thought I was in charge tonight."

"You're right. I apologize. What would milady like next?"

She circled him, boldly running her gaze up and down his body. "Are Therian males fitness junkies or are you naturally lean?"

"It's not just males." Her distraction allowed him to scrutinize her body as closely as she was scrutinizing him. "Your body is sleek and toned. Do you live at the gym?"

"Good point." She stopped behind him and pressed her breasts against his back. "I've always kept really busy, but I've never paid much attention to what I eat."

Her eager hands stroked his chest and sides as she rubbed against his back. He closed his eyes and enjoyed the heat of her soft body and the light stroke of her fingers. His cat tossed his head, restless and ready to pounce. He tried not to rush her, wanted her to explore and indulge all of her impulses.

She caressed her way around to his chest and bit her lower lip as her gaze zeroed in on his cock. He expected her to swoop down and fist his hard shaft. Instead she stroked his chest and squeezed his biceps while his cock bobbed between them, desperate for her touch.

Pushing up to the balls of her feet, she whispered in his ear, "Would you like me to touch you?"

He fought back a groan as desire constricted his balls. "You know I would."

"Then say it." She leaned in and his tip brushed against her soft belly. He caught her wrist and tried to bring her hand where he wanted it. She laughed and twisted out of his grip. "Now you have to say please."

How had she turned this around? Each time they'd touched before she'd seemed uncertain, almost afraid. Why was she so much more confident now? Jake and Ian. The thought made Kyle tense and his eyes stung as Therian light erupted in his gaze. Jake flirted with every female on the planet. Ian had been more subtle, but his desire for Ava had been easily interpreted. And she'd obviously enjoyed the attention.

He'd put a stop to this right now. Slipping his hand into her hair, he formed a loose fist and slowly tilted her head back. "I want your hands on me and only me. I want your lips so accustomed to my taste that anyone else is repulsive. I want—"

She placed her fingers against his lips as he had done with her. "Where is this coming from? I told you I don't want Ian."

"What about Jake?" He eased up on her hair but didn't remove his hand.

"Let go of my hair." Her tone was cold and precise, her gaze rapidly cooling.

He pulled his hand back and took a deep breath.

"Let's get one thing perfectly clear." She took a step back and snatched a bath towel off the rack, holding it in front of her as she went on. "You don't own me. No man ever will. It was only after my mother stopped depending on men and stood on her own two feet that she had anything resembling a real life."

"I'm sorry I upset you." Her gaze narrowed and he braced for the coming storm. That had obviously been the wrong thing to say.

"You're sorry *I'm* upset? How about being sorry for acting like a possessive asshole?"

He grappled for the right words while his cat roared, objecting to any compromise. She was his and his alone, challenging that fact only made him more determined to prove it. With any other female, he would have kissed her into submission. He'd have accepted the challenge and demonstrated his superior strength and the depths of his hunger. But Ava had been reared human. She didn't understand Therian ways. No matter how loudly his cat objected, he had to be patient with her.

"I don't want to own you, but the thought of another man touching you is...upsetting to me."

For some reason his explanation made her smile. "If this is you upset, I'd hate to see you get jealous."

"The only affective weapon against jealousy is trust."

Her momentary amusement evaporated and she was glaring again. "You don't trust me?"

"I don't trust anyone," he admitted. "I've been repeatedly betrayed by those I considered friends and more than a few lovers. I try not to expect the worst in people, but experience has taught me to be wary."

"That's sad." She draped the towel back over the rack and climbed into the bathtub. "Is there no one in your life you can relax with, no one who'll support you no matter what?"

"My mother and Quinn." He remained beside the tub, not sure if she'd welcome him in the water.

"I thought you were going to wash my hair."

Suppressing his relief, he climbed into the tub and settled against the molded end, facing her.

"Why have so many betrayed you? Are you that poor a judge of character?" She softened the question with a playful smile and sank to her chin in the water. Even though he could still see her clearly, the barrier seemed to make her feel more secure.

"My ancestors for six generations have held the position of network Prime. Both my father and grandfather resisted proposed changes to the Charter and stood in the way of much-needed changes. Suffice it to say, my family has many enemies."

"What's the Charter?"

He relaxed against the tub and spread his arms along the rim. Even keeping his gaze fixed on her face was doing little to curtail the hunger building inside him. But he needed her to understand the forces that shaped him. It would allow them to connect on more than a sexual level, and he sensed that she wanted that as much as he did. So he ignored the pressure in his groin and fought the urge to drag her back into his arms.

"It's a set of rules and policies governing the behavior of Therians, rather like the humans' Constitution." A nod was her only reply, so he went on. "Many of the alphas voiced their frustration with rules they considered obsolete or antiquated. My grandfather insisted there had been a concrete reason for each word entered into the Charter and gathered supporters who shared his view."

"And your father continued the fight?"

"Yes. The reformers—or rebels as they like to call us—grew in number, but the Prime council dug in their heels and refused to budge on even the most obvious changes."

"But you're one of the rebels, aren't you? That's what you said when we first met."

"I absolutely agree that the Charter needs to be updated, but the situation is more complicated than my beliefs. My mother comes from a long line of Historians. They are responsible for our historical relics and maintaining the journals containing our history."

Understanding narrowed her gaze and her shoulders gradually relaxed. "And these Historians have disagreed with their husbands' position?"

"My grandmother tried to remain neutral and concentrate on her responsibilities. My mother is too much like her father. Neutrality is just not in her character. She has distinct opinions and she's not afraid to voice them. She's been the driving force behind the rebellion for the past twenty years."

"That must have made their marriage harmonious."

"Their union was established by the rules she is trying so hard to eradicate. Father wasn't abusive, but theirs was not a love match."

She fiddled with the bottles on the shelf beside the tub until she found one that pleased her. "The history lesson is fascinating, but I'm not sure what it has to do with your unwillingness to trust." She poured some of the blue liquid into the water then reached over and activated the jets. The tub buzzed to life and water swirled all around them, rapidly forming fragrant bubbles.

"I'm the youngest network Prime in recorded history."

"How old are you?"

"Thirty-four. But my father's illness incapacitated him four years before he died, so I was barely thirty when I began acting in his place." He had to raise his voice to be heard over the motor, but she appeared to be attentive and interested.

"My mother's supporters were thrilled to have another voice on the Prime council, but Father's allies expected me to continue his positions."

"*Another* voice on the council? Who else supports the changes?"

"Ian."

"So the Rocky Mountain cats and the Minority Network are for changing the Charter while the Canines and the Southern cats want things to stay the same?"

"Exactly. Canine Prime is Nate Fitzroy, father of the wolf who tried to abduct you."

"I see. And the Southern Prime?"

"His name is Fredrick. Ian and I have some hope for converting him, but Nate is hopeless. He has a massive chip on his shoulder and he's unwilling to compromise on anything."

"So you never know when someone is genuinely interested in you or when they're trying to further some political agenda?"

"Basically. I've learned to search for ulterior motives and expect the worst. Unfortunately, people seldom disappoint me."

She pushed to her knees then crawled toward him, the bubbles clinging in the most distracting places. "What ulterior motive could I possibly have? You came after me, not the other way around."

"I never said you deserved my suspicion. I'm trying to explain why I reacted so strongly, even though you'd done nothing wrong."

"Careful." She straddled his hips, her warm ass cheeks lightly resting on his thighs. "That sounds precariously close to a genuine apology."

"I'm sorry I didn't trust you." He placed his hands on her hips, not wanting to risk the progress they'd made yet unable to go without touching her another minute. "You've given me no reason to doubt your..." He wasn't sure how to end the sentence. He didn't want to put words in her mouth.

"Attraction to you?"

He accepted the suggestion with a stiff nod. He felt far more than simple attraction to her, but this was a good place to start. She wasn't glaring at him anymore.

"I'm not attracted to Ian or Jake." She pressed her hand against the side of his face and smiled into his eyes. "I only want you in my bed and in my body. Are you okay with that?"

Rather than reply with words, he drew her head down and fit his mouth over hers.

Chapter Eight

Ava parted her lips at the first touch of Kyle's tongue. She ached for him, needed his fullness inside her core and his blazing presence inside her mind. Their bond strengthened and expanded each time they made love, yet she didn't feel encumbered by the connection, she felt protected and whole.

The kiss was slow and gentle. Their lips slid and pressed while their tongues tenderly stroked. His taste spread through her mouth and his scent filled her nose, more appealing to her senses than the expensive bubble bath.

She pushed her fingers into his hair as his hands drifted across her back and teased the outer swell of her breasts. His erection bobbed in the water between them, brushing against her belly as she began to roll her hips.

"I was going to wash your hair," he murmured against her parted lips.

"After." She nipped his bottom lip. "I want this more."

He chuckled then bent to her breasts as he whispered, "I'm at your command."

His lips fastened on to her nipple and sparks of pleasure zinged from her chest to her core. She arched her back and combed his hair with her fingers, noticing each texture and relishing each sensation. His hands were so strong, yet he touched her with such care. She felt special and adored in his arms.

She'd sensed desire smoldering in him, threatening to boil over and control his actions, but he'd restrained his need and shared more of himself with her. She rewarded him with open responses to his caresses. Not that she'd been able to hide how much she wanted him in the past, but now it was a conscious decision to bask in the heat of their desire.

Shifting back far enough to make room for her hand, she reached between them and found his cock. The shaft rose hard and thick, nearly breaking the surface of the churning water. She carefully squeezed him near the base then stroked from base to tip, sliding up and down with steady pressure.

His groan was muffled by her breast then his lips pulled harder on her nipple and she gasped, surprised yet excited by his aggression. His hands never stopped moving, gliding across her damp skin in hypnotic patterns.

Suddenly he tore his mouth away from her breasts, panting harshly as he eased her away. "We are not doing this here." His hands grasped her waist and propelled her upward as he shifted his legs beneath him. He opened the drain and turned on the long-handled sprayer, quickly rinsing the sudsy residue from both their bodies. Then he snatched one of the towels off the rack as he stepped out onto the thick bath mat.

"Maybe I wanted to play in the tub." She pouted, feeling wonderfully playful and free.

He lifted her over the side and shook out the other towel. "We were headed toward another fast and frantic ride and that wouldn't have fulfilled my promise." Starting with her shoulders, he dried her body with slow, caressing strokes.

"I'm going to explore every inch of your soft body with my fingers and my mouth." He moved behind her, brushing the towel along her spine and over her bottom. The gentle slide of his hands made the mental picture seem all the more graphic. "I'll make you wet and desperate for my cock." He whispered the claim into her ear as his hand eased between her thighs, separated from her sex by the plush towel. "You'll wiggle and beg and come over and over until you're mindless and wild." The towel moved against her, priming her body for the things he described. "Only then will I fill you." He reached around and slowly drew the towel out in front. The slow drag of the material against her sensitive folds made her gasp and tense. He brushed his thumb over her lower lip and produced a knee-melting smile. "You'll be so weak when we're finished, you'll sleep for days."

Her snappy rejoinder deserted her as he leaned down and licked her lips. The action was so unexpected and so *feline*, it was all she could do to keep her legs beneath her. "Fast and frantic" had just about blown her mind. How in the world would she survive a prolonged assault on her senses?

Dropping the towel to the floor, he took her by the hand and led her back into the bedroom. Moonlight spilling in from the windows was the only source of illumination and it took her eyes a second to adjust. He pulled the bedding down and folded it neatly over the foot of the bed. Then he picked her up and placed her on the bed.

"Any last requests?" He wiggled his eyebrows and made the question sound very dramatic.

She laughed and raised her arms, already missing the warmth of his body. He spread out on his side and slipped one arm beneath her neck. "Some women look best when they're all dolled up. You look amazing with no makeup and your hair wild about your face."

"You would know." She smiled, warmed by the praise. "I certainly haven't been at my best since I met you."

"I disagree." He ran his index finger along her jaw then down the side of her neck and onto the ridge of one collarbone. "I think you've been in your natural environment since we met. You just didn't know it until now."

His warm fingers cupped her breast as his lips slanted over hers. She raised one hand to the back of his neck and opened for the slide of his tongue. He was determined to go slow and easy, but already anxious energy thrummed through her body. She wanted him over her and in her, pressing her down into the bed as his hips moved strongly between her thighs.

As if sensing her longing, he crawled on top of her and settled on his knees between her legs. She bent her knees and opened wider, hoping he'd accept her invitation. His hand skimmed over her breasts, pausing every now and then to squeeze her nipples, but he made no move to enter her, kept his hips well back from hers.

The kiss deepened, his tongue boldly exploring her mouth. She clutched his shoulders, enjoying the bunch and flex of his muscles beneath her fingers. Heat spiraled through her body coalescing between her thighs. She wanted him there, inside her, sliding in and out, filling the emptiness.

Instead he kissed his way down her neck, tingles trailing in the wake of his lips. His warm breath wafted against her skin as his teeth gently scraped. She shifted restlessly beneath him, needing more specific touches. Tangling her fingers in his hair, she tried to guide his mouth to her breast, to her waiting nipples.

He wouldn't be rushed. With a deep chuckle, he licked and slightly sucked on the swell of her breasts, intentionally avoiding the needy tips. She tried to relax and enjoy the softer sensations, but each time her arousal ebbed, he brushed his thumb over her nipple or "accidently" brushed against her with his tongue.

"You're such a tease," she grumbled, and raised her arms over her head, knowing she had no choice but to accept what he gave her.

A low, sexy growl vibrated his throat. She looked into his eyes as he reacted to her words, or was it her submissive position? She'd thought his need to control her last night had been part of his ravenous hunger. He'd promised to give her anything she wanted tonight, but what if she wasn't sure what she wanted? She'd always thought that submission equaled weakness, that any woman who would allow a man to overpower her during sex didn't think much of herself. So why had she found more pleasure while she was at Kyle's command than during all of her other experiences combined?

With his gaze still fixed on hers, he licked one nipple and then the other. "Stay with me, sunshine. If you let your mind wander, I'll have a hard time keeping my promise." Golden light flickered in the depths of his eyes as he returned his mouth to her breast. Rather than closing his lips around the peak, he circled and laved. His tongue dragged across her flesh, the surface feeling oddly coarse. Was she just imagining the change in texture or was his cat pushing closer to the surface?

Rather than panic, she watched his eyes and opened her mind to his emotions. Desire burned within him, but it was tempered by his determination to protect and pleasure her.

He licked his way down to her navel, his tongue rasping over and into the small indentation. She grasped the sheet beside her head, ready to follow where he led. He nibbled and licked the soft hollow beneath each of her hipbones then licked his way down her inner thigh. Her fingers clutched the sheet as the tension between her thighs built and her clit began to twitch.

"You're scent is making me dizzy." He nuzzled her sex, brushing his lips against her folds. "Is there something you want from me?"

"There are lots of things I want from you." She canted her hips, bringing her slit into better alignment with his mouth.

His tongue teased her crease, tracing the sultry line without parting her folds.

"Please." Her inner muscles clenched and her thighs trembled as she waited for him to begin.

He slipped his hands beneath her and parted her with his thumbs, pausing to inhale before he covered her with his mouth. The first stroke of his tongue sent pleasure spiraling through her core and had her hanging on the verge of orgasm. But he carefully avoided her clit and kept her release just out of reach.

She wiggled and moaned, trying to bring his transient tongue in contact with her sensitive nub. One flick or a nice firm circle and she'd burst apart. He ignored her writhing and easily avoided her countermoves, so she held perfectly still and concentrated on the pleasure, squeezing her inner muscles as hard as she could each time his caress ventured near her swollen clit.

"What's the matter?" He slowly pushed one of his fingers into her tense passage but didn't move once it was deep inside her.

The hint of penetration was no more effective than his wandering tongue. "Please, let me come."

He pulled his hand back then smiled, his fingertip circling her entrance. "Anything you want."

Bending over her again, he slid his finger in and out then flicked his tongue against her clit. It took three flicks not one to set her off, but the result was still the same. She cried out and arched her back as her passage rippled around his finger.

Rather than allow the sensations to ebb, he added a second finger and built the pleasure to a second, even more shocking peak. He caught her clit between his lips and drew on the sensitive bud as he pumped into her with his fingers. She came again and again, body bowing each time the pleasure crested. She pressed her lips together, trying to muffle her screams, afraid someone would burst into the room thinking she was being murdered.

She gasped and shook as lights danced before her eyes. "No. More. I need..."

He draped her legs over his shoulders and sank to his stomach as he pulled his fingers out of her tight core. He slid down the bed and stretched out on his stomach then covered her slit with his mouth.

After that everything became a blur of pleasure and passion. He thrust into her with his tongue, swirling and stroking her inner walls as his lips drew her essence into his mouth. She lost count of her orgasms and stopped caring if anyone heard her cries of release. Not in her wildest dreams had she imagined that her body was capable of these sensations or that any man would forgo his own pleasure for so long.

He suddenly surged up along her body. Her legs slid off his shoulders, catching in the bend of his arms. His cock thrust home, filling her in one firm stroke. Her passage stretched around him, the pressure on her clit jolting her entire body.

He stared into her eyes as he drew back, making the connection even more intimate. She raised her hand to his face and he turned in to the touch, kissing the center of her palm. He'd done nearly the same thing in cat form while he'd been fighting for his life. The memory warmed her heart and made her want him even more.

His next stroke was slow and deliberate and she saw the strain on his face. He held back for her, battling his true nature at the expense of his own enjoyment.

"Faster. Please." She raised her hips to meet his next downstroke and Therian light burst within his eyes. "Your promise is kept. More than kept. I need you wild."

He released her legs and lowered his chest to her breasts, rubbing against her as his movements sped. She raised her legs against his sides, not wanting to restrict his range of motion. Firm and steady, he drilled into her ravenous body, his face hovering over hers.

She pulled his head down to hers and kissed him with all the passion surging within her. Their lips clung and their tongues tangled as their hips rolled and ground.

His breath filled her mouth and their psychic link pulsed with energy. She opened to him, taking him deeper into her mind as he steadily filled her body. Emotions flowed across the connection, a mesmerizing blending of his and hers. It was impossible to sort them out, they were so perfectly blended. Longing and tenderness, protectiveness and joy. Even the hint of possessiveness no longer upset her. She understood the emotion was part of his Therian nature, part of what made him so attractive and strong.

He tore his mouth away from hers as his strokes grew more demanding. Each forceful thrust pushed her arousal higher, keeping pace with his cresting desire. His hands clasped her hips, pulling her up as he buried his entire length in her snug heat. He threw his head back and cried out as his body shuddered and pulsed. She clung to his arms, riding out her own orgasm as he spilled deep inside her.

It was perfect, beyond anything she'd dare to dream. Her heartbeat gradually slowed and she blinked until her eyes focused. He looked just as dazed as she felt and she couldn't help but smile.

Bracing with his forearms and his knees, he kept the majority of his weight off her as he drifted back to reality. She brushed his hair back from his damp face and smiled into his eyes. "We're both covered in sweat. It's a good thing we waited to shower."

He slipped his arm beneath her neck then rolled to his side, taking her with him. "Let me catch my breath." He laughed. "I'm not sure I could stand right now."

The golden light was starting to recede from his eyes. She stroked her hand down his arm and searched his gaze. It felt wonderful to be held, to be sheltered from the dangers all around them, but a question had been nagging in the back of her mind all afternoon, and despite the warm security of his embrace, it shoved its way back to the surface.

"Bruce Fitzroy wasn't much of a threat, but what if he had been as badass as he thought he was?" She sighed then shivered, unable to meet his gaze. "He still had us at gunpoint."

He stroked the back of her hair and pressed his pelvis closer, maintaining the intimate joining of their bodies. "You were never in any real danger. If Natasha had thought differently, she never would have let him near you and I was standing in the kitchen long before you knew I was there."

She understood the concept, but she couldn't rid her mind of Bruce's semi-crazed expression or the gun pointed at her sister's head. "What if you'd both been wrong? Even cowards can snap. Can either of you outrun a bullet?"

"Ava..." He paused until she looked back into his eyes. "I could smell his fear and sense his anxiety. I have a sneaking suspicion that Nate set him up."

"Isn't Nate his father?"

"He is, but Bruce has been unpredictable for a long time." Kyle gently separated their bodies as the topic grew grim. "He's created more problems for Nate than anyone else in his pack. And unlike cats, wolves don't wait around for their alphas to step down or die off. Many, if not most, of their alphas are 'retired' by their sons as soon as the son realizes he's strong enough to pull it off."

"Nate sent his son here expecting you to kill him?"

"It's likely."

Anxiety crept through the afterglow. She wiggled away from him and sat up, dragging the sheet with her. So many Therian customs were truly savage. She'd almost adjust to all the changes and something like this would make her feel like an outsider all over again.

"As truly horrific as that is, it doesn't change the basic fact that I'm in danger."

He heaved a frustrated sigh and shoved a couple of pillows behind him so he could recline against the headboard. "There's no way to undo the danger. You are unique and highly desirable. We can be aware of the risks and surround you with people willing and able to protect you."

"Is this why Carissa agreed to the blood ritual so quickly? Was she trying to avert the danger?"

"I'm sure it contributed to her decision, but Carissa doesn't strike me as the type of a person who would bow to external pressures."

It was Ava's turn to sigh. He was right. External pressure tended to make Carissa contrary, not compliant. "Is there any way to release my abilities other than definition?"

"No, and definition can only be done once."

She'd suspected that's what he would say, but she'd needed to hear it. "Then teach me how to fight or at least let me practice with a gun. Mom made us both take firearm safety classes because we always had a loaded gun in the house, but it's been years since I fired one. There has to be some way for me to be less useless."

"You are anything but useless." He reached for her hand, but she kept it out of reach, not yet ready for his touch to distract her. "All right. Think about it like this. The president doesn't go anywhere without the Secret Service. They immediately surround him if there's a threat and they examine each situation before he's allowed to go near it. Does that make the president useless?"

She smiled. "Some would argue that his uselessness has nothing to do with the Secret Service."

Kyle chuckled. "Political frustrations aside, do you understand the parallel."

Holding the sheet with one hand, she finger combed her hair with the other. "I'm not the president."

"Your role is different, but to the Therian nation you are every bit as important as a president or prime minister. The clan leaders want you now because of your potential, and after your definition, you'll be pursued for your power. I could pat your hand and tell you everything's going to be fine, but you need to understand the reality of your situation."

"I appreciate your honesty and I don't want to be coddled. That's been my point all along. I want to be able to protect myself."

He leaned forward and caught her upper arms then dragged her into his lap. The sheet ended up tangled around her hips as she relaxed into the cradle of his strong arms. "Someday, not too long from now, you will be able to do all sorts of things you can't do now, but that doesn't mean I won't want to protect you." He paused for a long, lingering kiss. "Spend tomorrow with my mother and Carissa. They're here to answer your questions and help you adjust. But tonight belongs to me, belongs to us. And I'm tired of talking."

One of his hands covered her breast as his mouth took possession of her lips. Her troubled thoughts scattered and she raised her arms to circle his neck.

NATE SLOWLY CIRCLED his son, shaking with fury and frustration. The Clubhouse was silent, every person in the place anxiously watching the drama unfold. A tiny part of him had hoped Bruce would surpass his expectations and quietly return with Ava in tow. Instead a cold-eyed tigress had dragged Bruce into the bar in restraints, forced him to his knees and informed Nate that he had twenty-four hours to punish Bruce for attempting to murder the new Omni Prime or the cats would interpret his inaction as an act of war.

His guards had been so stunned by her arrogance that none of them had thought to detain her. She'd stormed into a wolf sanctuary, snapped out her ultimatum and departed while everyone looked on in shocked fascination.

"What the fuck happened?" He dragged Bruce to his feet but left the handcuffs and shackles in place. Muffled speculation rippled through their audience. He hadn't set up this ending, but it was perfect for what he had in mind. Bruce had failed his final exam and now he must pay, but there could be no doubt in anyone's mind that Bruce deserved what he was about to get. The pack could not think he perceived Bruce as a threat, just a failure.

"It was a setup." Bruce glared at him, yanking against the cuffs until blood trickled from his wrists. "Half the council was there to protect her."

"Why does that surprise you?" Nate faced his oldest son, hands clenched as anger churned within him. "Of course Kyle would have called in backup. You were supposed to sneak her out in the middle of the night or find a way to isolate her from the others."

Bruce looked around, his gaze blazing with anger and rebellion. "Don't you see what he's doing? *He* set me up," he called out to the room at large. "Your alpha is afraid of his own son!"

Nate backhanded him hard enough to knock him sideways. One of the guards stepped forward and steadied Bruce until he recovered from the blow. "I entrusted you with the most important assignment I've ever delegated to anyone." Nate sneered. "Don't attempt to mask your failure with ridiculous allegations."

"Why were we not included in this decision?" one of the elders asked from the far corner of the room. The question was met with nods and scattered mumbles.

"I learned of Ava's location and knew our window of opportunity was tiny." He stepped back from his trembling son and spoke loud enough for everyone to hear. "There wasn't time to gather the elders. I am alpha. I made the best decision possible under the circumstances. I sent the person I trusted most, our strongest hunter and a male whose dedication to this pack has never been questioned. I warned him that the situation required stealth and creativity. He assured me he was up to the task."

The crowd parted as the elder moved closer, but his hostile gaze was now focused on Bruce. "I can understand how you were discovered, but why did the cat accuse you of attempted murder? Ava is no use to us dead."

"She said he threatened the current Omni Prime," Nate reminded. "He must have threatened Carissa."

"I was trying to get Ava to come with me." Bruce rolled his eyes, belligerence the only weapon available to him now. "I wouldn't have hurt Carissa."

Nate crossed his arms over his chest and shook his head. "And the cats sensed your weakness so they charged you."

"I had no other choice! She was—"

"There are always other choices," the elder snapped. "Your father is right to be angry. Your actions have forced us to do the cats' bidding or prepare for war! Are you really so shortsighted that you risked this entire pack to further your own ambitions?"

"You're crazy, old man! I only did what I was told." The other guards emerged from the crowd, circling Bruce with grim determination.

Nate fought back a triumphant smile yet sorrow coiled in his belly. He'd wanted Bruce to succeed, had given him every opportunity to temper his aggression with reason. Besides, with Landon supporting the rebellion, Nate's only hope for a worthy successor was Dhane. And Dahane was still more child than man.

"If you'd done what you were told, you'd be fucking Ava right now." Nate moved to one side as the guards closed in, relieved that they'd taken the task out of his hands. Setting

Bruce up for failure was one thing, actually ripping out his heart was another.

Bruce looked at him as the color drained from his face. "Dad! What the hell's wrong with you? Do something!"

Someone touched his arm and Nate looked back and into Dhane's pleading gaze. "Can't you—"

Nate silenced his youngest son with a scathing glare. "He did this to himself. Never forget that."

"Dad!" Bruce screamed as the guards dragged him toward the back door of the Clubhouse. Stunned yet resigned, the crowd parted for them. When Nate failed to intervene, Bruce went wild. He twisted and jerked against the guards' restraining hands, screaming obscenities and hollow threats.

The back door slammed closed behind them and Bruce's indignation soon turned to screams of pain. Nate crossed to the bar and accepted the shot glass waiting for him. He'd known how this would end. Still, the sorrow twisting through him caught him by surprise. Landon had betrayed him, chosen the rebels over his own family. And Bruce had proven unworthy to take his place.

If two out of his three sons were failures, what did that say about him?

He motioned for the bartender to refill his glass and quickly tossed back the shot. Closing his eyes, he tuned out the room and waited for the fiery liquid to burn away the bitterness of regret.

AVA SPENT THE NEXT day with Carissa and Erin just as Kyle had suggested. Erin's stories still seemed a bit fantastical, but her knowledge was impressive. Every question Ava asked Erin answered with patience and thoroughness. Carissa added her perspective whenever she could and soon Ava felt less overwhelmed by the choices before her.

It really wasn't that complicated once she accepted the fact that she was part of a nation of shapeshifters. Erin would determine whether or not she was really a potential Omni Prime. Apparently, her bloodline wasn't the only prerequisite. The ancients needed to accept her into their ranks. If they did, she would choose six males she wanted to participate in her definition. The ritual would probably make her sexually aggressive, but she wasn't required to have sex with any of the men.

She would be safer once she chose her mate and the bonding would make her stronger, but she could take as long as she liked to make that decision. As long as they kept Osric away from her, of course.

"So what's my next step?" Ava asked after a long pause.

"When we return to the sanctuary, I'll take you to the vault," Erin explained.

"That's where you keep all the artifacts and your journals?"

"Yes. If you react to the artifacts as Carissa did and if you're able to read the ancient language, it will prove you're worthy of your calling." Erin didn't look old enough to be Kyle's mother. There wasn't a strand of gray in her brown hair and her face was still unlined. Her eyes were the same vivid green as her son's, but hers possessed a thoughtful wisdom Kyle had yet to achieve. Dressed in jeans and a fine-gauge sweater, Erin appeared far too normal to be clan healer and Historian.

Ava looked at her sister, amazed by the changes evident in her bearing and demeanor. Carissa had always been fun loving and adventurous, but the quiet confidence Ava sensed now hadn't been there before. "You just looked at the journals and suddenly you could read them?"

Carissa shook her head. "The change began as soon as I stepped into the vault. I could feel the power calling to me, stirring something deep inside. It'll be the same for you. I know it will. We've always done everything together." She smiled and playfully pushed Ava's shoulder. "Why should this be any different?"

They sat in Jake's living room, enjoying the fire's relaxing warmth. The day had turned out cool and rainy, and everyone was worried about Ian, who was gathering information at the secluded complex. The other men had split their time between strategy sessions in the kitchen and internet searches in Jake's office.

"Has anyone heard from Jake?" Ava asked after a short pause. "Or Enya, for that matter. They must both be going crazy by now."

"I spoke to Enya a couple of hours ago," Erin told her. "Jake and his men are still hunting, but so far, no luck."

"Did they call the police?" Even with her unusual up-bringing, it seemed like a natural reaction. When someone was in danger, the police were notified. "Even if they're only human, police tend to be aggressive whenever children are involved."

Erin shook her head. "Involving humans in our problems gives them access to our lives. We live among them, but we are not part of them. The less humans know about us, the better off we are."

A shiver slipped down Ava's spine and she rubbed her upper arms. Despite the crackling fire, she suddenly felt cold. "I'm going to go grab my hoodie and a pair of socks. I'll be right back."

"We should probably scrounge together something for lunch. I'm sure the men are getting hungry right about now." Erin and Carissa headed to the kitchen as Ava turned toward the stairs.

The upper level was quiet, almost eerily so. Ava hurried to the bedroom she shared with Kyle and found her favorite hoodie. Summit County Outfitters was emblazoned on the front of the bright red garment. She ran her fingers over the stylized letters with a sigh. All the time and energy she'd poured into the store seemed like part of another lifetime. Accounting anomalies and slow suppliers seemed extremely insignificant compared to kidnapped children and confrontations at gunpoint.

She found a pair of socks and crossed to the bed. One look at the rumpled covers sent heat cascading through her body. Her feelings for Kyle grew deeper and more specific with each passing moment. It wasn't just the pleasure they shared—though she'd never imagined sex could be so amazing. Each time they joined, their link expanded and she was drawn deeper into his mind. She shared his thoughts and memories and felt what he was feeling. His strength and nobility had been apparent from the start, but she also experienced his compassion and tenderness. He wasn't just protective of her. He jumped to the defense of any person in need of his strength.

With a dreamy smile curving her lips, she sat on the edge of the bed and pulled on her socks then wiggled into the hoodie. Noon had come and gone while she spoke with Carissa and Erin. Ian should return soon and she was anxious to hear what he'd learned. Kyle was sure her spontaneous teleportation had guided them toward something important and she was curious to find out if he was right.

She flipped off the light in the bedroom and stepped out into the hall. Blinking quickly as her eyes adjusted to the dark, she focused on the light at the top of the stairway and hurried down the corridor. One of the bedroom doors opened ahead of her and a tall man stepped out into the hall. For a moment she thought he was Ian then he turned and she caught a glimpse of his face.

Easily as tall as Ian yet more heavily muscled, the stranger stared at her with bright golden eyes. The rest of his features were lost in shadow, but there was no escaping his shimmering gaze. Ian's eyes were marbled with gold. Even Kyle's gaze had gold flecks. But no other color marred this man's irises. His hair swept straight back from his face into a thick ponytail and he emanated strength and menace.

She glanced behind her, looking for an escape route as she decided whether or not to scream. If she pushed her fear across their link, Kyle would come running.

"Name's Payne. You smell like Kyle." His rumbling voice was oddly accented and conveyed curiosity not danger. Still, she stepped back as he moved forward.

"How did you get in here?" She sounded more composed than she felt. The house had been locked down tight ever since they arrived, even more so since Bruce's failed attack. This man would have tripped an alarm unless someone let him in. So who was he and why was he here?

"Through the back door." He chuckled, the sound surprisingly warm. "Relax, *láska*. You have nothing to fear from me."

Swallowing past the lump rapidly forming in her throat, she nodded in reply and tried to rush past him.

He stuck out his arm, pressing his palm against the wall as he blocked her path. "You are Ava, yes?"

She turned her head and looked up into his face, trying to appear impatient not terrified. "I'd rather talk downstairs."

Angling his body toward her, he moved closer, surrounding her. "Erin's cub shares your bed. His scent is unmistakable. But I think your choice is not yet made. Will Kyle be your mate?"

"It's none of your business. Let me pass."

Someone flipped on the light and Ava glanced past his arm and found Carissa standing at the end of the hallway. "You all right?"

With obvious reluctance Payne lowered his arm and inclined his head toward Carissa.

"What are you doing here?" Carissa seemed surprised to see him, but she obviously knew him and wasn't threatened by his presence.

Now that Ava could see him clearly, she felt even more uncertain. With strong, masculine features and those strange golden eyes, he appeared more overtly feline than the other Therians.

"Ian told me to meet him here. It would seem I have arrived first."

Carissa accepted the explanation with a nod and motioned to the stairs. "Everyone's in the kitchen. We were about to make lunch."

He paused and looked at Ava again, his gaze caressing and warm. "This will end when you make your choice and not before." Not waiting for her reply, he ambled down the hall and disappeared into the stairwell.

Ava pressed her hand over her pounding heart and walked toward her sister. "Who is he? Why would Ian ask for his help?"

"Did he touch you?"

"No. I don't even think he was trying to scare me, he just..."

"Payne doesn't have to try." Carissa smiled. "He recently took over the largest lion pride in North America. I don't know why Ian called him. Let's go find out."

Ava followed Carissa down the stairs but froze in the archway as they reached the kitchen. Carissa crossed to the table and sat down next to Quinn, unaffected by the spectacle before her.

Ian stood near the sliding glass door leading out onto the deck. He was drenched, hair plastered to his head, and his *wings* were folded back behind him. Blood darkened the feathers of one wing and Erin examined the wound as Ian grimaced and grumbled.

Unable to help herself, Ava just stared. She'd seen him transform from eagle to man, but she'd had no idea he could do...this. His jeans hung low on his lean hips, leaving his sculpted chest and washboard abs bare. Even dripping wet and wounded, he looked like an angel. Or maybe a fallen angel. No messenger of God would appear so damn sexy.

She waited for the tingling rush or the warm tension Kyle always elicited in her, but all she felt was a superficial acknowledgment of his esthetic appeal.

The scraping of wood against wood drew her attention to the table. Kyle pushed back his chair and crossed to her. "Keep staring like that and he'll challenge me. He doesn't have to worry about us being in sync if I'm dead."

"Sorry." She pushed her emotions into Kyle's mind so he'd understand her reaction was platonic. "I've never seen anything like this."

He gave her a quick kiss then ushered her to the table.

"I didn't know he had wings." Then the more important issue pushed to the forefront of her befuddled mind. "How was he injured?"

"He was shot at," Ian supplied the answer with a knowing smile. Apparently he hadn't been oblivious to her rude behavior. "Bullet creased the top of my wing."

"You were searching the wilderness—like that?"

He spread his wings and lifted his chin, his gaze narrowed and bright. "Is there something wrong with 'this'?"

Erin slapped his chest and reached for the top of his wing, which now arched well above her head. "If you're finished *preening*, I'm sure Jake would appreciate me closing your wound. You're dripping blood all over his floor."

Ian folded his wings again and turned so she could reach the seeping wound. "I had a backpack full of equipment." He motioned toward the pack sitting by the door. "It's rather hard to strap that onto an eagle. I had to wear it backward, but at least I kept it on."

"Has anyone ever taken your picture when you're flying around like that?"

The phrase made him chuckle then Erin pressed some gauze to his wing and he hissed. "I try to be careful and I fly fast enough that the pictures tend to blur. If I have a long distance to go with little or no cover, I shift into a bird." He glared down at his nurse, obviously tired of her ministrations. "Are you about finished?"

"We both know what will happen if you put them away dirty."

He shuddered. "Definitely don't want to go through that again."

"What happened?" Ava whispered the question to Kyle, but again Ian answered. Damn the man had good hearing.

"I ignored several small wounds and just absorbed my wings. The next time I unfurled them they were both infected and excruciating. Worse, I couldn't absorb them again until they healed completely, which meant I was cooped up for almost a month."

"It's a raptor thing," Kyle told her. "If the rest of us are injured in one form, generally shifting to the other eliminates the wound."

"It works that way with me too if I transform into a bird," Ian corrected. "It's only the partial shifts that are tricky."

"It's not that I'm not entertained," Payne cut in, "but I do have other responsibilities." He looked at Ian expectantly. "Why have you summoned me?"

Erin finally pronounced Ian's wound clean. He furled his wings then slowly absorbed them. "Give me a minute to change and I'll explain everything."

"Would you like something to drink?" Erin asked their newest guest. Payne shook his head so she joined them at the table.

Ian returned a few minutes later in dry clothes, damp hair returned to some sort of order. He picked up the backpack and brought it to the table unzipping it as he began. "I entered the exact location into the GPS so we can use it to find the place tomorrow."

Tomorrow? They were going to raid the mysterious complex tomorrow? Dread washed over Ava. Even if she weren't directly involved in the raid, everyone else would be in danger.

"I took pictures of every room visible from the outside and I'm sure we can extrapolate the missing spaces. There are three teams of two guards. They rotate between interior and exterior positions with six hours off in between."

"Where do the guards go when they're off duty?" Quinn asked.

"The barracks are connected to the vehicle shed. I got a look inside the shed at one point and saw two Jeeps, several ATVs and various maintenance equipment."

"So, we take out the guards two at a time and—"

Ian stemmed Quinn's suggestions with an upraised hand. "Hear the rest before you plan a strategy." Quinn nodded, but tension arced between the two.

Do Quinn and Ian dislike each other? She looked at Kyle. *Long story. I'll tell you later.*

She nodded and returned her attention to Ian.

"The upper level is living quarters, the ground level offices and laboratories."

"Laboratories?" Erin sounded surprised. "As in microscopes and test tubes?"

"Yes, and pretty damn sophisticated from what I could see. I'd convinced myself we were wrong, that this place has nothing to do with us, then Osric stepped out of the elevator."

"Are you sure it was Osric?" Quinn asked the question they were all thinking.

"You tell me." Ian pulled a camera out of his backpack, scanned through several shots then slid it across the table to Quinn.

"That's Osric." Quinn handed it to Erin who looked at the picture then handed it to Kyle.

"Unbelievable," Kyle whispered under his breath.

Ava had no clear memory of Osric's appearance, so she didn't bother looking at the picture, wasn't sure she was ready for all the feelings his image might unleash. "You mentioned an elevator. Is there an underground level?"

Ian nodded. "I'm pretty sure there is and I'm just as sure that whatever they're protecting is kept down there."

"Is Osric working with the Abolitionists?" Carissa rubbed her upper arms, clearly upset by the possibility.

"I can't imagine what he would gain by indulging those lunatics," Ian said. "I think it's more likely this is something else entirely, a threat we were unaware of before."

"Wonderful." Erin sighed. "Devon may or may not be missing, Jake's sisters have been kidnapped, and the Abolitionists harass us at every turn. The last thing we need is a new enemy."

"We can't ignore this." Ian scooted closer to the table. "I'm just guessing at this point, but it's a pretty educated guess. Osric is obsessed with the possibility of creating a true Therian. He failed on his own, so he's recruited humans to help him."

"Or the humans recruited him." Kyle's anxiety spiked, rippling across their link and setting Ava on edge. "I don't think Osric has the connections to set something like this in motion. A secret lab in the middle of nowhere guarded by men with automatic weapons? Sounds military to me."

Ian didn't argue, nor did he agree. "We won't know anything for sure until we see what they're hiding."

"And how do we do that without getting ourselves killed?" There was a little less challenge in Quinn's tone now, but Ian still bristled.

"If you don't have the balls for—"

Quinn flew out of his chair and was halfway across the table when Carissa grabbed him. "Cut it out!" She didn't have the strength to pull him back, but she didn't let go. "If you two can't work together on this, we're all screwed."

Both men huffed, but Quinn returned to his seat and Ian proceeded to ignore him.

"You've been on-site," Erin prompted. "You know what we'll be facing, at least to some extent. What do you suggest we do?"

"Even if there's nothing but storage in the basement, we're outnumbered and out gunned. Trying to amass a larger force would take too long and compound the logistical nightmare. Our only hope is the element of surprise. We need to use distraction and deception to slip in under their noses. We strike fast and hard, preventing them from calling for backup."

"How well did the shooter see you? Haven't we already lost the element of surprise?" Quinn's tone was low and even while hostility still smoldered in his eyes.

"You got a better idea?" Ian snapped.

"It's a reasonable question." Erin's expression communicated warning even more eloquently than her words.

Ian sighed. "They were shooting at shadows. There's no way either of them saw me clearly."

"What if *we* need backup?" Kyle asked. "We have no idea what's waiting for us once we step off that elevator."

Clearly frustrated by the continued objections, Ian sighed. "So we'll have backup stationed far enough away to avoid detection yet close enough to assist if we're overwhelmed."

"Are you talking ground or air support?" Payne asked. He'd remained quiet through most of the conversation, silently watching as the others worked out the kinks.

"Air would be best, given the impossible terrain," Ian told him. "Do you still have access to those sorts of resources?"

"It will cost you, especially if you want them here by morning."

Ian looked at Erin and she nodded. "This thing with Osric has gone on long enough. Make the call."

"If that's all you needed from me, you could have told me on the phone." Payne smiled, his eyes shimmering like antique coins. "Am I distraction or deception?"

Ian returned the smile. "A little bit of both."

Chapter Nine

Kyle decided to barbeque for dinner, which drew all the men out onto the deck. "There is something about cooking over an open flame that men can't resist," Erin said with a chuckle.

"Brings out their inner caveman." Carissa laughed.

"That's not necessarily a bad thing, is it?" Ava wiggled her eyebrows and they all laughed some more.

"This feels so good!" Carissa wrapped her arm around Ava and squeezed. "I can't believe how much I missed you." They sat on the sofa in Jake's living room, enjoying the brief break in activity as the men bonded over burgers. Erin sat in an armchair facing them, a large window at her side showcasing the majestic mountains and deep blue sky.

"And I can't believe how much things have changed in so short a time."

"Do *I* seem different?" Carissa sounded hurt.

"You didn't until you turned into a... What the hell was that thing? I'm pretty sure I've never heard of a black tiger before."

"Nothing about Carissa is ordinary and I think her cat is beautiful," Erin objected.

"So do I. That's not what I meant. I'm just having a hard time believing that was her. With Kyle and the others it's easier to accept, but I grew up with Carissa. I remember her losing teeth and agonizing over her first pimple."

Carissa relaxed, even managed to smile. "It gets easier. Before long it'll all seem common."

Ava shook her head. "I hope not. I never want to lose that sense of awe. You guys are amazing."

Erin moved from her chair and joined them on the couch. "You are amazing too. Never doubt that for a minute. The blood that flows through Carissa's veins also flows through yours."

"That's not what's bothering me." Even as the words passed her lips they sounded hollow. "If the ancients accept me, I'll likely go through with the blood ritual. If they don't...I think I'm okay with that too."

"You're afraid." Carissa challenged her with a look. "It's understandable, but that's what this is. Good old-fashioned fear. You've always avoided change like the plague. You're comforted by routines."

Carissa was half right. She was definitely a creature of habit, but she wasn't afraid of becoming an Omni Prime. She was afraid of being left behind. Being surrounded by power and people with extraordinary abilities left her feeling useless.

"Which part of your new situation upsets you most?" Erin pivoted toward Ava, her gaze filled with compassion.

Rather than toss out a random concern, Ava took a moment to analyze each element of the conflict, trying to prioritize their effect on her life. Then she realized the answer was in her reaction to the question. "I'm analytical. If I can't weigh one thing against another and set priorities, I feel helpless. This situation isn't only filled with variables, but many of those variables haven't even been defined yet."

Carissa shook her head. "You're making this much too complicated. You need to trust yourself and the people around you and just enjoy the ride."

"That's your natural reaction to the challenge," Erin said. "Your sister's mind doesn't work that way. In fact, I'd like to speak with Ava for a few minutes alone."

"You're dismissing me?" Carissa sounded shocked.

"More or less." It was impossible to remain angry when Erin turned up the warmth in her smile.

Carissa huffed then pushed to her feet with a sigh. "Fine. I'll go supervise the men."

Ava waited until Carissa closed the door behind her before she spoke again. "She means well."

"I know she does. She loves you very much, but you're not Carissa. Your circumstances might be similar to hers, but you have different coping mechanisms. She relies on instinct while you prefer information." Erin turned nearly sideways, bending her knee against the sofa's cushion. "What else would you like to know?"

"There's so much I still don't understand. I'm not sure where to start."

"Start at the top. What thought won't leave your mind?"

Kyle's images flared within her mind, but she quickly hid her smile. Kyle definitely bothered her, but it wasn't the sort of bother that his mother could help her resolve. Carissa's image slowly eclipsed Kyle's and Ava felt a jolt of shame.

"Go on. Tell me what you're thinking. I'm here to help, not judge."

Ava looked at her new friend with narrowed eyes. "Are you the clan counselor or something?"

"At times. Maintaining an accurate history requires me to be more observant than most. Besides, I'm older than dirt." She laughed. "Age brings with it wisdom, if we're willing to learn."

Heaving a frustrated sigh, Ava looked inward as she shared her thoughts. "I know Carissa wasn't in control of a lot of what happened to her, but I can't help feeling like she..."

"Stole your thunder?"

"I'm not even sure I want what she has."

Erin's brow arched and her eyes gleamed. "We're being honest here."

"All right. Who doesn't want to learn that they're special? That their ancestors were unique and powerful. Carissa has embraced our heritage with open arms while I'm too afraid to even think about it."

Those perceptive eyes narrowed again. "Is that really what you're afraid of?"

"Now that the ancients have Carissa, I'm afraid they won't need me." Something inside Ava released and she exhaled as tingles crept over her arms. How had Erin known she was internalizing this fear? Was she just perceptive as she claimed or did her Therian nature allow her to see what others could not? "Wow. I feel like a weight has been lifted off my chest. You should charge money for this."

Erin wrapped her arm around Ava and squeezed her shoulder. "I don't want your money, but I might be able to answer your question. Would that help you relax?"

"What do you mean? I thought I needed to be in the vault to determine if the ancients would accept me."

"There are three tests used to determine if a potential Omni Prime is found worthy by the ancients. Two require you to be in the vault, but one can be conducted here. The test is not complicated and it can't be faked."

"All right. What do I have to do?"

"As you know, I'm the current Historian. I was taught the ancient language so I can make official entries in the sacred journals. Well, I keep a personal journal as well and once I realized many of my thoughts and observations could be potentially dangerous if read by the wrong person, I started using the ancient language for my personal journal as well."

"You want me to read your diary?" Ava smiled.

"Not for content, obviously. If the ancients empower you to read the language, it's almost assured that you'll pass the other tests."

"And if they don't, I'm probably out of luck?"

"The energy in the vault is far more concentrated, so don't lose hope if this doesn't work."

"But if it does, I'll have one less thing to worry about."

"Exactly."

Ava scooted to the edge of the couch and nodded. "I want to try. It would be really nice to know one way or the other."

Erin took Ava by the hand and led her to the only bedroom on the main level. Though smaller than the rooms upstairs, it was cozy and warm. Erin sat on the edge of the bed then patted the space beside her. "Have a seat. You need to be relaxed and open to their teaching."

As Ava sat down, Erin reached into the overnight bag beside the bed and pulled out a leather-bound journal. She handed the book to Ava then sat beside her. "Open it across your lap then run your fingertips over the page. If you don't feel anything at first, close your eyes and empty your mind."

Each line was written in a flowing script, not as decorative as calligraphy, but more stylized than cursive. "Carissa can read this?" Her uncertainty came rushing back and she sighed.

Erin touched Ava's forearm, drawing her attention to Erin's face. "I'm going to tell you something that I never mentioned to Carissa. Sam Collins was a gentle soul. Osric manipulated and used him, but Sam loved Willona with all his heart and she had grown to love him. If Sam had survived, I honestly think Willona wouldn't have run."

"What does that have to do with Carissa being able to read the ancient language?"

"You both received potential power from your mother. And though Osric's basic character is corrupt, his bloodline is old and powerful. Sam's bloodline, on the other hand, had been diluted and tainted so many times he was barely able to shift."

Ava stared at Erin, desperately trying to unravel her convoluted comments.

"Carissa told you about Sam, didn't she?"

"She said Osric convinced Sam to participate in Mother's definition, but..." Understanding shot through Ava in a sudden jolt. She gasped and pressed a hand over her heart. "The wolf-shifter was Carissa's father? How is that even possible?"

Erin laughed, the sound soft and infectious. "Cats do it all the time, my dear."

"Then we're not really twins. In fact, we're only half-sisters."

"I'm sorry. I didn't mean to derail your concentration. I only meant to explain that Carissa is the one I wasn't sure the ancients would accept. You have been infused with power from both your mother and father. I will be shocked if this doesn't work."

Pausing to rub her eyes, Ava took a moment to absorb this new information. It didn't really change anything. She still loved Carissa and always would. But another layer of deception had been peeled off her life. Was anything her mother told her true?

"Maybe we should try this after dinner. I've obviously upset you." Erin reached for the book, but Ava blocked her hand.

"I'm not upset. I'm just adjusting my thinking—again."

"All right. But remember, if this doesn't work, it's not a definitive fail. This is more of a prescreening than one of the official tests."

Ava smiled. "Each time you prepare me for failure, I'm more convinced you think I can't do it."

Erin pressed her lips together, pulled an imaginary zipper across the seam then motioned toward the book.

Import hung in the air like static electricity. If the stories were true, this is what Ava had been born to do, what her ancestors had done for generations. She would not doubt herself or think about Carissa. Or their mother. The past could not be changed. She needed to focus on the future.

Ava closed her eyes and took a deep breath, releasing all the details while she exhaled. Then with her mind clear and accessible, Ava slowly opened her eyes.

The book rested on Ava's thighs, black ink contrasting sharply with stark white pages. She ran her fingertips over the first line, her gaze following the motion of her hand. Should she...

Before the speculative thought could fully form, her fingertips began to tingle. Rather than analyze the sensation, she let instinct guide her and pressed her palm against the page. Warm currents flowed up her arm and swirled through her chest. Her heartbeat sped, but her lungs felt heavy.

She pressed her other hand against the opposite page and closed her eyes. Tingles became prickles and warmth turned to heat. She opened her mind and surrendered to the sensations, thrilled by her body's immediate reaction.

Lines of script scrolled through her mind, but the words were still unreadable to her. *Show me. Please allow me to understand.* She didn't know if she was supposed to interact with the spirits directly or if she should remain silent and still, but they were here. She could sense them and feel her body reacting to their presence.

Her eyes burned and she pressed her lids tighter as tears escaped the corners of her eyes. The lines of script in her mind slowly blurred, becoming shapeless blobs before reforming in crisp, clear English. "'Osric has thrown down the gauntlet, dared us to react. His selfish abuse has already set us back by decades. We cannot allow his challenge to go unanswered.'"

Erin's happy cry echoed in the distance, but the connection sank deeper into Ava's mind. Ava raised her hands to her head and moaned. The journal's weight was lifted from her legs and Ava fell back onto the bed.

"Ava? Are you all right."

The fear in Erin's tone sent a shiver through Ava. She hadn't been afraid until she heard Erin's voice. She tried to speak, to reassure the other woman, but she couldn't move, could barely think beyond the roaring in her head.

Images swirled, disconnected and dizzying. The harder she fought the current the more disconcerting the sensations became. She bobbed and rocked, twisted and soared with no control, no specific destination. Like the steady pull of a vacuum, the trance drew her deeper and deeper into its power.

The mattress dipped as someone sat down beside her. Then warm fingers brushed her hair back from her face. "We're here, sunshine. If you need our help, let me feel your fear."

Kyle. Her protector, her lover, her...mate? The thought wasn't nearly as upsetting as it had been the first time the possibility popped into her mind. But he was afraid for her, as was his mother. She needed to let them know she was all right.

But was she all right? She was paralyzed and helpless, yet she felt no threat, no menace within the tranquility.

Locating her link with Kyle, she sent him a pulse of calm, curiosity. *Not sure what's happening, but I don't think I'm in danger.*

She wasn't sure if the thought had reached his mind until he said, "She's not afraid, but she's not sure what this is either."

As if in response to their exchange, the pulling sensation increased, rushing her toward a looming void. She struggled against the hold, frightened for the first time.

She plunged into darkness like a tunnel in the middle of a roller coaster. Then she burst out the other side and sensations bombarded her consciousness. Fear and delight, excitement and dread, all compressed into one overwhelming moment.

Hovering above the scene, disembodied yet connected, she watched what was happening to the other Ava. She could feel what her other self felt, yet she saw the events from outside her body.

Her other self sat on the edge of a highly carved pedestal table, the wood darkened as if by age. All the chairs had been stacked off to one side and six people stood around the oval table. To her right stood Kyle, his handsome features stern while excitement burned in his gaze. Payne stood at her left, his strange golden eyes glowing. No one moved. No one spoke. And tension increased with each frantic heartbeat.

Ava looked at the other shifters, suddenly understanding what she was witnessing. Three men and a woman. They were strangers to her now, but she would know them well by the time this scene took place.

"Are you ready, my love?" Kyle asked her, his voice hushed and filled with love.

"Finally." Her future self smiled. "I'm sorry this took so long."

"No." Kyle reached over and took her hand. "You were right to wait. Your certainty will make the bonding that much stronger. Besides, you'll always be worth the wait."

"Will you go first or last?"

"Last." A slow, sexy smile parted his lips. "Once our bonding is complete, I won't be able to hold back. I don't particularly want an audience for what I have planned."

"I wouldn't mind." Payne's tone was surprisingly playful.

"Not in your wildest dreams." Kyle growled out a warning and Payne laughed.

"If you two are finished posturing, I'm ready to begin."

Ava felt the suction reverse, drawing her back into the present. She quickly shifted her focus to the unfamiliar faces, doing her best to memorize their features.

The return trip was far less gentle. Her consciousness was hurtled back into her body and she arrived with a startled cry.

"Are you all right, love?" Now Kyle sounded scared.

Ava blinked until her eyes focused and then she smiled up at him. "I'm fine. The ancients just wanted to silence my doubts once and for all."

"What happened? Where did you go?" Erin stood beside the bed, still looking rather worried.

With Kyle's help, Ava sat and shook off the last of the muddle. She blew out a shaky breath then recalled the specifics of the vision. "I saw myself, sometime in the future, preparing for the blood ritual. I was sitting on an antique table with Kyle on one side and Payne on the other. There were four other people there, three men and a woman. I don't know them now, but I will know them then."

"Describe them," Erin suggested. "Maybe we can tell you who they are."

Ava shook her head. "I don't think it's supposed to happen like that. I'll know them when I see them, and when I meet the last one, I'll know it's time for the ritual."

Kyle looked at his mother then back at Ava, clearly confused by her explanation. "What were you two doing? Was this some sort of vision quest?"

"Ava has been distracted by all the unknowns in her life. We were trying to determine whether or not the ancients would accept her." Erin held up her journal and Kyle nodded.

"Did it work?" He looked at Ava and asked, "Were you able to read the ancient language?"

"I think so." She smiled at Erin, feeling hopeful for the first time in days. "Were the words I spoke correct?"

"Absolutely." She opened the book and held it so Ava could see it. "Can you still read it?"

It was rather like looking through 3D glasses, but as soon as the image focused, Ava was able to read every word.

"How far in the future was the vision?" Kyle stood and helped Ava to her feet.

"I have no clue. We didn't look significantly older, so I suspect it was months not years from now. But I did apologize for making you wait so long."

"Wonderful," he grumbled, and his mother laughed.

"The blood ritual has nothing to do with your personal relationship," Erin reminded them. "Were you still lovers or perhaps even more?"

It was impossible to miss the hopeful catch in Erin's voice. "We were still together," Ava assured her. "But I'm not sure if we were bonded mates."

Her answer seemed to please Kyle, but his gaze remained thoughtful.

Erin stashed her journal back in her overnight bag then motioned toward the door. "Dinner was ready a while ago. I told them to start without us."

"I want to tell Carissa I was able to read the journal, but the vision felt personal. I'd rather not share that information with anyone but you two."

They both nodded then Erin said, "I consider anything I hear private unless I'm told otherwise."

"Thank you."

"We'll be right there." Kyle pulled Ava into his arms as his mother slipped out of the room. "You're really all right?"

"I'm fine. Honestly."

He leaned down and kissed her, his lips warm and tender. "Then don't scare me like that again. I don't like feeling helpless."

She drew his mouth back to hers as a smile curved her lips. She understood what he was feeling all too well.

ZOPHIEL STARED AT HER sister with a mixture of fear and loathing. Nehema was weak and Zophiel had no tolerance for any form of weakness. Zophiel liked to think blood ties accounted for something, but she wouldn't hesitate to end Nehema if her theatrics drew any more attention to their operation.

If it had been Zophiel's choice, their road to justice would have been more direct. The atrocities perpetuated by Therian males had been concealed and excused for centuries. Retribution was long overdue.

Nehema agreed with Zophiel that Therian males needed to be punished, but Nehema was obsessed with "saving" innocent females. Zophiel's thinking was less complicated and much less forgiving. Any female who didn't openly rebel against the injustices was enabling her own mistreatment. If they were foolish enough to allow their own abuse, who was she to interfere? Zophiel preferred to focus on the males and let Nehema play hero with the females.

"Osric told that bitch everything," Nehema lamented, baby-blue eyes wild, pale features tinged with gray. Though Zophiel was older than Nehema by almost ten years, Nehema had allowed herself to age while Zophiel culled enough energy to maintain her youthful appearance. They now looked more like mother and daughter than sisters. Another sign of Nehema's inevitable decline.

"We don't know that for certain. All Barns said was Carly spoke with Roberto after spending the night with Osric. Barns wasn't able to unscramble the transmission, so we have no idea what they said."

"What else would Carly have told Roberto? The only thing Osric knows that he hasn't already told the backers is what he knows about you." Nehema wrung her hands and Zophiel wanted to shake her.

When Zophiel first learned that a Therian was assisting the backers, she'd been appalled and enraged. Traitors existed in any society, but this betrayal was exceptionally crass. She'd found out everything she could about the traitor and set out to end his miserable life, but something about Osric had been so dark and twisted that she'd decided to toy with him instead.

She arranged an "accidental" meeting then allowed him to believe he pursued her. It had been many years since she indulged her sexual appetites and Osric was perfect for her unconventional needs. He wasn't afraid of pain, enjoyed giving and receiving it to enhance his partner's pleasure. And he was oh so trainable.

Fascinated by his obsessive appetites, Zophiel cultivated his devotion into something akin to worship. She was his guardian angel, his provider, his Mistress. She used her empathic abilities to anticipate his every need then amplified the pleasure, allowing her to fulfill his most twisted desire. No one could satisfy him the way she did because no one else possessed her abilities.

But if he displeased her in anyway, she would punish him with pain every bit as intense as the pleasure. Then she would disappear for weeks, sometimes months, leaving him aching for a level of satisfaction impossible to attain without her.

Shaking away the distraction, she refocused on the present complication. "The conversation Barns reported to you might not have had anything to do with Osric." If Carly were a more effective spy than they'd thought, they would simply have to deal with her. All this worrying was a waste of energy.

Nehema's brow arched as a bit of her spirit returned. "If the backers know about you, it's only a matter of time before their investigation leads them to me."

"They already know who you are. If they'd wanted you dead, you'd be dead."

The reminder earned Zophiel an impatient glare. "The only thing they can prove about me is that I've been helping females escape their abusers."

"Tell that to Gage Seaton." Zophiel laughed. "I'm sure he's given the cats quite an earful by now."

"*You* approved his actions. I had nothing to do with it."

"We know that, but Gage has no idea he was talking to me not you."

Nehema stomped her foot and started pacing, fists tightly clenched at her sides. "You intentionally complicate things. I've done everything I can to avoid violence, but you seem to crave it."

Zophiel had had enough of Nehema's denials. Their tactics might differ, but they were both equally guilty in the eyes of the Therian nation. "You'd rather kidnap children and terrorize adolescents with tales of demon possession and evil spirits."

"The spirits are real and you know it." Her steps sped as her agitation mounted. "How can you speak such blasphemy?"

Zophiel stepped in front of Nehema, grasped her shoulders and gave her a good hard shake. "Snap out of it! Osric knows nothing but my name and how to make me come. Even if he did run his mouth to Carly, we are not in danger."

"I want to believe it's that simple, but things never work out that well for us."

Ignoring her sister's pessimism, Zophiel went on. "Even if the backers miraculously connect you and me, I'll kill them long before they harm either of us."

Fear flickered in the depths of Nehema's eyes. "Is violence your solution for everything?"

"Pretty much." Nehema gaped and Zophiel laughed. "Relax, little sister. You'll end up with an ulcer if you keep tying yourself in knots."

"We need to know how much the backers have pieced together, which means you need to search one of their memories."

Zophiel tensed as she searched the depths of her sister's gaze. "You know what happened last time I tried to probe that deeply. Do you really want me to try again?"

Nehema sighed then squared her shoulders. "I don't see that we have any other choice. I will not allow us to be blindsided. It's time for the Angel of Justice to make another house call. I'll let you choose which one you visit."

AVA'S VISION LEFT HER with a sense of belonging that she'd never experienced before. She'd always been close with her family, but the safety precautions that shaped her childhood had kept her isolated from everyone else.

To begin with, the easy camaraderie the Therians shared had made Ava feel isolated and sad. But now there was no doubt left in her mind that this was where she belonged and she would one day be as exceptional as the others.

Her buoyant mood lasted through dinner and well into the evening. Yet by the time Kyle made their excuses and led her upstairs, some of her old uncertainty had starting bleeding through her newfound calm.

Kyle closed the door to their bedroom and leaned back against the sturdy panel. "You've been talkative and smiling all evening. Why are you so tense now?"

She averted her face as she considered the question. Trying to think clearly while she looked at him was an utter waste of time. He attracted her physically, challenged her mentally and complemented her emotionally. How was she supposed to resist him?

Or why did she feel the need to try to push him away? Most people spent their entire lives searching for that one special person who was compatible with them in every way. If she'd been lucky enough to find hers, why should she fight the attraction?

She licked her lips and glanced away, not sure she could make him understand her hesitation. Not sure she understood it herself. "This has always felt sort of...preordained."

"Is that a bad thing?" His tone was quiet, nonconfrontational.

"I hate being manipulated." She looked at him, needing to see his reaction to the statement.

His brows drew together and his lips thinned. "Do you feel like I've manipulated you?"

She shook her head. He'd been nothing but gallant. "That's not what I meant." She sat on the edge of the bed and pulled off her boots. "You haven't had any more of a choice in this than I've had. I don't blame you for any of it."

His gaze gleamed like expensive emeralds and the soft lighting in the room accented the lighter streaks in his tawny hair. He watched her with the lazy intensity of a predator that had already cornered his prey. "Many things in a Therian's life are triggered by instinct and seem 'preordained'. I suppose I'm just used to being manipulated by forces more powerful than myself."

"Well, I don't like it." Before he could react to her statement, she pulled her shirt off and let it drop from her fingers. "I won't pretend I don't want you. Hypocrisy is not in my nature, but the vision gave me a glimpse into the future. It assured me that this is my chosen path, but it also gave me back control over when and with whom the bond is formed." He started to reply, but she unzipped her jeans and wiggled out of the snug denim. "I know it's your nature to take control and I'm not trying to change you. But tonight I need to reclaim control over my desire."

His gaze meandered from her face to the swell of her breasts. "What'd you have in mind?"

"I want to make the decisions." Adorned in her bra and panties, she crept toward him, pulse increasing with each step. "I need you to follow my lead. Just for tonight."

His gaze locked with hers, fierce yet amazingly tender. "You can have whatever you need, as long as I'm the one who gives it to you."

"I don't want anybody else." She tugged his t-shirt out from inside his jeans and slipped one hand under the soft cotton. "I don't think I ever will. I just need to remain in control tonight, to know this is something I've chosen."

"I'm yours to command."

A sexy growl threaded through his voice, making her nipples tingle. "Take off your shirt." His fast, focused movements pushed his body against hers, further arousing her senses and accentuating the ache rapidly building between her thighs. His torso was corded with well-defined muscles, compact and lean.

He didn't touch her. Instead he silently waited for her next move. She ran her hands across his chest then down his arms, enjoying every dip and curve of his amazing body. As her hands explored, she pressed her lips to his chest, absorbing the heat of his skin and the steady thumping of his heart.

She kissed her way to one of his nipples, wondering if he'd enjoy the firm pull of her mouth as much as she enjoyed his. Closing her lips around the tiny peak, she could barely form a circle. Rather than abandoning the task, she used her teeth, nibbling and pulling until he pushed one hand into her hair and released a throaty moan.

Excitement rushed through her body and she switched to the other side, determined to hear the sound again. Responding to Kyle's skill had been easy. All she'd had to do was surrender and receive the most powerful orgasms of her life. Giving him pleasure might require more concentration, but each time he tensed, each gasp and groan sent desire cascading through her body.

Her hands drifted downward as her mouth continued to play. His hand remained in her hair, yet he didn't tighten his grip or try to control her. She wasn't sure how long his mood would last, so she took full advantage of his willingness to indulge her.

Slipping to her knees, she kissed her way farther down. Each quiver and hiss fueled her determination to watch him lose control. She slowly unzipped his pants, freeing his cock from its denim prison. His shaft was thick and hard, the flared tip deeply flushed and weeping.

She caught a drop of clear fluid as it escaped and smoothed it over his sensitive crest. Her thumb glided across his velvety flesh and his fingers slowly tightened in her hair.

"This is hard enough." His voice sounded gravelly. "Don't tease."

"But I like teasing you." She wrapped her fingers around the base and slowly stroked up and down. "Isn't that what you said the last time I begged you to let me come?"

With their gazes still locked, she pumped him, swiping the moist tip at the apex of each stroke. His other hand clenched and unclenched as his cock grew harder within the circle of her fingers. He closed his eyes and rested his head against the door. And she stopped.

He muttered a curse and opened his eyes.

"Finish undressing. I want you naked." She stayed on her knees as he frantically tugged off his boots, socks and jeans. Knowing her touch had created his urgency empowered her to be even bolder. She pointed to the bed as she stood and unfastened her bra. "Sit on the edge and spread your legs."

"You better be careful, sunshine. Payback's a bitch." Golden flecks shimmered in the depths of his eyes, revealing the heat of his desire and his cat's restlessness.

"I'm not worried." She smiled, high on feminine power. "Sit on the bed and show me how much you want me."

He sat and moved his legs apart then rested back on his elbows and flexed his abdomen, making his cock jerk before it came to rest against his flat belly. "I'm all yours, sweetheart. What are you going to do with me?"

"I think I'll just enjoy the view." She stepped closer but stopped well out of reach. "You have an amazing body." She skimmed her hands up her sides and cupped her breasts. "Makes me hot just looking at you."

His gaze narrowed, but he didn't move.

She rolled her nipples, enjoying the tension in his thighs and the flush crawling across his skin as much as the pressure of her fingers. Suddenly their link expanded and scalding need saturated her mind. She groaned, pressing her thighs together.

"That's not fair." She gasped.

"You're the one who wanted to play." One of his tawny brows arched, emphasizing the challenge in his tone. "You told me to show you how much I want you."

Determined to remain in control as long as possible, she caught the sides of her panties and pulled them down as she spun in an undulating circle. Her panties briefly caught around her upper thighs then fell to her ankles and she kicked them aside.

"Very nice." He licked his lips, gaze boldly moving over her naked body. "The back view is just as appealing as the front."

Twinges of pleasure raced from her nipples to her clit and back, each sensation compounded by the emotions flowing across their link. She approached him one step at a time, pausing in between to touch herself in progressively bolder places. By the time she stood between his legs, her fingers were buried between her thighs, rubbing with almost frantic urgency.

"Your scent is driving me crazy." He inhaled deeply, his hips bucking. "Let me touch you."

She drew her fingers out and smiled into his eyes. "Is this what you want?" She brought her fingers to his mouth and painted his lips with her cream. He licked his lips, eyes half closed as he savored her taste.

"More."

"Not yet." She put her fingers in her mouth and shivered as her taste spread across her tongue. This was what he wanted, what he craved whenever they made love. Would she find his taste as evocative? She looked at his straining cock and smiled. There was only one way to find out.

Kneeling between his spread thighs, she cupped his balls with one hand and gripped his shaft with the other. His legs flexed and he groaned. "If you do this, I'm not sure I'll be able to stop."

She ran her tongue around the head of his cock then caught the bead of moisture perched on the very tip. The salty-sharp taste sank into her tongue and stirred a primal hunger for more. "I don't want you to stop, so don't hold back."

Her lips formed a firm circle as she slowly sucked him into her mouth. She cradled him with her tongue, absorbing his heat and the contrasting textures. He was hot and soft, warm and moist, and she couldn't get enough of him.

He let her set the pace, remaining as passive as his consuming desire allowed. His hand steadied the back of her head, but his hips stayed nearly still as she slid her mouth up and down the length of his shaft.

She released his balls and stroked his legs, his hips, his sides. She wanted to touch him everywhere, know every contour of his strong body by heart. His chest heaved as his breathing sped. She slid her knees outward, lowering her mouth and tilting her head to a better angle. She took more of him, felt him bump the back of her throat with each rotation.

"Oh!" He framed her face with his hands and helplessly rocked into her mouth.

Thrilled by his urgency, she relaxed her throat and tilted her head back even farther. *Come for me*. She pushed her excitement across their link, showing him how eager she was to know his taste.

He cried out and pushed to the back of her mouth, shuddering violently as his seed released in rhythmic jets. She swallowed and swallowed again, taking as much as he had, unwilling to let him go until he'd surrendered every last drop of his pleasure.

They stared into each other's eyes as she licked him clean. He brushed her hair back from her face, his hands trembling and careful. "I love you," he whispered. "You know that, don't you?"

She pulled back, releasing his semi-hard cock into her waiting hand. "I love you too."

He chuckled, pulling her up until their faces were on a level. "You sound surprised."

"I didn't think I believed in love at first sight. In fact, I wasn't sure I believed in romantic love at all, so how can I be in love with you? We've only known each other a few days."

"But look at all we've been through in those few days." He brushed her mouth with his. "Don't try to analyze it. Some things can't be explained. You either accept them or you don't." He curved his index finger beneath her chin and looked deep into her eyes. "Do you accept me?"

Chapter Ten

Kyle held his breath as he waited for Ava to respond to his question. She'd just pleasured him with utter self-lessness. Why was he pressuring her? She knelt in front of him naked, his scent still clear on her breath. She'd never denied her desire for him. She'd just been overwhelmed by the changes and the pace at which everything was happening.

He was about to offer her an out when she pushed to her feet and smiled. "I can't guarantee I'll never bombard you with questions again, but I accept you. I accept that the Creator has a plan for my life and you are an essential part of it."

He stood too, wrapping his hand around the back of her neck as he bent to kiss her. "I'll spend the rest of my life making sure you don't regret that decision."

Their lips met, pressing and sliding as they enjoyed the simple intimacy of sharing each other's breath. Then he parted her lips with the tip of his tongue and explored the underside of her lips. They'd felt so soft against his cock. Just the thought of it sent blood rushing to his groin.

Her tongue curled around his, drawing him deeper into his mouth. His taste lingered on her tongue and his cat stretched and growled, ready to imprint her body with his mark. She clutched his shoulders and rubbed her soft breasts against his chest. He wrapped his arms around her and eased his knee between her legs.

A vivid image formed within his mind, provided by his restless cat. He had her pressed against the wall with her legs wrapped around his waist as he drove into her with fast, deep strokes. She moaned, her fingers digging into his shoulders and he realized she'd seen the image too.

He tore his mouth from hers and picked her up. "My cat might be ready to take you, but I promised you payback. Remember?"

"I think your cat's got it right." She was panting softly, her breasts quivering with each ragged breath. "Payback can wait for another day."

"Don't think so." He placed her on the bed then knelt on the floor and pulled her hips toward the edge of the mattress. She only resisted a little when he parted her thighs and draped one of her legs over his shoulder. Her scent sank deeper into his consciousness with each indrawn breath. "You smell so damn good."

She canted her hips, silently offering her creamy slit. He bent lower and traced her seam with the tip of her tongue. Her folds parted for him and he circled the entrance to her body. "Is this where you want me?" He pushed his tongue right into her core and she arched off the bed with a muffled cry. "Or would you rather have my mouth here?" He closed his lips around her swollen clit and gently sucked.

"Yes! Oh Kyle, please."

He chuckled against her damp flesh. "Yes to which one?"

"Either. Or both. Just don't stop until I come."

Even after the powerful release she'd given him, his need had returned with a vengeance. He licked her from front to back then returned to her sensitive clit. She pushed up against his mouth, rocking her hips as she whispered his name.

He pushed two fingers into her core and flicked his tongue against her nub. Her inner muscles tightened around his fingers as he slid his hand in and out. Her cream was intoxicating. He wanted to drink her down and feel her spasm against his lips.

Desire thrummed across their link, making his body pulse in time with hers. He withdrew his fingers and shifted both her legs over his shoulders. Then he raised her to his mouth and fucked her with his tongue. She cried out, shaking as an orgasm claimed her. He stayed inside her as her inner muscles rippled and her cream flowed into his mouth.

She started to relax and he lowered her hips to the bed as he raised his head from between her thighs. "Now we can indulge my cat," he said with a grin. "This is your night to call the shots. How do you want me?"

A fresh wave of desire sparked within her eyes and she let her gaze wander over his body. "On your back. I want to ride you again."

"Fair enough." He climbed onto the bed and spread out on his back. She'd offered him her acceptance. The least he could do was allow her one night of control. Rather than reach for her as he wanted to, he folded his arms and tucked his hands beneath his head.

She crawled toward him, eyes glowing with desire and a triumphant smile parting her lips. "It's just killing you, isn't it?" She swung one of her legs over and settled astride his hips.

"If this is what you need, I'll deal with it."

Her smile softened as she reached down and guided his aching cock to the center of her body. "Just tonight," she whispered as she slowly sank onto his length. She dropped her head back and moaned. "That feels so good."

His fists clenched then he interlaced his fingers, anything to keep from grasping her hips and going wild. She felt hot and firm around his shaft as she paused to savor the fullness. Then she rocked forward and dragged her body up with the same torturous slowness.

"Come on, sunshine. You're killing me."

She braced her hands against his shoulders and slid up and down with the rolling motion of her hips. "Better?"

"Faster."

She moved faster, but the new pace made her breasts sway and bounce. "Let me move." He ground out the words, unable to ignore the demands of his nature any longer.

"Okay." She pressed her mouth over his and surrendered control.

He rolled, sweeping her beneath him as he pinned her arms to the bed. She drew her legs up against his sides as he shifted to his knees. Then he released her arms and lifted her hips to better accommodate his first deep thrust. She kept her arms raised and stared into his eyes as he began to move.

Her core clung to him, caressing his entire length as he shuttled in and out. The longing in her gaze warmed and excited him, mocking his determination to make it last. It always felt so perfect when he was inside her. He wanted it to last forever, but the perfection of their joining was generally what pushed him over the edge.

She ran her hands down his sides then cupped his flexing ass, pulling him closer, taking him deeper. Her inner muscles tightened, assuring him that she was as close as he was.

"Now, Kyle. Now!"

He rode her hard, head thrown back as sensations bombarded his body. Her pleasure poured across their link, compounding the pressure ravaging his composure. He jerked her hips up off the mattress and spilled deep inside her. His pleasure shot across their link and triggered her orgasm. Each of her gasps and rhythmic spasms in turn heightened his enjoyment and prolonged his release.

They clung to each other, fighting for breath as the bliss slowly receded. "You're right," she whispered against his throat.

"About what?" He pulled back far enough so he could see her face.

"It's better when you control the ending."

He rolled to his side, taking her with him. Then he pulled one of her legs up to circle his waist. "Therian males are dominant by nature. It wouldn't be honest if I pretended otherwise."

"Well, thank you for indulging me tonight."

"My pleasure." He kissed her with the patient tenderness he knew she craved. "Any other desires you need to get out of your system before tomorrow?"

Mischief erupted deep in her eyes. "Tomorrow I need to be as in touch with my Therian self as possible. Maybe we should let your cat control what we do next."

Kyle's cat surged toward the surface with such violence it was all he could do to fight back the shift. His recent orgasm might have satisfied the man, but the cat was still restless and ready to prowl. "That's a dangerous offer to make if you don't mean it."

Ava had never meant anything more. Kyle continually held back, suppressed his primitive nature and struggled with his cat. He didn't want to hurt her or frighten her. But until she was able to shift, they had to compromise. He'd allowed her control tonight, had demonstrated his devotion with restraint and tenderness. Now she wanted to give him something in return.

Wiggling out of his embrace, she groaned as their bodies separated. She felt so empty without his cock deep inside her. How had she ever lived without the reassurance of their passionate joining? It seemed almost impossible now.

She moved to the middle of the bed and folded her legs beneath her, angling her body so he could see her rounded behind.

"This is how he likes it, isn't it?" She leaned forward and rested her forearms against the bed then lowered her head. She couldn't see him now, but lust surged across their link, assuring her that he appreciated the brazen display.

For a long, anxious moment he didn't move and all she could hear was the steady beating of her own heart. Then the bed dipped as he moved in close behind her.

"You sure?" The hushed urgency in his tone made her smile.

"Oh yes."

Rather than slam into her as she'd expected, he eased his hand between her thighs and traced her slit. She was slick with their combined pleasure. The creamy liquid had even lubricated her inner thighs.

"You're so wet." He caressed her, teasing her folds without pushing inside.

"In me," she whispered, not sure why he hesitated.

"Like this?" He pushed his long middle finger into her center, sliding slowly in and out.

"No."

"No?" He withdrew his finger and brushed his thumb across her other opening. "Like this?"

His thumb pressed against the stubborn little pucker and she gasped then twisted away. "Not like that!"

He laughed. "Are you sure? My cat would love to introduce you to some of the more exotic pleasures."

"I just meant..."

His hands steadied her hips and he pushed his cock between her thighs. "I know what you mean and I know what you want." Reaching beneath her, he found one of her nipples and firmly squeezed. Pleasure-pain sliced through her chest and sent a fresh rush of desire deep into her groin. "I thought this was about what I want."

He was right. She was doing this for him. Even though her body was already humming with anticipation, she wanted to give him anything he desired. "If that's what you need, I'll try it. At least once." The dark temptation hovered in the distance, forbidden yet intriguing. She trusted him with her pleasure, trusted him with her life. He would never do anything to intentionally harm her.

"I'll take you up on that offer, but not tonight. I'm too wound up to make it good for you." He pulled her up and pressed against her back while his shaft slid between her folds.

She wiggled and rocked, trying to bring him into better alignment with her aching body. He refused to cooperate. He squeezed one breast, his fingers splayed against the soft mound while he teased the other nipple. The firm, rolling motion of his fingers drove her pleasure to the very brink of pain before easing and letting blood return to the pebble-hard tip.

Then his fingers tangled in her hair and he pulled her head back, turning her face sharply to the side. He brushed his mouth over hers, making her crave the deep, tongue-tangling kiss he refused to deliver. She arched and wiggled and finally twisted around far enough to hold his head still so she could take what she wanted.

Her mouth meshed with his and her tongue pushed boldly past his lips. His fingers tightened in her hair and a feral growl vibrated his throat. They'd barely begun and already he was wild and demanding—and she kept up with him kiss for kiss.

Pressure built between her thighs, her inner muscles clenching in on themselves. She whimpered into his mouth, unable to plead with their tongues curling around each other but unwilling to lose the sweet intimacy of their kisses.

Touch yourself. He went right on kissing her, but his thought was clear in her mind. *Let me feel your release and maybe I'll give you want you want.*

Was he serious? She could feel the considerable thickness of his erection between her thighs and he wanted her to masturbate?

He pinched one of her nipples hard enough to make her cry out. "Decide." He whispered the word against her kiss-dampened lips. "Touch yourself or I'll go take a shower."

And then she understood. This wasn't about patience or prolonging pleasure, it was about control. He needed her to obey, to willingly surrender to his will.

Slowly easing her hand between her legs, she moaned as her fingers were surrounded by heat and softness. Her folds were slick and warm as they curved around the head of his cock.

"That's right. Feel what I do to you. What we do to each other." His voice was deep and caressing and his arms encircled and supported her trembling body.

She rested her head against his chest as she found the strength to explore. She'd never been uninhibited before she met Kyle. He made her feel sexy and confident. She caressed him softly then rubbed her folds over him, stimulating herself in the process.

He shifted his hips, positioning his cock at the entrance to her body. "I'm not going to wait all night." His arm wrapped around her waist, yet he didn't thrust into her. He was waiting for her to accommodate his needs as he'd accommodated hers.

Hesitantly, she circled her clit with her middle finger. Sensations spiraled through her abdomen, but mostly she just felt tension. Her thighs quivered and she rubbed a little harder, over, around and across. "I need you inside me." She blew out a shaky breath. "I don't think I can come like this."

"That'd be a shame because you're not getting *this* until you do." He pushed a bit deeper then withdrew.

She let out an exasperated cry then focused on pleasuring herself. She always used a vibrator because it took forever to rub herself off. But she wasn't alone right now. Kyle held her, poised ready to take her, and his scent was still heavy in the air.

He squeezed one nipple and then the other, and her inner muscles tightened.

"I'm trying," she whispered. "Don't leave me, please."

"Never." His mouth opened against the side of her neck. His teeth scraped then he sucked hard enough to draw blood to the surface.

His hand covered hers and she whimpered. She was still technically touching herself, but he controlled the motion and speed of each caress. Her body came alive, tingling and pulsing. She rotated her hips, unable to keep still.

The pleasure crested suddenly, dragging a cry from her throat. Her core rippled with long, deep spasms as Ava shook in his arms.

Before the last pulse faded, he urged her forward and she lowered her forearms to the bed. His hands swept along her sides until he grasped her hips. Then he thrust his cock deep into her center and moved one of his hands to the back of her neck. The sudden fullness kept the spasms coming. She cried out, clawing at the bedding as he began to move.

He pounded into her relentlessly, the momentum reverberating through her entire body. She came in a violent burst of sensation and the bedding muffled her screams. He released her neck and moved both hands to her shoulders, holding her in place to maximize the depth of each penetration.

So deep, so demanding. She felt as if each individual thrust was an attempt to claim her body and soul. She moved her knees farther apart and pressed up into each stroke. She wasn't afraid of his aggression. In fact, knowing how wild she made him felt liberating and empowering.

He moved his hands to her waist as his hips maintained the steady rhythm. Then he opened his mouth against her shoulder and held her firmly with his teeth. It wasn't a bite, exactly, but the savagery of the act, combined with the shockingly intense sensation catapulted her to an even higher peak. She bucked and trembled as wave upon wave of dizzying pleasure crashed over her.

Their link dilated and his cat growled in her mind. He ground his groin against her ass as his seed burst deep inside her. She collapsed on the bed and he followed her down, pulse after pulse of sensation flowing across their connection, leaving them breathless and weak.

He used the last of his strength to roll off her then gather her against his side. "Did I hurt you?"

"No." She smiled, the expression downright dreamy. "Does your cat forgive me for continually shoving him into the background?"

"You're still latent, love. Someday it will be different, but for now we are both content." As if to prove his point, Kyle's cougar began to purr.

THE FOLLOWING MORNING Kyle shifted restlessly on the passenger seat as Quinn's truck bumped and jerked its way along the barely discernable trail. In many places the path was overgrown or obscured by landslides and upended trees. Quinn used the GPS to navigate around the obstacles and followed the contour of the land.

"This should go a little faster now that we know where we're going," Kyle said to no one in particular.

Carissa and Ava were strapped securely to the backseat, each looking a bit unnerved. The blood ritual might have given Carissa access to her Therian abilities, but she had no more experience in battle than Ava did.

Therians expected their Omni Primes to be competent and brave in the face of danger. This mission should be contained and controlled. It was a good opportunity for the sisters to prove themselves to supporters and doubters alike.

Following close behind in a rugged SUV, Payne, Ian and Erin were likely more composed. Potentially violent conflicts were nothing new for any of them. Erin's role would be indirect. She had been included as a precaution in case anyone was badly injured during the confrontation. If the plan was executed without a hitch—which was a damn big if—no one would fire a shot and not a drop of blood would be shed. They would attack fast and stealthily, overtaking the complex in a matter of minutes.

"Hold up," Payne's voice came over the two-way radio. Kyle adjusted the volume and reseated the tiny transceiver in his ear canal. "Ian's going to fly ahead and make sure the situation hasn't changed."

"Copy that," Quinn replied then found a relatively safe place to stop.

Ian climbed out of the passenger side of Payne's SUV and took off his shirt. After tucking his earpiece into the pocket of his jeans, he spread his wings and leapt into the air.

"Why'd he take off his radio?" Ava asked after Ian disappeared above the trees.

"Didn't want the wind to blow it off," Carissa guessed. "I flew with him once and it's really windy up there."

"You flew with Ian?" There was a little too much envy in Ava's voice for Kyle's comfort. He had no doubts about Ava's loyalty, but her fascination with the raptor was still annoying. "When? Why?"

"Long story," Quinn grumbled, and Carissa laughed. Apparently, Kyle wasn't the only one annoyed by their interest in Ian.

"I'll tell you later," Carissa promised. "We better focus right now."

Quinn took off again, his pace slow and steady. Suddenly the truck lurched violently to one side and then the other. Kyle bumped his head against the window before he positioned his hand against the dashboard. "Take it easy."

"Tell that to the trail. What little there is of it." Quinn wrestled the wheel with both hands and shifted his gaze between the truck's mirrors. "They must fly in and out. This is painful!"

Silence spread as the climb grew even more treacherous. Several times the trail was so steep Kyle was tempted to get out and steady the truck. Tree branches scraped against the windows and the seat belt bit into his chest. He glanced at Ava and Carissa, finding each pensive and still.

He accessed his link with Ava, knowing there would be little time for reassurances once the raid began. Despite the looming danger, her emotions were remarkably grounded. An occasional spike of fear flared through her determination, but overall she was calm and—ready. He pushed affection across the connection and she responded with a smile.

"There's a small clearing after the next descent. We'll hike in from there," Ian directed. "We don't want them to hear our approach."

Quinn turned the truck around and backed into the cover of a leafy tree. Payne followed suit, positioning the SUV for a fast getaway.

Ian was waiting by the time everyone climbed out. Erin handed him his shirt and he pulled it on as he explained, "The guards work in pairs and follow predictable patterns. This shouldn't take long."

Anything involving Osric was never that easy. Kyle reviewed phase one in his mind, trying to anticipate complications. They'd done their best to cover all bases, but there were still so many variables. He gave Ava a quick hug as protectiveness welled within him. She'd outsmarted her wolf pursuers. In fact, he wouldn't have been able to find her without Carissa's help.

His people would never accept a leader who had yet to be tested in battle. Like it or not, Ava needed this opportunity. "Keep Erin company for now." He brushed his lips against Ava's then stepped back. "We'll need you soon enough."

"Let's do this thing." Payne wasn't armed with conventional weapons. Anything he carried into the fight would have to be abandoned once he transformed into one of the guards.

"Follow me." Ian headed off through the trees and the others fell in behind him. Each of them was more accustomed to giving orders than receiving them, but Ian was the only one with firsthand knowledge of the situation. They hiked up a rise and remained within the trees near the crest until the hill dipped suddenly. Hustling down at an angle, Ian gradually slowed their pace.

Kyle spotted the guards off to his left and Ian motioned for them to fan out. Skirting the target, Kyle crept along, giving the others time to reach their positions. Ian sent a telepathic pulse, signaling the charge. The guards snapped to attention, shouldering their weapons as they scanned their surroundings.

Ian dropped down from a tree, knocking one guard to the ground and kicking his rifle out of reach. Stunned and confused, the guard thrashed. Ian easily deflected the blows. A well-placed punch rendered the guard unconscious then Ian reached into his pocket and withdrew a couple of oversized zip ties so he could restrain his prisoner.

Reaching the second guard a moment later, Kyle and Quinn coordinated their attack. Quinn ripped the rifle out of his hands as Kyle jerked his arms behind his back, preventing him from activating his radio.

"You can't do this!" The guard yanked against Kyle's hands, arching and twisting in a futile attempt to escape. "They'll kill me this time! Please let me go."

Kyle had been so focused on the task that he'd barely glanced at the guard's face. Motioning Quinn forward he traded places with the other Therian so he could move in front of the guard. This was one of the guards he'd run into when he was lost on this mountain with Ava. "Who are 'they'?"

The guard shook his head and panic clouded his gaze. "No one fails them twice. I'm already dead."

"Heard enough?"

Kyle nodded and Quinn punched the guard then steadied him as he collapsed onto the leaf-strewn ground.

"Which one was in charge?" Payne moved closer, looking at one guard and then the other.

"I'm not sure, but I had a run-in with this one already. He'd be more than happy to get his hands on me and Ava."

Quinn bound the guard's wrists and ankles with zip ties as Payne knelt at his side. Kyle had heard of skinwalkers, had even known Payne inherited the rare ability from his mother, but he'd never seen the transformation before. Was the process significantly different than any other Therian shift?

"I need his uniform."

"That would have been nice to know *before* I restrained him," Quinn muttered then snapped the sturdy plastic so he could undress the guard.

Ian held his position, but he was obviously curious as well. Payne took the guard's head between his hands and closed his eyes. For a moment it seemed as if nothing happened. Then the wind stilled and silence spread over the area like an insulating blanket. Kyle felt energy streaming around and into Payne. The currents were warm and softly sizzled.

Bending closer to the guard, Payne whispered words Kyle didn't understand. Payne repositioned his hands as his arms began to tremble. The chant grew louder, his lips moving faster.

A spark, like an ember escaping a campfire, floated out of the guard and into Payne's mouth. Kyle thought he'd imagined the manifestation until it happened again. Payne inhaled deeply and more sparks followed, forming a shimmering stream. His features blurred, the angles smoothed and his skin paled.

This must be how Ava felt when she saw a Therian shift for the first time. His respect for her grew with each passing moment. It was amazing that she hadn't run screaming in terror. It really was rather grotesque. Kyle watched the undulation of Payne's flesh, heard the crack of joints and crunch of bones as he assumed the guard's smaller shape.

Payne finally released the guard's face and struggled to his feet. Though he was shaky and a bit dazed, the likeness was absolute. Quinn handed him the uniform then knelt and restrained the guard as Payne put on the uniform.

"We'll carry these two closer to the vehicle shed then incapacitate the rest of the guards," Ian told Kyle then he turned to Quinn and added, "I know you'd rather keep Carissa out of this, but we could use the cover."

Quinn reluctantly nodded and they turned their attention to the unconscious guards.

"You good to go?" Kyle asked Payne. "We need to secure the complex before they reach the shed."

Payne rolled his shoulders and stretched out his back. "Lead on."

Rather than backtrack, Kyle reached across his link with Ava and told her they were ready for phase two.

Chapter Eleven

A va looked at her sister and smiled with a little more confidence than she felt. "Time to go. Kyle needs me."

"Yeah, Quinn just called me too. Be careful." Carissa hugged her tightly.

"You too."

"You're both in good hands," Erin stressed. "Trust your men and trust yourselves. You'll be fine."

"Says the woman who's staying behind."

Rather than being insulting, as Ava feared, Carissa's comment made Erin laugh.

"Get!" Erin waved them on. "They're waiting for you."

Using their link like a beacon, Ava followed the signal to Kyle. He stood with a uniformed guard in the trees to one side of the complex Ian had described. Her steps faltered and her gaze shot back to Kyle.

"It's all right." Kyle looked at the guard and smiled. "Damn convincing, isn't he?"

"Payne?" The guard inclined his head and a shiver raced down her spine. He looked exactly like one of the guards they'd encountered during their first trip to this area. No visible trace of the lion-shifter was left. It would be so easy to misuse such a powerful ability.

"Remember, we're his prisoners." Kyle coached. "Don't fight your nerves too hard. You should be afraid and upset." He took out his pistol and handed it to Payne, who also held the guard's rifle.

"Walk in front of me with your hands in the air," Payne told them.

"This guard has an ax to grind with me, so don't hold back."

Payne chuckled. "I didn't intend to." Even his voice had transformed. Gone was the unusual accent and the deep rumbling tone. He tucked Kyle's pistol into the back of his pants then repositioned his rifle.

They stepped out of the trees and headed across the grassy clearing, making a beeline for the nearest exterior door. It was safe to presume someone was watching, so Payne fell into character. "Not too close and keep those hands up!" He poked Kyle in the back with the barrel of his rifle. "I can't believe you had the balls to come back. I'd be impressed if it wasn't so *stupid*."

There was no keypad or scanner to trigger the door so Payne told Ava to try the handle. It was securely locked. *Should we try a different door?*

Camera at ten o'clock. Give it another second. Kyle projected the thought without shielding it, so Payne could hear him as well.

Payne looked into the camera and called out, "Open up. I've got a present for Osric."

Ava heard the subtle pop as the lock released, but Kyle stopped her before she could try the handle again. *Don't seem too eager to get inside.*

"Open it, bitch!" Payne nudged her with the rifle, the contact far more careful than it had been with Kyle.

"Wrong shifter, asshole," she returned, and he kicked her in the butt, propelling her toward the door. The handle rotated and she slowly pulled the door open.

Kyle stepped through first, but the caution seemed unnecessary as the hallway was empty.

Someone was monitoring that camera. There's likely a guard headed our way.

It felt odd to have anyone other than Kyle in her mind, but she heeded Payne's warning. They proceeded cautiously, Kyle moving beside her as they turned a corner and entered a wider corridor. There was nothing unique or menacing about the building. They passed an office on the right and approached what appeared to be a lab on the left. The bottom portion of the wall was obscured while the upper half was transparent.

A guard came into view as he rounded a corner. "You're out of luck, Carvel. Osric left this morning with Barns. I'm not sure who the backers summoned. They both seemed mighty jumpy."

"Shit. Then who's on duty."

Ava couldn't see Payne's expression, but he certainly sounded petulant.

"Daniels, of course." The guard's impatient sneer made it obvious the real Carvel would have known.

"Then I'll ask Daniels what I should do with these two. I'm not sticking my neck out again."

"Whatever you say." The guard turned around and Kyle lunged for him, trapping his arms against his sides as he wrestled him to the floor. Careful to keep the guard's hands away from his weapons, Kyle dragged his arms behind his back and pinned him to the floor with his knee.

Payne approached and the guard renewed his struggles. "You fucking coward! Are you working with them?"

"Close enough." Payne disarmed the guard while Kyle secured his wrists and ankles. Good thing they had lots of zip ties.

Ava looked around, belatedly checking for cameras. There were so many details, so many things that could go wrong. How did these men keep track of everything?

"Where's Daniels and are there any other guards in the building?" When the guard didn't reply, Payne pulled up on his bound wrists, twisting his shoulders. The guard cried out between clenched teeth. "If you don't tell me, I'll scan your mind and I'll make it hurt worse than anything you can imagine."

The guard stilled, color draining from his face. "You're one of those freaks, aren't you?"

"Speak!" Ignoring the question, Payne yanked on the guard's hands for emphasis.

"Control room." The guard panted and turned his head, looking away from his tormentor.

"Which is where?" Payne grabbed his wrists but waited for his answer.

"Turn right, second door on the left." He sounded so dejected, Ava almost felt sorry for him. Then she remembered he was in league with Osric and the spark of pity sputtered out.

Kyle opened an office door and dragged the guard inside. Ava heard the familiar smack of flesh hitting flesh and a muffled groan.

"He was already restrained. Was that necessary?"

"Yes!" The men answered as one.

Trying not to be distracted by their aggression, Ava fell into step beside Kyle. Payne resumed his role as antagonistic guard and they headed for the main corridor. There was a dark-haired woman and two young men in the laboratory. They watched with obvious curiosity as Payne marched his prisoners down the hall, but none seemed interested enough to interfere.

The control room door was unmarked. Payne knocked with the butt of his rifle. "Daniels, open up! I've got my hands full."

After a short pause, the door swung inward and Kyle grabbed the guard by his shirtfront and yanked him into the hall. Payne caught the door before it swung shut and Kyle went to work on the guard. Daniels put up more of a fight than his comrades, punching and kicking with obvious skill. Kyle absorbed a few blows while Ava moved out of the way, then he unleashed his Therian speed and strength.

The guard reached for his pistol as he executed a flashy jump kick. Kyle grabbed his ankle and swept his other foot out from under him. Daniels went down hard on his back, his head slamming the floor with enough force to knock him out.

"Now you don't have to punch him." Payne chuckled.

Kyle rolled him over and zip tied his wrists then pulled his sidearm out of its holster. Leaving him on his stomach,

Kyle secured his ankles then tucked the gun into the back of his pants.

Ava stepped into the doorway as Payne moved farther into the control room. A wide console had been mounted below a large, oblong monitor. The monitor was divided into six sections, three on top and three on the bottom. The first two sections displayed external shots of the complex while the other four were internal.

"Let me see if I can find a full list of the cameras. There has to be more than six." Ava sat down at the keyboard, feeling useful for the first time since the mission began. The operating system was familiar, but the program itself was not. It took her a few minutes to find a main menu, but the rest was pretty straightforward. "Here we go."

"Is the lower level available?" Kyle moved up beside her chair while Payne returned to the doorway.

"Lower *levels*. There are two." There were thirty available cameras, so Ava took them level by level. There were no surprises on the first two levels or in any of the exterior shots. She selected the first six cameras on sublevel one and sent their signals to the monitors. Images of identical cell-like rooms filled the screen, each containing at least one captive. "Oh my God." Her stomach clenched and her heart thudded in her chest. "What is this place?"

Kyle moved to her other side and touched the upper corner of the monitor. "Is that..."

Two girls huddled together on the narrow bunk, their images so small they were barely visible on the cluttered screen. Pity and anger twisted through Ava's chest. What the

Cyndi Friberg

hell were innocent children doing in a place like this? She selected the camera again and the image filled the screen.

Without explaining his excitement, Kyle tapped his earpiece and began to pace. "Ian, call Jake. We've found the girls!"

Ava looked at the screen with new interest. These were two of Jake's nieces? How wonderful! But weren't there three missing? And who were the rest of these people? She returned to the divided screen and Kyle pointed to one of the other rooms. "Show me this one."

She toggled the image and Kyle let out a happy cry. "That's Cheyenne. We have all three!"

"Not yet we don't," Payne said from the doorway. "There have to be guards down there and what about the lab rats? They're the ones doing the experiments. They have to be held accountable for their actions."

Quickly selecting the other images on sublevel one, Ava determined that there were six holding cells, a treatment room and two guards. The second sublevel was basically a duplicate of the first.

"Go through all the images again," Kyle told her. "Make sure we didn't miss anything."

The upper level housed living quarters and none were occupied at the moment. She located two additional teams of scientists, but no more guards on the main level.

"Let's leave Quinn and Carissa in the shed as planned," Payne suggested. "But we could use Ian. Especially if anyone manages to sound an alarm."

All was quiet right now, but they were rather outnumbered.

Kyle nodded and tapped his earpiece. "We need you inside," he told Ian. "Come to the east door and Payne will let you in."

Payne jogged off down the hall, not needing further instruction.

Kyle moved back in front of the monitor. "As soon as we lose the element of surprise, we're screwed."

"So let's not lose the element of surprise." Ava smiled, hoping to encourage him. She brought the lab they'd passed on the way to the control room to screen and went on. "They were curious as we walked by them, but they shrugged it off and went back to work." She brought up images of the other two labs. "Payne can round up one group of the 'lab rats' and you and Ian can round up the other. Then bring them all to the woman's lab. She's already seen us, so she'll be less shocked when something else happens."

"Any panic button in the lab will probably notify the control center. It's not like calling the police would do any good."

Ava swiveled her chair so she could look up at him. "Then once all the scientists are in one place, you guys can start rounding up—or knocking out—the remaining guards."

"Would you rather we have snapped their necks? That's the easiest way to prevent an enemy from sounding an alarm."

"Put that way, I guess you guys have been remarkably restrained." She turned back to the computer and checked then rechecked the images. One misstep would send their plans toppling like a row of dominos.

"What's the plan?" Ian asked as he returned with Payne.

"Payne, head straight down this hall and collect the three lab rats on your right. Ian, you're with me."

"What do I do once I've collected them?" Payne asked.

"Keep them from doing anything stupid and bring them to the first lab we saw."

"Got it."

Ava took a deep breath and pushed to her feet. "Where do you want me?"

Anywhere and everywhere. He grinned and then said out loud, "Wait for us near the first lab, but don't go in until we join you."

Ava nodded. It was unlikely the scientists would give her any trouble, but she was much more comfortable behind a keyboard than pointing a gun. She quickly propped open the door to the control room with a book then headed for the lab.

Watching the workers from an adjacent hallway, Ava waited for Kyle's return. They moved about at a leisurely pace, apparently unconcerned with what they'd seen earlier.

Payne arrived first, marching his three lab rats in front of him like obedient children. He winked at her as he passed and she followed as he ushered his group into the lab.

"What the hell is this?" the female scientist asked, hopping down from her stool. She spoke with obvious authority, her dark eyes sweeping the entire scene before focusing in on Payne. "Carvel, explain."

Payne's explanation was interrupted by Ian and Kyle's arrival. One of the scientists had his hands bound behind his back and his mouth taped shut. Apparently he had tried to be a hero.

"What is this?" The female scientist crept toward the end of her workspace.

Ava rushed to the counter and ran her fingers along the underside, easily finding the woman's destination. "A panic button's not going to help you now." She didn't want to provoke the woman, but she couldn't forget the captives waiting below.

Kyle looked around the room then pointed to the back corner where there wasn't any furniture or outlets of any kind. "Everyone over there. Sit down against the wall."

"Want me to secure them?" Payne held up a fist full of zip ties.

"Probably wouldn't hurt."

Ian helped Payne, and all of the scientists were soon contained in a nice cluster, wrists securely bound. Except the woman. Kyle had stopped her when she started to join the others. "How many holding cells are there total?"

According to the security feeds there were twelve, but there could be more if they weren't under surveillance.

"Six on each sublevel." There was no hesitation in her tone and she seemed almost excited by the intrusion of armed strangers. Who was she?

"Don't help them, Carly. The backers will kill you."

She glared at the speaker, one of the young men who had been assisting her. "Thanks for telling them my name."

"So, *Carly*," Kyle paused for effect. "Tell me about 'the backers'?"

"I'm not telling you anything." Then she moved closer to Kyle and whispered, "Unless you take me with you."

"And why would I do that?" Kyle's brows arched, but his expression remained cold. "We both know you've been abusing the people in those cages downstairs. Why would I deal with someone like that?"

"Can we talk somewhere away from them?" She nodded toward the other scientists.

"She's Osric's lover," a thin man with balding hair warned. "Don't believe anything she tells you."

"He's my professional rival." Carly glared at the outspoken man then returned her gaze to Kyle. "And he doesn't know half of what I know."

"We don't have time for this." Payne growled and rubbed his forehead. Then he looked at Ian and asked, "What did Quinn do with my clothes? I need to...change into something more comfortable."

Ian shrugged, yet his focus remained on the huddled scientists. "He either threw them in the back of his truck or left them in the woods. Maybe she can find you a set of scrubs."

"May I?" Carly asked Kyle. He nodded so she crossed the lab and opened one of the cabinets. "What size?"

"As big as you've got." Payne's voice sounded tenser by the moment.

She walked back across the lab and handed him the garments. "Anything else?"

"Take her up on it," her rival sneered. "She can be *very* accommodating."

"Take them out to the shed," Kyle directed. "If Quinn needs help, one of you can stay, but I need the other back as soon as possible."

The scientists were helped to their feet and marched out of the lab in a line. Ian led and Payne took up the lead. More than a few glares were tossed at Carly as the room emptied.

"Are you Osric's lover?" Before she could answer, Kyle added, "Don't lie to me. I can hear your heartbeat and smell your fear. I'll know if you're lying."

"I have sex with him but it's not by choice. I've been spying for the backers." She squared her shoulders and shoved her hands into the pockets of her lab coat. "My assistant wasn't exaggerating. The backers will kill me if they think I helped you."

"Do you know where Osric is or when he'll return?"

"He left early this morning with our head of security. They both think the other is in trouble, but I suspect Osric is in for a rude awakening."

"Meaning?"

"The backers will probably kill them both."

He rubbed his chin and stared at the nervous hostage. "I'll take you out of here, but your fate has yet to be determined. The more valuable you can make yourself, the more likely it is you'll survive."

Carly's lips trembled while desperation burned in her eyes. "There are two guards on each of the sublevels. I could sound an alarm and two of the four would run up the stairs to help me. They won't desert their posts. You'll have to deal with the other two."

"Why are you so anxious to turn traitor?" He stalked toward her, gaze narrowed and assessing.

"I'm a survivor, and right now you're my best chance of coming out of this alive."

Payne walked back into the lab. He'd returned to his natural form and was now dressed in the borrowed scrubs. "What's next, *boss*?"

Carly just stared at him, mouth gaping as he strode across the room. "You're... How did you... Where is Carvel?"

"In the woods where we found him," Kyle told her. "As of right now, we haven't killed anyone. If you help us, that statistic might remain the same."

"Are you all Therians?" Her anxious gaze kept drifting back toward Payne. "I don't think the backers know you can imitate people too."

Imitate people? As if we don't deserve the title. Ava clenched her hands into fists. She was rapidly developing an extreme dislike for this woman.

Relax, sunshine. Our first priority has to be evacuating the captives. He glanced at her to make sure she'd heard him, so she nodded.

"We really are going to have a nice long talk about these 'backers,'" he said to Carly. "But right now we have more pressing concerns. How many captives are downstairs?"

"Eleven, no ten. I almost forgot they moved Devon."

"Devon?" Dread, anger and fear twisted through Kyle so powerfully Ava groaned. "You had a prisoner named Devon? What did she look like? How long has she been here? Where did they take her?"

"Black hair, big green eyes, very pretty." Carly stared into his eyes and her gaze narrowed. "Is she related to you?"

He grasped her upper arms and lifted her off her feet. "Where did they take her?"

"I honestly don't know. I didn't even know they had other complexes until Roberto mentioned it."

"Roberto is one of the backers?"

"We need to get moving," Payne reminded. "You can interrogate the little turncoat later."

Reluctantly, Kyle released Carly and stepped back. "No alarms. Use a radio to call two of the guards, so I can hear what you're saying."

"The intercom is hardwired. Radio reception is sketchy belowground."

"Fine. Use the intercom."

They escorted Carly to the nearest intercom and she contacted two of the guards, asking for their help moving a filing cabinet. After some grumbling about useless females, they agreed to help.

Kyle hurried Carly toward the elevator in time to hear the distinct hum of the motor. There was no way to know if one or both of the guards were contained within the car, so they prepared for a dual attack. Carly stood in front of the elevator while Kyle and Payne flanked the door.

The car contained both guards and one greeted Carly with a flirtatious smile.

"Thanks for helping me, guys."

Neither of the guards had drawn their weapons. They moved out of the elevator in close succession and the confrontation was over as quickly as it began. Kyle disarmed one while Payne wrestled with the other. Even the second guard's fiery determination was no match for Payne's calm strength. Payne twisted his arm behind his back and forced him to his knees. Kyle had already incapacitated his guard, so he helped Payne secure the second man.

Carly watched it all with morbid curiosity. "What do they change into?" she whispered the question to Ava. Ava's only reaction was a silent glare.

"Two to go," Payne muttered. "Then what? How do we get off this mountain with ten extra passengers?"

"Let's worry about that once the complex is secured," Kyle suggested. "There's one left for you and one for me."

"They'll presume we're the returning guards. Let's get this done."

Kyle kissed Ava and said, "I'll let you know when it's safe to come down." Then he stepped into the elevator with Payne and the door slid closed.

"I told him radios don't work down there."

Ava looked at Carly, suppressing the urge to gloat. "Who said anything about radios?"

"You *are* telepathic. I knew it." Carly covered her mouth with one hand as her gaze moved over Ava's face. "Did Devon signal your... Is he your mate or just your lover?"

"It's none of your business." She took a deep breath and widened her stance as she glared into Carly's eyes. "You experiment on children. I find you detestable."

"The children weren't touched and I had nothing to do with their capture."

"How long have you been experimenting on the others or are you going to deny that too?"

Carly started to say something then shook her head and looked away as she sighed. "I know you won't believe me, but I'm as much a prisoner as they are."

Ava laughed, hands clenched so tightly her nails bit into her palm. "Sure you are."

Kyle signaled Ava a few minutes later and told her to bring Carly down with her. The conditions below were not nearly as bad as Ava had feared. There was no excuse for treating these people like guinea pigs, but it didn't appear as if they had been overly abused. Beyond long periods of incarceration and numerous medical procedures, of course.

Kyle had opened Cheyenne's cell and let her go in to her nieces. The two girls clung to their aunt, all three sobbing.

"Do you have a laptop?" Kyle asked Carly. His expression hadn't changed significantly, but Ava could feel the hatred seething beneath the surface. Carly's chances of coming out of this alive were shrinking by the minute.

"Why?"

"I want you to gather as much of your research as you can carry. Samples, reports, whatever."

"Samples are a good idea, but the rest is documented in the database, which is backed up remotely. I can access it with any computer." Carly licked her lips and slipped her hands into her pockets, clearly sensing the change in his attitude.

"Payne will accompany you to your lab. If you're not ready in ten minutes, we'll leave without you."

Ava waited until Payne and Carly were on their way up in the elevator before she asked Kyle what he and Payne had decided. "How are we going to get all these people off this mountain?"

"You, Carissa and Erin will have to drive while Quinn and I escort you."

"What about Ian and Payne?"

"They're going to wait for backup."

"Why do we need backup? Don't we control the entire complex?"

"We do, but we have several tasks still to be completed. First, the doctors must be taken to the council for judgment. Their actions cannot go unpunished."

"What about the guards?"

"It doesn't appear that the guards had any direct interaction with the captives. We're going to leave them bound in the shed and let the backers deal with their inability to protect the facility."

"Why did you want Carly to gather her research?"

"We need to know how much they've learned and what they intend to do with the knowledge. Besides, once everyone is evacuated, Payne and his friends are going to blow this place sky high."

"I see." She was pleased by the outcome but tension still gripped her belly. If the women were going to drive, how were the men going to "escort" the vehicles? "You're going to shift, aren't you? You'll escort us in cat form."

He nodded. "It's the best option. We need every seat we have for the captives."

"We only have two vehicles. How will that be enough?"

He finally smiled. "I guess we'll have to borrow one of their Jeeps."

Kyle made it sound so simple, but Ava gripped the steering wheel with both hands and reminded herself to breathe. The terrain had seemed treacherous while she was a passenger. Now that she was driving an unfamiliar Jeep filled with frightened strangers, she wasn't sure she would survive the dangerous descent. But the former captives watched her with a mixture of hope and fear. She couldn't fail them now. They were counting on her to deliver them safely into the arms of their loved ones and she intended to do just that.

Kyle, in cougar form, darted in and out of the trees, scaling rocks and navigating slopes with agile strength. He looked completely at home in this inhospitable setting. Quinn ran on the other side of the vehicles, his large black jaguar blending with the shadows.

The trail dipped suddenly, pitching the Jeep dangerously to the side. One of the young women in the backseat cried out and the others quickly shushed her.

"It's all right," Ava assured them with a smile. "We'll be on a real road soon."

Erin led the three-vehicle convoy in Payne's SUV. Ava drove in the middle and Carissa brought up the end in Quinn's truck. The pace Erin set stretched the boundaries of Ava comfort zone, but she understood time was of the essence. Payne and Ian were waiting for word that all the captives were safely away before they blew up the lab and made their own escape.

The "real road" was more like a winding dirt trail, but Ava was thrilled to leave the worst of the obstacles behind.

"Where are you taking us?" The speaker, a dark-haired woman in her mid- to late-thirties, sat in the middle of the backseat and appeared to have appointed herself spokesperson for the other three.

"I'm not sure. I doubt they'll want to keep everyone together, that would be too dangerous."

"Who organized the escape?" the woman in the passenger seat asked. She was pale and gaunt. Had she been in captivity longer than the others or had her testing been more invasive? "I know no one was looking for me. Everyone thinks I'm dead."

"There's no way my family has given up on me," the outspoken brunette bragged, drawing glares from the others.

"The escape was the combined effort of a variety of cat clans," Ava replied, hoping to defuse the budding argument. "Oh and Ian. He's a raptor."

"How did you find the lab? What will be done with the employees and the people who financed the place? I've heard them called 'the backers' or something like that."

Ava wasn't sure who rattled off the question and she wasn't sure how much she should share. She knew they were Therians, but she had no idea if she could trust them. Not all the clans were friendly. "It's probably best if we let one of the others explain. I don't know what happens next and I don't want to mislead you."

"In other words, she's a grunt. Don't waste your time."

That had definitely been the argumentative brunette, but Ava kept her gaze fixed on the road and pretended not to have heard the spiteful comments.

They continued in relative silence for the remainder of the trip. The ex-captives spoke to each other, but none of them attempted to include Ava in the conversation.

Ava didn't breathe easily until they reached a paved road and even then she found herself checking her rearview mirror far more often than necessary. A deep, rumbling sound drew her attention to her right.

"Was that thunder?" someone asked.

"There's not a cloud in the sky," someone else pointed out.

The lab. Ava couldn't contain her smile. Payne and his friends must have blown up the lab.

"That wasn't thunder," the snooty brunette said. "And it looks like our driver knows exactly what it was."

Before they could pressure her for specifics, Ava followed Erin onto a side street. They drove along a narrow access road that led to a vacant parking lot beside a small lake. A dark blue SUV and two midsized trucks were clustered in one corner of the lot. Ava recognized the SUV as Jake's but had never seen the trucks before.

She parked beside Erin and left the keys in the ignition, not sure what the men would do with the pilfered vehicle.

A happy squeal guided her gaze back to the SUV in time to see Jake embrace his sister with one arm and his nieces with the other. She had never seen him look so happy. A blinding smile showcased his even white teeth and unshed tears made his eyes shimmer.

Her passengers piled out of the Jeep and gravitated toward Erin. Ava looked around, wondering where Kyle and Quinn had gone. The crisis was nearly over, but she still hoped they'd return soon.

Carissa motioned her over to Quinn's SUV and they watched the happy reunion while trying not to intrude. "He must be so relieved. Nothing is worse than not knowing where a loved one is." She shot Carissa a knowing smile then gave her a quick hug.

"I'm thrilled we found the girls, but what the hell are we going to do with all the others?" Carissa whispered. "Jake only has so many bedrooms."

Quinn and Kyle stepped out from behind the SUV. Kyle tucked his t-shirt into his jeans while Quinn quickly buttoned up his shirt. They were both barefoot.

"Your boots are on the floor in back." Carissa motioned toward the SUV.

By the time Quinn and Kyle finished dressing, the ex-captives had congregated near the Jeep and Erin was deep in conversation with Jake. Quinn hung back with Carissa, but Kyle took Ava by the hand and crossed the parking lot to find out what his mother was plotting.

"Has anyone heard from Ian or Payne?" Kyle asked. "Were there any complications once we took off?"

Erin shook her head. "Everything went as planned. The lab is destroyed and Payne will deliver the other two doctors to the council as soon as they're ready to deal with this mess."

"What do you mean the 'other two doctors'?" Jake asked.

"We have one of the doctors with us," Erin explained. "She's promised to cooperate and her information has proved valuable so far, so we're going to hold on to her for a little while longer."

Jake tensed, his expression suddenly grim. "If she touched my kin, I have a say in what happens to her."

"Carly can wait," Kyle interjected. "The others can't. We need to decide what to do with the rest of our guests."

"That's what we were talking about while you dressed." Erin looked at Kyle as she went on. "Liz is on her way here to pick up Cheyenne and the girls. Jake has agreed to take three of the former captives and I'll take the other four."

"And then what?" Ava didn't want to be difficult, but her passengers had given her a good idea of the complications they were facing.

"If they have no family or friends who can come get them, it will be their clan alpha's responsibility to provide for their needs until they're able to provide for themselves." A certain coldness in Jake's tone made Ava wonder if he was quoting rules he didn't agree with.

"And if their clan alpha is someone like Osric?"

"We'll make sure they're safe and entering a situation they welcome." When Ava offered no more objections, Erin turned to Kyle. "Do you think Quinn and Carissa could hold on to Carly until we're ready to interrogate her? It shouldn't be more than a day or two. I don't want her in the same house as any of the people she abused. That's just asking for trouble."

"If he won't, I will," Kyle said.

"No." She smiled at him then winked at Ava. "We all agree that you two need some time alone. Carissa and Quinn have had a few days to themselves already. It's your turn to focus entirely on each other."

"What about Devon?" Kyle flared, obviously upset by his mother's plan. "Carly rode down with you. Didn't she tell you about Devon?"

"Ian went after Devon. And I intend to learn everything Carly knows with or without her cooperation. If there is anything we can do to help Ian's search, he'll let us know."

"You're kicking me to the curb?" Kyle shook his head, disbelief clear in his expression.

"No, I'm freeing you to solidify your personal life so you can be a more effective network Prime."

"Sounds much better the way she put it." Jake laughed. "Take one of the trucks. I'll send someone back for the Jeep."

"None of us are safe. You realize that, don't you?" Kyle grumbled. "We know more now than we did yesterday, but they still know a whole hell of a lot more about us than we know about them."

"Before Ava zapped you to their backyard, we had no idea this threat existed," Jake argued. "I refuse to think of this as anything but a win."

"Cheyenne and the girls are safe. That's an undeniable blessing." But Devon was still out there, still at the mercy of the ruthless monsters who'd kidnapped Jake's kin. Erin didn't come right out and say it, but everyone knew what she was thinking.

"Ian will find Devon." Jake looked from Erin to Kyle and back. "We all know how stubborn he is."

Erin accepted the assurance with a stiff nod. "We better get moving. Our guests are growing restless."

"Keep me updated and I'll do the same." Without further ado, Jake walked away.

Erin gave Kyle a firm hug. "I'm serious about this. You and Ava need this time to yourselves. Unfortunately these mysteries are going to take more than a day or two to unravel. There will be plenty of work waiting for you when you return."

"I hear and I obey." He kissed her forehead then wrapped his arm around Ava and led her back toward Quinn's SUV. "Better say good-bye to your sister, sunshine. I guess we're going home."

She smiled as joy swelled within her. "Even if it's just for a few days, home has never sounded so wonderful."

THE END

Please Leave a Review

If you enjoyed this book, could you please take a minute and write a review? Reviews have become an important way for readers to find new authors and evaluate new books. I know your time is valuable, but I'd really appreciate your help.

Thanks, Cyndi

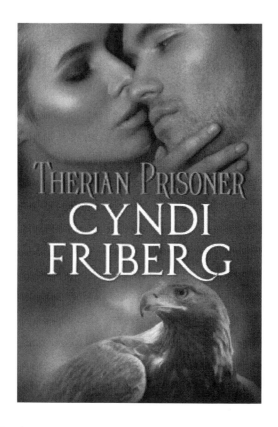

THERIAN HEAT, BOOK Four: Though Devon comes from a line of cougar-shifters, her own animal nature has not yet been defined. The mysterious "backers" have captured her, intent on using her untapped Therian abilities for unknown ends. She escapes from their prison, but not from the emotional scars left by their abuse.

Ian, an ancient Therian raptor, offers her protection and encouragement. Devon has always wanted Ian, always felt a connection deeper than friendship. But Ian insists he's too old and jaded to make Devon an honorable mate. If she hopes to feel whole again, she must regain control over her emotions and desires. And she desires Ian.

At first, Ian resists Devon's attempts at seduction. She needs a shoulder to cry on, not a demanding lover, and Ian is never satisfied until his partners surrender unconditionally. But Devon stirs primal instincts and awakens ravenous longings he has suppressed for centuries. He wants her, but he fears the darkness inside him will destroy her.

Printed in Great Britain
by Amazon